MW00790366

HER PRETTY LIES

ANGELA HENRY

Storm
PUBLISHING

This is a work of fiction. Names, characters, business, events and incidents are the products of the author's imagination. Any resemblance to actual persons, living or dead, or actual events is purely coincidental.

Copyright © Angela Henry, 2024

The moral right of the author has been asserted.

All rights reserved. No part of this book may be reproduced or used in any manner without the prior written permission of the copyright owner.

To request permissions, contact the publisher at rights@stormpublishing.co

Ebook ISBN: 978-1-80508-515-7
Paperback ISBN: 978-1-80508-516-4

Cover design: Lisa Horton
Cover images: Shutterstock

Published by Storm Publishing.
For further information, visit:
www.stormpublishing.co

ALSO BY ANGELA HENRY

The Perfect Affair

Kendra Clayton Series

The Company You Keep

Tangled Roots

Diva's Last Curtain Call

Schooled in Lies

Sly, Slick & Wicked

Doing it to Death

Xavier Knight Series

Knight's Fall

Knight's Shade

Maya Sinclair Thriller

The Paris Secret

Middle-Grade as Angie Kelly

Labyrinth Society: The Versailles Vendetta

PROLOGUE

I'm sitting at the back of an ambulance as the flashing lights of police cars illuminate the night sky. My arms, legs, and hands are covered in blood. I think there may even be a smudge of blood on my face. Whose blood is this? Is it mine? I can't be sure. I feel so numb and detached it's like I've stepped out of my body and I'm watching myself and the scene in front of me from a distance. What time is it? I was told I can't leave until the police have talked to me. But that felt like hours ago.

The door to the apartment opens, and two men bring a body bag on a collapsible wheeled stretcher down the apartment steps. Instantly, I remember whose blood is all over me, and the horror of what I came home to comes flooding back. I'm suddenly freezing cold, despite the muggy August heat. I shiver uncontrollably as my heart races.

"She's going into shock."

Seconds later, the female EMT who'd checked me for wounds wraps me in a shiny thermal blanket that does little to stop my chattering teeth. I stand abruptly and take a step forward, not sure of where I'm trying to go.

"Kendall, please sit back down."

How does she know my name? Then I remember giving it to her when the ambulance arrived. I was sitting on the steps in front of the apartment with a uniformed officer, mute and covered in blood. "Have you remembered what happened to you?"

I'm still standing and merely stare at her.

"Kendall?"

The concern on the EMT's face is obvious. And just like that, I remember it all. Everything. Down to the coppery smell of the blood and the shoe. Oh my God, the shoe! And I know in that moment how bad this looks for me.

Instead of answering her, I take a step back as if retreating from the horror of what happened in that apartment, as a wave of dizziness hits me. The world tilts crazily, and I fall into the welcome abyss of unconsciousness.

ONE

COLUMBUS, OHIO

Franklin County Family Court
1999

Custody cases were their own special kind of hell for the Honorable Judge Iris Hanson. She had just awarded temporary custody of an abandoned three-month-old baby girl to her foster parents.

"No! They tricked me!" screamed the child's young mother, jumping up from her chair. "You're letting them steal my baby! Do something!" She shoved her hapless attorney, a newbie lawyer, who sat pale and silent next to her and was probably rethinking his chosen profession.

"Mr. Cassell, please control your client."

Mr. Cassell could surely tell that Judge Hanson had had enough of his client's excuses. The mother had left her child in the care of her cousin and her cousin's husband for what was supposed to be a weekend, but no one had seen or heard from her for more than a week while she'd supposedly partied in Cancun.

"They're lying! I'd never abandon my baby!"

"Miss Reynolds, calm down!" Mr. Cassell hissed under his breath as he grabbed his semi-hysterical client's arm and pulled her back down into her seat. "Acting irrationally won't help your case. This is a temporary arrangement. Nothing permanent has been decided."

Even as inexperienced as he was, he must have known Judge Hanson had a bias against single mothers who neglected their children. His client most likely would not be getting her baby back. But as he glanced over at Miss Reynolds' cousin and her husband, sitting with their attorney at the table next to them, and witnessed the sly smile that passed between the couple, a chill went down his spine. His client was telling the truth.

And her baby had just been legally stolen.

2011
Twelve Years Later

The girl hurt everywhere. It even hurt to breathe. Warm blood trickled down her forehead. She tried to open her eyes, but even that slight gesture made the searing pain in her head worse. Muffled sounds floated around her like she was underwater. Breaking glass, screaming, music, more screaming...

No... not screaming exactly. A man was yelling. A woman was sobbing. She finally opened her eyes to see a woman leaning over her. Tears streaked the woman's swollen face. Just beyond her stood a man. His face was so contorted with rage that his neck veins bulged. He grabbed the woman by her hair, yanked her head violently backward and yelled in her face.

"This is all your fault!"

The girl tried to speak. She tried to reach out and stop the man from hurting the woman. But no words would come out. And then everything went black.

TWO

Enlightened Path Rehab Center

2023

It took two orderlies to subdue her. But who could blame her for putting up a fight? She'd been lured to the rehab facility under false pretenses. It hadn't been a complete lie because she did, in fact, get the tour of the facilities she was promised. She'd made polite small talk and admired the tennis courts, and the Olympic-size indoor swimming pool, and the massive vegetable garden. But when the time had come for her to leave, her phone, which the director had asked her to surrender upon arriving, for issues of privacy, hadn't been returned. It was only when they gave her a set of powder blue scrubs and slippers to change into that she realized, with horror, that they were not going to let her leave.

"Call my mom!" she screamed as she frantically fought to escape the grasp of the orderlies. "I don't belong here! I didn't agree to this!"

"Calm down, miss. This will all go so much smoother if you

quit fighting," said a female nurse in a deceptively calm voice that didn't match her hard eyes or tight smile.

"Don't touch me! I'm an adult! You can't do this to me!" She managed to get an arm free and swung her hand out, so it almost connected with the nurse's face, causing the woman to flinch and throw her arm up to shield herself. That's when she took out the hypodermic needle.

"Hold her still," commanded the nurse.

"Please don't do this!" she sobbed. The nurse ignored her and nodded to the two orderlies. They kicked the girl's feet out from under her and slammed her down onto the hard linoleum floor. "Call my mom! She'll tell you I don't belong here!"

"Honey," the nurse lifted her skirt and jammed the needle into the meat of her upper thigh, "who do you think admitted you?"

THREE
ADDISON, OHIO

Three Months Later

"What do you mean there's no money for my fellowship?" My throat was so dry the question had come out as a strangled squeak.

Eli Brogan, the Dean of Arts and Sciences at Bellbrook College, took a deep breath, then cleared his throat before answering.

"Because of unforeseen circumstances, the funds for the fellowship are no longer available." He was talking to me softly and slowly, like a doctor giving a patient a terminal diagnosis. Either that or he thought I was a total idiot. Brogan had a reputation for treating anyone without a PhD like a product of inbreeding.

"But... I... I don't understand," I persisted. "I thought Lena Bennett left the money to the college in her will to create the Bennett Fellowship. How can the money no longer be available?" I suddenly realized I'd been gripping the arms of the chair I was sitting in so hard my nails had left indentations in the leather.

"We got word just yesterday from Mrs. Bennett's lawyer that the fellowship won't be funded after all. Apparently, her widower is contesting her will and all of Mrs. Bennett's assets, including the money allocated for the fellowship endowment, were frozen."

"But—" I began feebly before he cut me off.

"I'm so sorry, Ms. Good, I wish there was something we could do, but this is a legal matter, and I'm afraid the college's hands are tied." He didn't look sorry. He looked like he wanted me gone and for this awkward conversation to be over and done with.

"What am I supposed to do?" My voice trailed off into a whisper because I already knew the answer to my question. I'd either have to come up with the money myself or drop out.

Fall semester at Bellbrook College, the small liberal arts college I attended in Addison, Ohio, started the week after next. It was too late to apply for another fellowship or even financial aid. To make matters worse, I'd just quit my library job, thinking the fellowship would pay my tuition and living expenses for the next two years while I worked on my master's degree in psychology. I'd even blown my savings by treating myself to a trip to Europe to celebrate being the first ever recipient of the Lena Bennett Memorial Fellowship. I was broke. I'd have to drop my classes, sit the semester out, and try to pull a financial miracle out of my ass before the start of the spring semester, which would put my perfectly laid out plans on hold for another year. Tears welled in my eyes. I couldn't help it. How could this be happening to me?

Dean Brogan's assistant poked her head into the office to tell him that his next appointment had arrived. He cleared his throat again and looked at the ornate silver clock on his desk. And then, to make sure I was getting the message, he glanced at the expensive gold watch on his wrist. My time was up – and in more ways than one.

On my way out, I passed by Brogan's next appointment who was sitting on the loveseat in the reception area, applying a thick coat of lip gloss. I took in her pink pixie haircut, magenta lips, and flawless brown skin. She wore workout clothes, a tight black sleeveless crop top and matching leggings with gold trainers and a leather Gucci fanny pack around her narrow waist. She looked familiar, but I couldn't quite remember where I'd seen her before. I was pretty sure she hadn't been in any of my classes because I would have noticed someone as gorgeous as her. She winked at me with a smile before standing and heading toward Brogan's office. It wasn't until I reached the front steps outside that I finally realized who she was. Mackenzie Burk. The *It Girl* of Bellbrook College, who documented her every move for her thousands of TikTok and Instagram followers. As I headed across campus, I wondered what it felt like to have such a wealthy family that you never had to worry about money.

I was so deep in thought about my troubles that I wasn't watching where I was going. So, it shouldn't have been a surprise when I rounded a corner and slammed into someone so hard I lost my balance. As I fell backward, I didn't think about hitting the pavement or how much it was going to hurt, or how embarrassed I'd be when my flowered skirt flew up, exposing the most boring panties on the planet. Instead, I hoped my meeting with Brogan had been a bad dream and that maybe hitting the ground would wake me up. Only, I didn't hit the ground because the person I'd ran into caught my arm and pulled me gently to an upright position.

"Easy," said a deep voice.

Suddenly, I was staring into a pair of warm brown eyes framed by laughter lines. My gaze traveled down to a smiling mouth of perfectly straight white teeth and a squared chin. He had dark bronze skin and thick, black hair that had just a hint of curl around his ears, both of which were pierced, with a silver hoop in one. Easily six two, he wore a pair of faded jeans and a black Henley shirt that was molded to his muscular arms and chest. He smiled at me, and a warm knot formed in the pit of my stomach.

"You okay?" he asked as I continued to gawk at him. Was he a student? I'd never seen him before. I'd remember if I had.

"Sorry," I said, flustered. "I didn't hurt you, did I?"

He must have thought my question was hysterical because he threw his head back and laughed so hard it annoyed me. But then again, I understood why he found it funny; short of shooting the man, I couldn't have put a mark on him.

"I think I'll live," he finally said. Then, noticing my red-rimmed eyes, he added, "Are you all right? You look a little shaky."

Of course I looked shaky. I just had the rug ripped out from under me. My life was in the toilet, and the last thing I had time for was small talk with a stranger, even a hot one.

"Sorry," I said again as I pushed past him. "I gotta go. But thanks for... um... catching me." As I rushed off across the college green, I heard him calling out.

"Hey! Can't I even get your name?"

Kendall, I wanted to yell back. But I thought better of it. Instead, I kept right on moving. He didn't need to know my name. I had a boyfriend. After the events of that morning, I may not have had much else, but at least I still had Byron.

"There has to be something you can do," said Liv as I sat slumped on a lumpy brown couch in the graduate students' office in Clayton Hall.

Olivia 'Liv' Bryant, a fellow psychology grad student, was the closest thing I had to a best friend. Liv was a GTA, a graduate teaching assistant for a member of the psychology faculty, and taught Psych 101. For this, she received a monthly stipend and free tuition. Not that she needed it. Her wealthy grand-mother had been paying her tuition since her freshman year. I'd been offered a GTA position as well but had been relieved to turn it down when I was awarded the Lena Bennett Fellowship. Plus, the thought of having to stand in front of a classroom full of freshmen and teach a class terrified me.

"It's too late to do anything," I wailed. "I'm screwed, Liv. I'm going to have to drop out."

Liv looked alarmed. She handed me a box of tissues, then watched as I blew my nose. Sitting in a leather-backed chair, she looked intense and cerebral as usual, with her long brown hair, bangs and black cat-eyed glasses. She wore a faded denim jump-suit with bright yellow platform high-tops. Liv always dressed like she was cosplaying the stylish older sister of Velma from *Scooby Doo*.

"Have you been to financial aid to see if there's some kind of emergency fund you can apply for?"

"Unless they have a fund with a hundred grand in it, they can't help me."

The Lena Bennett Memorial Fellowship was supposed to pay two years' worth of tuition at Bellbrook – which was thirty-five grand a year – plus living expenses. Nothing financial aid had to offer was going to help me out. I'd planned the next two years of my life around being the Lena Bennett Fellow. And now it was ruined. What was I going to do?

"How about talking to Mrs. Bennett's husband?" she offered.

"The man just wants his wife's money. He has no interest in helping me." Now I was lying down on the couch with the tissue box balanced across my chest.

"He might let you know what the status of his lawsuit is, so you'll know whether you should try to wait it out or make other arrangements."

Liv was just trying to be helpful, but I wasn't in the right frame of mind to appreciate it. All I wanted to do was be mad at the world and wallow in self-pity. But if I saw the world as a glass half-empty, Liv was the poster child for the glass half-full. She always saw the bright side of everything and planned on working with children with emotional problems after getting her masters.

"He'll probably just refer me to his lawyer, who'll tell me that because of the lawsuit, he can't give me any information."

"What about your mom?" she asked.

I didn't even want to think about asking my mom for the money. I'd gotten a small scholarship for my undergrad degree, but she'd paid for everything else, and she never missed an opportunity to remind me how she'd driven a fifteen-year-old car and hadn't taken a vacation for five years while I was in school.

"I know!" she said brightly when I didn't respond to her last suggestion. "Byron works at a bank. Why not get a loan? Then you could use the money you get from the fellowship to pay it back once Mrs. Bennett's estate is settled."

That didn't sound half bad. Though I wasn't thrilled about the idea of borrowing money, this option was at least worth checking out. I'd go home and cook Byron his favorite dinner, or more likely reheat leftovers from last night, and wait for him to get off work. Then I'd tell him what happened. Once it sank in that I'd now have to live with him for the unforeseeable future, making his very religious mom's head explode because we weren't married, he'd come up with a plan to solve my problem. Why hadn't I thought of it before? I sat up and handed Liv the tissue box.

"Thanks, Liv," I told her as I headed out the door.

"Keep me posted!" she called out after me.

. . .

On the walk home, I kept my head down so no one would see my puffy, tear-swollen eyes. Not that many people were around. The campus was still mostly deserted after summer break, and there were only a handful of clueless-looking freshmen wandering the college green having been dropped off early by their parents.

I live a block from campus in an apartment with Byron. This wasn't a permanent arrangement. I had a beautiful apartment picked out in a nearby Victorian mansion that had been converted into four units. My fellowship had meant I could afford the top floor unit overlooking the college green – a spacious one bedroom apartment with high ceilings and hardwood floors and an entire wall of bookshelves. I was supposed to move in this weekend. The thought of having to call the landlady to tell her I couldn't take the place made me cry again. The thought of having to call my mom to ask for money, if I couldn't get a loan, practically sent me into shock.

My mom and I have a strange relationship, which relies on me not rocking the boat of her carefully laid-out plans for me. She started bugging me to major in psychology when I was in high school, and I finally gave in during my junior year of college. The plan was I would finish graduate school and then join Mom in her occupational psychology practice, consulting with businesses all over the globe on how to hire the best people, before eventually taking over when she retired. Everything had been carefully planned out, and now I was looking at a least a yearlong setback. I already knew how she'd react when I told her. She'd sigh that heavy sigh of hers and tell me it wasn't my fault and not to worry. Then, in every conversation from then on, she'd casually mention how all her plans were ruined and how inconvenienced she was.

As I let myself into the apartment, this thought made me want to curl up in bed and never get up again. I hung my winter coat on the hook by the door and crossed the apartment to the bedroom. I was so wrapped up in my misery that it didn't occur to me to wonder why there were clothes all over the apartment floor, or why I smelled the familiar scent of Gucci *Guilty* perfume. I paused outside Byron's closed bedroom door and heard deep passionate moans of pleasure.

"What the hell?" I whispered as my whole body tensed. My hand trembled on the knob for only an instant before I turned it and flung the door wide open. The people in the bed were so wrapped up in their passion that they didn't realize I was there for what felt like a full minute.

"Kendall!" was all my man of three years could say when he finally noticed me standing open-mouthed in the doorway.

He'd spotted me in the mirror on the wall behind the bed. His companion was on her hands and knees and her long, shiny, dark weave fell into her face, obscuring it. But I already knew who she was. Byron's ex, Kayla Perkins, aka the chick he told me I didn't need to worry about.

Byron froze on the spot with his hands still gripping Kayla's hips. Kayla, wondering why he'd stopped pushing her toward the exquisite orgasm she was about to have, looked over at the door through the veil of her hair. Her eyes widened in surprise. She immediately pulled away from Byron and rolled over, pulling the sheet – my sheet that I'd bought on sale at Target the last time Byron and I had gone shopping – up over her big boobs.

"Shit!" was all she said. But whether she meant *shit, I just got caught fucking my ex-boyfriend*, or *shit, I didn't get to come*, I'll never know.

"What the fuck, Byron?" I said in a voice shaky with anger.

They just looked at each other and then back at me. I balled my fists so tightly I was sure I'd cut my palm with my nails. Closing my eyes, I took a deep breath, hoping maybe it was just a bad dream. How much more messed up could this day get? But when I opened them, Byron and Kayla were still there; only

Byron had now put on a pair of jeans that had been lying on the floor.

Nobody said anything. Neither of them offered so much as an explanation, or tried to convince me it wasn't what it looked like.

"Kendall, I'm so sorry," said Byron, coming toward me. I backed away and rushed out the door.

Kayla stayed behind, still undressed, lying in the same bed I'd rolled out of not two hours before.

"I swear I never meant for you to find out like this. I was going to tell you tonight."

"How long?" I demanded. My voice was thick with tears.

"Kendall, I..." he began before I cut him off.

"*How long?*" I insisted.

"Two months," answered Kayla, appearing in the living room, still wrapped in a sheet. While she looked a little embarrassed, she hardly looked ashamed or remorseful, and why would she? She'd made no secret of the fact that she wanted Byron back.

"You've been lying to my face for two months!"

Byron took a step toward me. "We never planned this, it just happened," he insisted in a low, calm voice, like he was afraid I'd explode.

Three years of dating and he didn't know me well enough to know I never exploded. I might raise my voice and cry a lot. But explode? Never. I didn't have it in me to lose control like that. I'd suck up the pain, saving it for later when I could write it all down in my diary. My mom had given me a diary at thirteen to write all my messy, negative thoughts and emotions that she didn't have the time or desire to deal with. I was now twenty-four years old and was on my eleventh diary.

"You two make me sick." My voice sounded so hollow I didn't even recognize it.

I turned to go and caught a flash of emotion on Kayla's face.

It wasn't a look of remorse. It was a look of pity. This bitch felt sorry for me. The strength of that look propelled me out the door.

From the diary of Kendall Good:

April 4, 2011

Dear Diary,

My name is Kendall Good and today is my birthday. I'm 13 years old, and my mom gave me this diary because she's tired of me talking about my dad and everything else she doesn't want to hear about. Ever since my accident, she's been so weird. Maybe it was because I was in a coma for three days. But who knows? All I know is that now I get to talk to you. Today my dad's been in prison for a month, and Mom still won't take me to see him. She says he doesn't want to see me, and I should just forget about him. But I don't believe her. He would never forget my birthday. Never. But don't worry. I'm going to write everything down so I don't forget and when I finally see Dad, I will tell him everything.

FOUR

ADDISON, OHIO

The next morning, when I arrived back at Byron's apartment to get my things, I was relieved to find he wasn't there, and the only trace of Kayla was the scent of her expensive perfume. I'd booked a room for two nights at campus guest housing, but I didn't know where I was going to live when those two days were up.

I got busy packing, ignoring the still rumpled, unmade bed and my memories of the day before. Bending down to retrieve the box I kept my diaries in, I spied something under the bed. It was a gold bangle bracelet. The bands of the bracelet met on either side of a heart-shaped ring in the middle. It had to have been Kayla's because it sure as hell wasn't mine. At least it wasn't until now. I slipped it into the pocket of my sweatpants without a second thought. Some people eat when they're stressed, others drink. Me? I steal shit. Normally, it's nothing too valuable, always small things that I could quickly and easily put into my purse or pocket. Things people rarely miss right away, if at all. But this bracelet was beautiful and looked expensive, and I'm sure Kayla would miss it, and I was happy to cause her a bit of distress.

The last time I stole anything was a year ago. My mother wanted me to quit my library job to come home and work for her, completing my master's part-time at the college in my hometown. We had a raging argument, during which she called me ungrateful and lazy, claiming I enjoyed working at the library because it was unchallenging. I stormed out, drove to Walmart and stole a pair of earrings. I instantly felt better, then came home and confessed in my journal. Applying for the Bennett fellowship was a desperate act to keep myself from being under my mother's thumb for at least two more years. I was stunned when they chose me and even more stunned now that the party was over before it had even begun. I needed a plan B that didn't involve selling feet pics.

As I cleared all my stuff from the bathroom cabinet, I spied Byron's blue toothbrush in the holder. Feeling petty as fuck, I took his toothbrush and scrubbed the toilet with it before drying it off with his towel and putting it back in the holder. I hoped he'd get some kind of horrific bacterial disease that would rot his teeth out of his lying mouth, but not before passing it on to Kayla. The thought of them both toothless made me grin.

I was finished packing in no time. Everything I owned fit neatly into two large suitcases. I didn't even have a car since I'd been planning to buy a used one with some of the fellowship money. I was lugging my suitcases through the door of the apartment when Kayla showed up, probably looking for the bracelet that was now burning a hole in my pocket.

She leaned against the hallway wall, a blank expression on her face while she watched me struggle with the suitcases. She looked as perfect as she always did, wearing black skintight jeans, high-heeled sandals and a baggy leopard print shirt that hung off one shoulder, exposing perfect golden skin. Even though I'd showered and changed, my gray sweats hung off me like elephant skin and my hair was pulled into a bushy topknot.

"You know this is all your fault," she said matter-of-factly.

Instantly, I dropped the suitcases, not believing I'd heard her right.

"What did you just say?"

"You heard exactly what I said. This is your fault." She tossed a lock of her long hair over her shoulder.

"You screw my boyfriend and it's all my fault?"

"When was the last time you screwed him? When was the last time you cooked for him or asked him about his day and really listened to what he had to say? When was the last time you played hooky and stayed in bed all day making love, or went away for the weekend, or took a drive in the country?"

"None of that makes it my fault," I blurted. But did I really believe it? Was it really my own fault?

Byron and I were busy people. His job had him working sixty-hour weeks, and when I wasn't busy working every hour I could at the library, I'd been studying for the GRE to get into grad school. We barely saw each other, but we both knew it wouldn't be like that forever. Hadn't we? Or maybe I was the one who thought that way.

"Get out of my way, Kayla." I grabbed the suitcases again and tried to brush past her.

She laughed and my face burned. "I knew this was how things were going to be when you found out. You'd never see what you'd done wrong to bring this on yourself."

Anger bubbled up in my chest. "Get out of my way."

"I'm not in your way. You're in your own way. You practically handed Byron to me on a silver platter. Look at you. Why wouldn't he cheat on you when you dress like you're collecting for a church can drive?"

At that, I dropped the suitcases again, and before I could stop myself, my hand swung out and cracked her hard against the side of her face. The sound echoed in the narrow hallway. Her hand flew to her cheek in shock. I stepped right up to her, backing her against the wall, and got in her face.

"You want Byron. He's all yours. I wouldn't take him back if you put a gun to my head," I spat out in a venomous voice I didn't recognize. "He stuck his dick in toxic waste when he fucked you, and now he's damaged goods."

To my surprise, Kayla scurried off, nearly tripping in her heels with her hand still pressed to her face.

"You're a crazy bitch!" she called out once she'd gotten far enough away.

And she was right; I was crazy. Crazy for ever trusting another man after my father hurt me. It wasn't a mistake I would make again.

Hours later, my hand was still sore from where I'd slapped Kayla. Smacking the gloss off her lips should have made me feel better, but somehow, I felt worse. I was Kendall Good, future psychologist, not some reality show contestant brawling over a man for fifteen minutes of fame. Besides, if anyone needed the snot slapped out of them, it was Byron.

Had it really been my fault they'd hooked up behind my back? Had I really been neglecting Byron that much? True, it had been about a month since we'd made love, and I'll never claim to be the world's greatest in bed. Byron was my first, and I still felt a little uncomfortable doing certain things. It had only been in the last year that I could do it with the lights on without feeling self-conscious. But Kayla hadn't been self-conscious. The image of Byron taking her from behind while she moaned like a porn star would be forever burned into my retinas and imprinted on my eardrums.

I couldn't change what had happened between Byron and Kayla, but there was one thing I could do. Slinking back to ask for my old job at the library after I'd left riding high on the wave of the Bennett Fellowship was embarrassing. I felt like a colossal failure, but I couldn't worry about what people would think now. I had to keep moving, and the only way to do that was to work out an alternate plan. If I could get my old job back, at least I'd have an income. Maybe I could take one graduate-level class and not have to drop out entirely. Maybe I could even afford the apartment I was supposed to be moving into this weekend. I was feeling more confident until I arrived at the library.

"I am so sorry, Kendall," said Mrs. Tate, my old supervisor. "But we've already filled your position. Your replacement started today. If I'd known what happened, I might have been able to rehire you, but it's just not possible now." She seemed very sorry, which somehow made it even worse.

I'd quit last week, and they'd already replaced me? I hoped this wouldn't become the story of my life. First Byron and now this.

"That's okay." I forced a smile. "I knew it was a long shot, but I just had to check." I got up to go, and she followed me out of her small office.

"Keep checking back, I may have something for you next semester."

"Thanks, Mrs. Tate. I appreciate you keeping me in mind."

"Of course. You were easily one of our best workers. We could always count on you, Kendall. You were one of the few people who would drop everything and be here at a moment's notice."

And just look where that had gotten me, I thought as I walked down the library steps. To my surprise, Liv was heading up. Her face lit up when she spotted me. I wanted to go back to the guest dorm and cry, but she insisted on buying me a latte at the B&C café on campus.

"Well?" she said once we'd settled at a table at the small café at the bottom of the steps. "How'd it go with Byron?"

"It didn't," I replied flatly, and then explained what had happened since I'd seen her last.

Liv's eyes grew big and round behind her glasses. Today's glasses were pink with rhinestones to match her hot pink high-heeled ankle boots. Whenever I got some money, I needed to rethink my footwear.

"That grimy shit stain!" Liv exclaimed, not bothering to lower her voice. Good old Liv. I knew I could count on her for some righteous indignation to make me feel justified in my murderous thoughts. "And why didn't you call me? You know you can stay at my place, right?"

She meant well, and the thought had crossed my mind, but Liv's place was a cramped studio apartment that she shared with Spanky, her French bulldog, and a boa constrictor named Spike. I'd either have to share the futon with her and Spanky or sleep in a sleeping bag on the floor under Spike's tank.

"Thanks for the offer. But I'll figure something out."

"Like what?" Liv persisted, and I felt myself getting annoyed with her before quickly realizing she was one of only a few people in my corner right now. I gave her a big smile.

"That, my friend, is the million-dollar question."

"I still say you should talk to Mrs. Bennett's husband. If you threaten to sue and make a big stink, he might figure out a way to fund the fellowship just to get rid of you."

"I don't think it would be that easy. Besides, I don't have money for a lawyer," I said, uneasy at the thought of a legal confrontation.

"I didn't say to actually sue him. I said to threaten a lawsuit." Liv must have noticed my flushed face and instantly looked contrite. "I'm sorry, Kendall. This is just so messed up." She sat back in her chair, with a disgusted expression. "I want to bitch-slap Lena Bennett's greedy-ass husband and kick Byron's balls through the roof of his mouth."

I let out a loud snort of laughter at the thought of Liv's pink boot connecting with Byron's crotch. Finally, something I agreed with her about.

"Well, enough about me and my pathetic problems. What's going on with you?"

"Not a lot." Liv shrugged. "Just getting ready for the new semester and then heading home this weekend to be with my mom. It's the anniversary of Dad's death, and she always has a hard time with it. Which reminds me." She jumped from the table. "I need to go home and pack. Promise me you'll keep me posted?"

"I will," I promised and watched her go, envious of the close bond she shared with her mother.

After Liv left, I sat in the café and nursed my iced matcha latte until the ice had melted as multiple notifications popped up on my phone, showing various bills hitting my bank account. After paying for guest housing and a few meals, my account had exactly $72 in it that morning and now had an overdraft of more than $200. I was supposed to receive my first installment of $50,000 from the Bennett Fellowship the day before Dean Brogan had broken the bad news. I could feel the latte curdling in my stomach as panic tap-danced up my spine. The old scar along my hairline throbbed, signaling the beginning of a raging headache. I retrieved my migraine medicine from my purse and popped two pills in my mouth, washing them down with a swig of my watery latte. That's when the call I was dreading came in, and I reluctantly answered it.

"Hello."

"Kendall?" came the voice of a woman.

"Hi, Mrs. Reinhart, this is Kendall."

"Kendall, the check for your first and last month's rent and deposit bounced, and I need to know if you're going to take the apartment."

"I am so sorry, Mrs. Reinhart. There's been a mistake with my account and I'm trying to get it fixed as soon as possible." Why was I lying to this woman? There was no money forth-coming to cover any of my incoming expenses, let alone the twenty-five-hundred-dollar check I'd given Mrs. Reinhart two days ago when I was still the Lena Bennett Fellow. I should have stopped payment on the check immediately following my meeting with Dean Brogan. But after what had happened with Byron, I'd totally forgotten about it.

"I'm sorry, Kendall. You seem like a nice person, but I have a long waiting list for the apartment, and unless you can bring me the cash within the hour, I'm going to have to give it to the next person on the list."

"That won't be possible. I'm sorry for the inconvenience." I told her, trying to keep the tears out of my voice.

"Would you like me to add your name back to the list when it becomes available in the future?"

"That would be great. Thanks, Mrs. Reinhart," I told her and hung up as the reality that I was officially homeless finally hit me.

What the hell was I going to do? I needed a job. And I needed it now. I noticed a HELP WANTED sign next to the café's register and was about to get up to go to ask for an application when a pretty brown-skinned girl with a pink pixie cut slid into Liv's recently vacated seat. She wore ripped denim shorts so short the pockets hung out of the bottoms and a red and white short-sleeved Cincinnati Reds jersey knotted at the waist. White Nike slides showed off her metallic black toenail polish and a large tattoo of the number fourteen almost covered her right thigh. It was Mackenzie Burk. I wasn't surprised she'd grabbed my table before I'd even left; the café had filled up in the hour I'd been sitting here, and there were no available tables. Still, I was annoyed she couldn't have waited a few more seconds until I was gone. I'm not sure what look I gave her, but she burst out laughing, making my cheeks flush with embarrassment.

"Chill, sis." She slung a quilted red Chanel backpack under

the table. "I just came over to see if you were okay. You're Kendall, right?"

"Uh, yeah," I replied, looking around because I wasn't sure she'd been talking to me even though she'd just said my name. "Have we met?"

"Don't move. I'll be right back." She reached down to pull a wallet from her backpack. "If I don't get some caffeine in me right now, I'll be a zombie for the rest of the day."

I looked at her properly and noticed she looked tired, probably from all the partying she did. If I were to pull up her Instagram or TikTok accounts, I'm sure they'd show curated pics of whatever she'd been up to last night, and she'd look fabulous in all of them. As she headed up to the counter to place her order, I saw the name Burk in big red letters as well as the number 14 on the back of her jersey. It must have been her father's number when he'd been an outfielder for the Reds.

Mackenzie Burk was the only child of Marcus and Blessing Burk. Marcus had turned his salary from one season playing with the Reds before a back injury ended his career into a luxury car empire. Burk's Luxury Auto Mall had locations in every major city in Ohio and a few in Indiana. His wife, Blessing, a former Grammy-winning gospel singer, was the daughter of Pastor Augustus Grimes, head of Blood of Christ Ministries, a mega church in Columbus. Mackenzie had grown up with money, and it showed in the way she'd tossed a backpack that probably cost a few grand under the table like it was a plastic grocery bag. How did I know all of this about a chick I didn't know? Because I was one of her many followers on TikTok and Instagram, or at least I used to be.

After living by my mother's strict rules until college, I went a bit wild my freshman year, partying and bar hopping most nights of the week, not because I enjoyed it, but because I could finally breathe. And because I was trying to emulate what I saw the

Mackenzie Burks of the world doing online, I ended my first semester at Bellbrook with a 2.4 grade point average. My mother was incandescent with rage. I was told I had spring semester to turn it around or she would not only stop paying my tuition, but I'd have to work for her to pay back the money she had already paid. There was no way I was going to let her pull me out of school. So, I got busy. I ditched the party girls and befriended Liv. I got a job at the library and buried myself in my studies. And more importantly, I abandoned all my social media accounts. By the end of the fall semester the following year, I was on the dean's list.

Still, from what I remember, Mackenzie may be a hard-partying rich girl, but she was never boring. Her social feeds consisted of luxury clothing hauls, learning to surf in Bali, exploring the Paris catacombs, partying in clubs in South Korea, and doing yoga on the summit at Machu Picchu. For someone like me whose whole life revolved around not taking too many risks and trying to make my mother happy, her life was #goals.

"Here." She snapped me out of my thoughts as she put a fresh iced matcha latte in front of me before taking a seat. "You look like you need it."

"Thanks." I took a small sip to show I was grateful. But I was still confused. How in the world did Mackenzie Burk know who the hell I was? We didn't exactly travel in the same circles.

We sipped our drinks in silence for a minute, and I was aware of eyes on us. Mackenzie, aka Mac, attracted attention wherever she went. And today was no exception. People were glancing over at her and whispering to each other and pointing. But, if the attention was bothering her, I couldn't tell.

"You never said if you were okay." She'd already sucked down half her iced double espresso. The shot of caffeine must have done the trick because she was sitting up straighter and looking more alert.

"And you never said how you know me." I tried to give her a smile but only ended up grimacing.

"Hello? We met in Brogan's office yesterday. Remember?" She tilted her head to one side, looking at me like I was slow.

"I remember passing you on my way out. But we never met. How do you even know my name?"

"Don't get mad." She laughed, which immediately told me I was about to be mad. "But when I got to Brogan's office for my appointment, I had to pee. So, I used the restroom right next to his office, and when I was in there, I overheard what he told you." She gave me a sheepish look as she drained the rest of her drink.

"You mean you eavesdropped?" I sat back in my chair as blood rushed to my face and pounded in my ears. At this point, I wanted nothing more than to bolt, but I wouldn't give her the satisfaction. Why was she telling me this? Had this chick who'd never had to worry about money a day in her life come to gloat over my no good, very bad day?

"No!" she insisted, throwing her hands up, probably to shield herself from the venomous look I was giving her, before lowering her voice. "I was just sitting there peeing and minding my own business and I could hear your conversation through the vent in the wall."

"*And?*"

"And that was seriously fucked up how they did you."

To her credit, she looked genuinely sorry for me. But it was still embarrassing and still none of her business. And it didn't answer my question. "How did you find out my name?"

"From the sign-in sheet on Brogan's admin assistant's desk."

"Okay," I said slowly, still eyeing her skeptically. "But why do you care how I'm doing? You don't even know me."

Mac looked around the room before leaning forward and whispering, "Because I think we can help each other out."

"How?" What the hell was she talking about?

She didn't respond right away. Instead, she let out a heavy sigh and pulled a pen from a pocket in her backpack. She scribbled something on a napkin, then shoved it across the table at me before getting up. It was an address and phone number. "I can't talk about this here. But come by my house for dinner tonight around eight, please. I promise it'll be worth it."

She got up, turned on her heel, and left before I could tell her no. Mackenzie Burk didn't strike me as the kind of person who heard that word often – and she clearly didn't want to hear it from me.

From the diary of Kendall Good:

October 13, 2011

Dear Diary,

I got into a fight at school today and I got sent home. But it wasn't my fault. Cinda Patterson lost her stupid butterfly ring in gym class. She told everyone I took it because my dad is a criminal and that means I'm one too. So I punched her in the stomach. And I don't feel bad about it because she deserved it. She pulled my hair, and I slapped her face, and then it was on. Miss Farrelli broke it up and sent us to the office. Cinda cried like a baby the minute our parents showed up. Big fat faker. We both have detention every day next week and Mom is mad. She won't talk to me or look at me. She never even asked me why we were fighting. She doesn't care. I miss my dad so much it hurts. Why won't she let me see him?

PS: I did steal Cinda's ring, and I'm not giving it back.

FIVE

ADDISON, OHIO

Mackenzie Burk lived in an apartment two blocks from campus on a quiet, tree-lined street. It was a squat, square red-brick building with a flat roof divided into six units, and it didn't look like it belonged amongst the turn-of-the-century mansions that lined either side of the block.

I stood in front of the burgundy door of Mackenzie's ground-floor apartment at 8:05 p.m. My fist was raised, poised to knock, as I wondered what I was doing here, when she whipped the door open, startling me.

"Hey, thanks for coming, Kendall." She stepped aside so I could enter and then quickly glanced up and down the street before closing the door. "Where'd you park?"

"I walked. I'm between cars at the moment." This made her smile, and I wondered again for the millionth time why she'd invited me here.

I followed her through a narrow foyer into a brightly lit and airy living room with white walls and shiny hardwood floors and barely anything else. Against one wall was a vintage-looking blue brocade couch opposite a metal rack full of clothing. On the coffee table sat an open laptop, and a glance at the screen showed editing software. A camera mounted on a tripod with a ring light faced a freestanding full-length mirror with gilded trim. There were no rugs on the floor. No books. No plants. No pictures on the walls, not even a flat screen TV. And from the looks of it, she only used this room for work. I smelled the aroma of food and glanced around briefly, hoping she hadn't heard my stomach growl.

"Sorry about the mess. I was filming some clothing hauls."

"If you think this is a mess, you should see my place." I had no place. Not anymore. But somehow, I didn't want her to know that. I already felt sure she'd invited me to dinner because she felt sorry for me, and I didn't need to add to her pity by letting her know I was currently homeless.

"I didn't think you were going to come." She headed into the kitchen, and I followed behind. "I hope you like Thai food."

"I almost didn't come, and I love Thai food."

The kitchen was tiny with outdated white appliances and a small table. Sitting on it were food bags I recognized from a local Thai restaurant. She began pulling cartons and then looked at me with horror.

"Oh my God. You're not vegan, are you? Because I can order something different if you are."

"No," I assured her because she seemed suddenly nervous. "This looks great."

We sat down at the table and began spooning food onto our plates. I was starving since I hadn't eaten all day. Truth be told, I'd only showed up for the free meal, since the $2.78 in my purse wouldn't even buy me a Happy Meal. I had devoured half of my Pad Thai and was spooning coconut chicken curry into my mouth when I noticed that Mackenzie had barely touched her food. I slid my plate away. I'd been avoiding the inevitable long enough; now I needed to know why she'd summoned me to her place. Her discomfort was telling me this wasn't about her feeling sorry for me.

"So, what's this all about?"

She put her fork down. "I know why you were in Brogan's office yesterday. But you didn't ask me why I was there. Aren't you curious?"

It never occurred to me to wonder why Mackenzie Burk had an appointment with the Dean of Arts and Sciences. I had my own issues to worry about.

"I was preoccupied."

"Yeah," she said, giving me an embarrassed look. "Sorry."

"So, why were you there?"

"I was there because I needed to get Brogan's permission to retake a class I flunked last semester. I'm on academic probation."

I have no clue what I had expected her to say, but I certainly hadn't expected her to say that. It really shouldn't have surprised me because, as I remembered from when I kept up with her social media, her life was all parties and clothes and travel.

"Wow," was all I could manage because I didn't really know what else to say.

I will admit to experiencing a small sense of satisfaction that this rich girl's life wasn't as perfect as it seemed. I might have been homeless and about to drop out of all my fall semester classes, but at least I had a perfect 4.0 grade point average. Not that it was going to pay my rent or buy me some food in the immediate future. "And how'd it go?"

"Brogan agreed because he had no choice. My father donates a lot of money to this school, and if I flunked out, the college is SOL."

"But what does any of this have to do with me?" Was she bragging to my broke ass to make herself feel better?

Mackenzie stared at me for a few seconds before getting up and going into the living room. She came back and sat down, put an envelope on the table and shoved it across at me.

"Go ahead." She gestured for me to pick up the envelope. I did so reluctantly, then looked inside and almost dropped it. It contained a thick stack of one hundred-dollar bills. I looked at her in alarm.

"It's $10,000 to start. Then I can pay you two grand a month for the rest of the school year. It's not what you would have gotten from your fellowship, but it's the best I can do."

"For what? Why are you handing me all this money?" I stared at the envelope for a long time. I'd never seen so much money in my life and holding it made me instantly wary.

"Look." Mackenzie got up from the table. She was agitated, wringing her hands as she spoke. "I have to graduate next spring. My entire future depends on it."

"And I still don't understand what this has to do with me. What are you giving me money for?"

"Seriously?" She gave me an incredulous look, like I was the stupidest person on the planet. "Why are you asking me all these questions when it's obvious I need your help."

I must have been in a food coma or maybe I *was* just stupid because it took me several long seconds to realize what she was asking me or rather, paying me to do.

"You want me to take your class for you?"

"Yes. It's online, and it doesn't meet every day. We're talking a couple of hours of work per week and you're a grad student. It should be a piece of cake for you."

"And you can't take your own damn class because...?"

"Are you kidding me? I didn't even want to come to college. I didn't need to come to college. Do you know how many brands are chasing me down for collabs and deals? I haven't had to pay for my own clothes, makeup, or travel since before my freshman year."

"Then why are you even here?"

"Because my dad told me that unless I got a college degree, he was cutting me off financially."

I closed my eyes and rubbed my temples. "And why do you need his money if you've got it going on and everyone's chasing you down to work with them?"

She rolled her eyes, clearly annoyed that I wasn't falling in line with her a little scheme.

"I make decent money being an influencer, but there are things I want to do with my life that I need big investors for."

"Such as?"

"Burk Beauty," she said proudly. "I want my own fashion and makeup brand. My dad said he'd invest. And if Marcus Burk invests, then other investors will be easier to come by. But only if I graduate next spring with a business degree. If I flunk out, I'm on my own."

Like all the rest of us, I thought bitterly. "Why not get a business loan? Why depend on him at all?" I saw the irony of advising her to get a loan when less than twenty-four hours ago Liv had suggested the same thing to me. I'd probably given her the same annoyed look Mac was giving me now.

"I don't want some tired ass small business loan with high interest rates when I could pull in investors. My dad's influential and having him in my corner would make the difference between Burk Beauty merely existing on a shoestring budget or *thriving*."

"You're talking about just one class, right?" I immediately realized my mistake in asking this question. The hope in her eyes and the smile that lit up her face made me cringe.

I should have left before this chick got me expelled on top of every other shitty thing that had happened to me recently. But I won't lie. Being the broke bitch that I currently was, the sight of all those hundred-dollar bills was casting a spell on me big time, and my bank overdraft had climbed to $640.

"I'm proposing a semester-by-semester arrangement."

Now it was my turn to get up and start pacing. I couldn't believe I was considering this, but at the same time, it didn't hurt to weigh all my options, of which there were few. "If you don't have the money to start your own business, where are you getting the money you're offering me now?" I gestured toward the bulging envelope on the kitchen table.

"Come with me." She headed out of the kitchen, and I followed her around the corner and up a flight of carpeted stairs to the second floor.

The second floor showed more personality than the first. The hall was painted black like the kitchen cabinets. Gold lighting fixtures were mounted along the walls, highlighting photos of Mac as a chubby-cheeked baby and of her high school graduation. I noticed there was only one picture of her with her parents, which hung at the end of the hall. As I got closer, I realized it wasn't a photograph but a painted family portrait, with Mac's parents sat in black leather high-backed throne chairs. Mac looked about fourteen and sat between her parents on a golden stool, staring straight forward and not smiling. Her hair was in an elaborate updo of tiny gold beaded braids like a crown. Her dress was black with a high waist and short-puffed sleeves that seemed too old for her, while on her feet were gold high-top Converse tennis shoes.

Her mother, Blessing, also sported long thin gold beaded braids, but hers fell past her shoulders. Her black halter neck dress was long, with a slit up the side showing off an abundance of toned thigh and her four-inch gold platform pumps. The plunging neckline of her dress was surprising for a gospel singer. A ruby and gold tiara sat atop her head and the knowing smirk on her bright red lips gave the impression she knew a secret no one else knew. In keeping with the black and gold theme, Marcus Burk's suit was also black, and he wore a gold shirt open almost to the waist, revealing a thick gold link chain resting against his light brown, muscular chest. A gold crown sat askew on his bald head. His solemn expression and heavy-lidded eyes made me wonder if he was high when the picture was taken, or just bored. For the first time, I noticed that Mac's hands rested stiffly on top of each of her parents' hands.

"I call this my 'blink if you need help' painting." Mac stood beside me.

"Well, it's... um..." My voice trailed off and Mac finished my thought.

"Pretentious as fuck? Sad? Soulless? Trying too hard? *The Addams Family* meets *Game of Thrones*?"

I couldn't help but smile. "I was going to say interesting."

"Liar," she said with a humorless laugh. "And it's okay. I know it's horrible. My mom decided she wanted to help me decorate, but we don't have the same taste." She brushed a speck of dust from the gold frame. "I'd only let her do the hallway, and she brought this from home where it used to hang in the first-floor bathroom because my father hates it, too, and said the only way he can look at it is if he's taking a shit."

I burst out laughing without meaning to, making Mac smile as well.

"This mausoleum-look isn't my vibe at all, but it made her happy."

We stared at the picture for a few seconds before I asked, "Is this what you brought me up here to show me?"

"No. Sorry. This is." She opened the door to the left of the portrait, and I followed her into a large walk-in closet. I gasped and Mac looked pleased.

"Go ahead. You can look around."

Unlike the dark hallway, this space was bright and decorated in cream and blush striped wallpaper with flecks of gold glitter. The shelving unit built into the wall held clothing arranged by color. There was even a separate section for hats and belts. Three rows of shelving underneath displayed shoes. On the top shelf were heels, the middle row held casual shoes, sandals, and flats, while the bottom row stored trainers. None of it looked like it had come from Target where I shopped. Many of the clothes still had tags on them showing prices that made my head spin.

In the adjoining room was a queen-sized bed with an abundance of pillows of different shades and sizes.

"I flipped the room," Mac said, looking around proudly. "My bed is where the closet used to be, and all this space out there was the bedroom."

"And your landlord let you do all of this?"

"My landlord is my dad. He owns the building. So, yeah. Anything to make his little girl happy," she concluded dryly.

But I'd stopped listening to her the second I noticed the wall of designer purses. Besides the red Chanel backpack I'd seen her with earlier, I recognized a brown Ralph Lauren Ricky bag, a black and tan Dior saddle bag, a burgundy Prada mini handbag, and a gray Celine luggage bag. There must have been at least three dozen bags totaling well over $100k, but the star of the show sat in the middle shelf compartment.

"Is this what I think it is?"

"If you think it's a Birkin, then yes, it's what you think it is." Mac walked over and took the black bag down from the shelf and handed it to me. "Go ahead. It won't bite you," she said when I hesitated.

I'm not sure what I thought was going to happen when I took the Birkin from her, but it felt just like a regular bag. In fact, it was just like holding a purse I'd bought from a thrift store.

Mac smiled. "You're holding my first lesson in investing in your hands."

"What do you mean?"

"My mom gave me that bag for my high school graduation present. She was on a waiting list for two years to get it. And being the spoiled bougie bitch I've always been, I was mad at her because I'd wanted a Tesla and instead, I got a purse that cost more than most people's car."

I could have told her I'd gotten luggage from my mom for my high school graduation. Not just a practical gift, but a message that I wasn't going to lie around her house doing nothing with my life. She expected me to leave and make something of myself. But I kept that story to myself and let Mac finish hers.

"Mom let me pout for a few days before she finally pulled me aside and explained why she'd given me the Birkin."

"Which was?"

"A car loses its value the minute it's driven off the lot. I'd never get out of it what was paid for it. But a Birkin holds its value. In fact, they grow in value, and a woman should always be able to get her hands on ready cash at any moment."

"Makes good sense." I felt stupid for having put all my eggs in one basket with the Bennett Fellowship, and yet I was confused why she was telling me all of this.

"There have been a few times since I got this bag that I needed to get my hands on some cash in a hurry. This Birkin is a fake because my mom likes to pop in unexpectedly and I didn't want her to know that I'd sold the original."

And that's when it finally hit me. "You sold your Birkin to pay me to take your class for you. Are you crazy?"

"I'm paying you for your time and your expertise and that's worth something. And don't get your panties in a knot, sis. This is the second time I've sold that Birkin."

I gaped at her, too incredulous to speak.

"My dad lets me live here for free and he gives me an allowance and pays for my tuition and books, but everything else I want is on me. I've sold all these bags at least once. And then as soon as I get the money, I buy it back or I get a replacement."

"Are all these bags fake?"

"A few of them are. But the only one I need to always have on display is the Birkin because it was a gift from my mother, and she'd ask too many questions about why I'd sold it."

"And she's never noticed?"

"She has no reason to look that closely, and I buy good fakes. Even some experts can't tell the difference."

I handed her back the Birkin, and she put it back in its place on the shelf. "Do you need some time to think about it?" She gave me a hopeful look, and I glanced away. This was such a colossally bad idea. We could both be expelled from college, or worse, be charged with fraud.

"I'm sorry, Mac. I just can't help you out." I walked out of the room and headed down the stairs.

"It's not just the money I'm offering you," she said in a frantic voice as she trailed behind me.

I stopped and turned to look at her, eyebrows raised. "What?"

She opened the door at the end of a hallway and gestured for me to come look. Reluctantly, I headed back up the steps and joined her in the doorway of a large bedroom.

"Earlier today I overheard your conversation with your friend. I'm not just offering you a job. I'm offering you a place to live rent-free. You can come and go as you please, and you don't have to worry about me bothering you. As long as you give me space to do my thing, I'll give you space to do yours. The only thing I ask is that you don't bring dudes here."

I was confused. She was making this sound way simpler than it was. My college career meant everything to me, and she was offering to pay me to commit academic fraud. My masters was my stepping-stone to the future I wanted.

"Sorry. I need to get out of here." I rushed back to the stairs, down the hallway and was halfway out the front door when Mac caught up with me.

"Can you at least think about it? Please, Kendall, I need your help."

Mac must've mastered the art of getting her own way because I could feel myself wavering. I had to get out of that apartment so I could think straight. My answer hadn't changed, but I couldn't bear to hear her pleading. So I took the coward's way out.

"I promise I'll think about it and let you know." Translation: *I'll tell you no again in a text and then block you.*

She merely nodded and let me leave, which I did without a backward glance.

Instead of going back to my room at guest housing, I swung by Byron's apartment. I still had my mail key, and since I had no intention of ever talking to him again, I wasn't about to ask him to bring me my mail. I was about to insert my key into the mailbox for apartment 18B, when I heard familiar voices and ducked behind the vending machines. I peeked around the corner to see Byron and Kayla arguing by the elevator.

"Why would she steal your bracelet? That doesn't sound like something Kendall would do," insisted Byron.

"Well, she took it. I left it on your nightstand the other night and now it's gone, and I met her coming out of your apartment and then she assaulted me. I should have called the police. I still might."

"Come on, Kayla. We're talking about Kendall. The chick is so uptight, the only way she can express herself is in a damned diary. You want to me to believe mousy ass Kendall clocked you in the face?" Their voices faded as they stepped into the elevator and the doors closed behind them.

My face burned with embarrassment and tears pricked my eyes. How could I have been so wrong about the man I'd been in a three-year relationship with? Had he always been an asshole and I'd been in denial? Or did he turn into a bastard because he was involved with that bitch? He was wrong, in any case. I wasn't repressed. I was controlled. I was also tired. I quickly retrieved the only piece of mail in the box that had been for me, a small manila envelope with no return address. On my way out, I tore it open and pulled out a single item.

It was a faded 4x6 photo of a tall handsome man holding a little girl of about three. The man wore a brown suit, and the little girl wore a yellow Easter dress with white rabbits frolicking around the hem. It was a picture of my father and me.

It slipped out of my suddenly nerveless fingers and fluttered to the pavement. I couldn't breathe and sank down to sit on the top step, wondering how the man who'd almost killed me had found out where I lived.

From the diary of Kendall Good:

December 10, 2011

Dear Diary,

I tried to go see Dad. I used my birthday money to buy a bus ticket to Lucasville. I was just going to see him and then come home. But Mom found me at the bus station and dragged me home. She screamed at me the entire ride home and I screamed back. I told her I'd just do it again. She told me he was dangerous, and I kept asking her what she was talking about, but she wouldn't answer me. That's okay. I'll just have to find another way to see him.

SIX

ADDISON, OHIO

I'd tossed and turned all night trying to figure out how my dad could have gotten a hold of that photo of us and found out where I was staying. Mom would have chewed her own arm off rather than give him the time of day, let alone share anything about me. I hadn't seen my father in twelve years. He'd left with only the clothes on his back and certainly hadn't taken any photographs as far as I knew. When had he gotten out of prison?

The next day, I was jumpy and paranoid, looking over my shoulder every few minutes. My time was up at campus guest housing. I had no money to stay another night and my one and only credit card was maxed out. I found some change in the bottom of my purse and paid for a locker at the bus station to store my largest suitcase and had no choice but to bring the smaller one with me. I could have called Liv and asked to stay, but if my dad had managed to track me down at Byron's, then he probably knew about Liv too. I camped out at the college library in a deserted corner on the sixth floor, purposefully avoiding the second floor where I used to work. I was tired, hungry, broke, and homeless. I could have just called my mom to come get me. If she knew about the picture, she'd be on the highway in minutes. But I couldn't go back to the way things were when I was younger, after Dad did what he did. She'd use this as an excuse to keep me under her thumb for the foreseeable future. Tears filled my eyes and I willed myself to calm down. I was an adult, and I should be able to figure out what to do, but instead, I closed my eyes wondering how the hell this had become my life.

A sharp nudge to my shoulder woke me, and I realized I'd fallen asleep in the lumpy, pleather library chair.

"Miss," said an elderly black security guard I'd never seen before. "We're closing in five minutes."

"Five minutes?" I sat up and looked beyond the guard out the nearest window and saw that the sun had set. Checking my watch, I saw it was almost seven o'clock. I'd forgotten about the library's shortened hours between semesters. I'd been asleep all afternoon. Hastily I gathered my things and got up to go, ignoring the loud growl of my stomach, when the guard stopped me.

"Miss?" He gave me the once over.

I couldn't quite meet his eyes. "Yes?"

"St. Mark's church over on Stanton serves hot meals. They close their doors at eight, so you better be quick." He didn't wait for my reply and turned to go.

I was about to protest that I wasn't homeless when I caught a glimpse of myself in the glass of the display case next to my chair. My clothes were wrinkled, and my hair looked like a bird's nest. I let out a sigh. It would take a good fifteen minutes to walk to St. Mark's. I got going.

Half an hour later, I was eating a lukewarm bowl of vegetable beef soup and a peanut butter and jelly sandwich. I was one of two dozen people sitting at a table in the church's community room. I ate slowly knowing as soon as I was done, I'd have to leave, and I had no place to go. Then I spotted one of the nuns across the room talking to another nun and pointing in my direction. They must have realized I wasn't one of the regulars. I wasn't up for answering any questions, and despite the fact that I was here eating a free meal and my fellow diners looked like they came from every walk of life, my ego wouldn't allow me to think that I was like the rest of these people. I didn't need charity, even though I was currently filling my stomach with it. When another nun joined the other two, I quickly got up and bolted from the church, angry that I hadn't gotten to finish my meal.

I had walked two blocks by the time I noticed the beat-up white Honda Accord following me. I picked up my pace and turned the next corner. The car turned, too, following slowly behind me. Who was this? Was it my dad? I couldn't see the driver because the windows were tinted. My heart pounded wildly as a trickle of sweat rolled down my back. Finally, I reached the corner and whirled around. The car had parked in front of a house and a teenage girl got out with a bag from Taco Bell, not my father or some other maniac out to do me bodily harm. The tears came anyway. I quickly wiped them away and looked around, realizing I was half a block from Mac's place. Was this the universe's way of telling me that her offer was the answer to my problems?

Ten minutes later, I knocked on her door. Mac stood aside wordlessly as I entered her house with my suitcase. She guided me into her living room and onto the couch and poured me a glass of red wine. I drained it, my hands still shaking over my ordeal with the white car. I didn't even notice Mac leave the room until she came back with the same envelope she'd offered me the night before. She placed it on the coffee table and sat down next to me.

"There are fresh towels in the upstairs hall closet. You look like you could use a hot bubble bath, sis. I've got some filming to do in my room. So, help yourself to anything you want in the fridge. But if this money isn't on this table in the morning, I'll know you've accepted my offer." She left the room. I was too busy staring at the thick envelope of one hundred-dollar bills to watch her go.

There were a million reasons not to take this money. I could end up so much worse off than I am now. Expelled, my academic career and future ruined, and living back at home with my mom who wouldn't miss an opportunity to remind me of what a disappointment I was. And would Mac want her money back if I got caught? I glanced toward the window in the front door, catching a sliver of night sky through it. I couldn't go back out there. The white car hadn't been following me this time. It wasn't my father. But what about next time? I reheated some of last night's Thai food, and when I finished eating, I drank another glass of red wine. Then I picked up the envelope and headed upstairs to take a bath.

"Why are you asking me about some old picture album?" asked Mom two days later as I sat in Mackenzie Burk's guest bedroom.

"I was thinking about having some of my old photos blown up to decorate my new place." It wasn't a complete lie, I convinced myself. I could absolutely use those pictures. It just wouldn't be in the apartment she thought I was living in.

"All that stuff's in the attic, and I don't have time to go sorting through that mess. You should have gotten it when you were home last month."

"I meant to, I just forgot. Are you sure it's still up there? When was the last time you saw it?"

"As far as I know, it's still up there, Kendall. But I have no reason to go up in the attic, so I can't be positive."

She sounded annoyed, but that was nothing new. She always sounded annoyed, like whatever she'd been doing when I'd called was ten times more important than talking to me. Unless she called me. Then, of course, I was supposed to drop everything.

"Well, I was just checking. I didn't want to come all the way home and it not be there."

"What's your new address? You never gave it to me."

"I'll email it to you so you won't lose it," I blurted. "I know you're busy, so I'll talk to you later." I hung up before she could say anything else. Besides, I was still trying to figure out how my father could have found me.

A quick internet search revealed my address listed in an Ohio Residents database as my mother's address. How would he have known I was living with Byron? Had he been watching my mother's house and followed me back home when I'd visited her? But that couldn't be right because I rarely went home to see my mom. Now that I'd had time to calm down and think, I realized that anyone could have sent that photo, and agreeing to take Mac's class was an impulsive mistake. A mistake I couldn't undo, as not only had I already used some of the money she'd given me to pay off my bank overdraft; I'd also ordered my books for the semester.

"Everything okay?" Mac had appeared in the doorway of the guest room so suddenly I jumped. "Sorry. You alright?"

"All good," I lied because nothing had been *all* good for as long as I could remember. I saw Mac had a shopping bag with her.

"What's that?"

"Now don't freak out, but my online class has a mandatory final on campus."

"*What?*" I spun around to face her. "You never said anything about me having to show up on campus as you. I thought these classes were completely online." Hiding behind a computer and taking someone's class was one thing, but cosplaying as Mackenzie Burk was out of the question.

"I thought it was," she insisted. "It was a last-minute change. Seriously, I just found out about it."

She avoided my gaze, and a sinking sense of doom began forming in the pit of my stomach. I didn't believe her for a minute. I sat down on the edge of the bed and ran a hand over my face, kicking myself for being in a position where I had to trust a chick that was already lying to me. I planned on examining every single hundred-dollar bill in that fat stack of cash she'd given me to make sure none of it was monopoly money.

"It'll be okay. I promise."

"How the hell am I supposed to pass for you in person?"

"It's only once. And don't worry. I got you, sis." She began pulling the items out of the bag and laying them out on the bed.

The first thing out of the bag was a purple wig cut into a blunt cut bob, followed by an assortment of makeup, foundation, primer, blush, contouring sticks, lipsticks, gloss, eyeliner, mascara, powder, and highlighter.

I eyed the pile she'd just dumped on the bed with growing anxiety. "What's all this?"

"Makeup is magic, and I can make you look like anyone. All this is what I'll be using to turn you into me."

"And all this is necessary? Can't I just wear the wig and a baseball cap and sit at the back of the lecture hall?"

She gaped at me before bursting out laughing. "Necessary? It's probably not even enough."

"And why is that?" I asked coolly.

"Because I don't leave this house without my face beat to death. Plus, there's no way you're going to pass for me slinking into the back of a lecture hall. I don't sit at the back of rooms. I sit up front. People will get suspicious if I sit in back."

"But this is an online class. These people won't know who you are and won't wonder why you're sitting in the back."

"You're kidding, right? I'm the only black girl on this tired ass campus who wears bright colored wigs. I'm *Mackenzie Burk*. As soon as someone spots you with this wig on, they're going to think it's me and start watching you, especially the professors."

For someone who was used to lurking at the back of every room and going through life unnoticed, my anxiety shot me up off the bed. "Why would the professors be watching?"

"Like I said," she replied, looking at her bright pink nails. "My dad donates a lot of money to this college, and because of it, a lot of my profs are extra nice to me. They notice when my name turns up on their class rosters and they treat me accordingly. They may not like it, but they don't want to be the one who caused a million-dollar well to run dry." She said it with a smirk and a sideways glance that irritated me more than if I'd wiped my ass with sandpaper. Why she was proud of people being nice to her because of her daddy's money, I couldn't say.

"You know what?" I asked, not bothering to keep the sarcasm out of my voice. "I love that for you. But there has to be a way to pull this off without me having to act like you in front of students and professors. Like you said, I'm a grad student. Not an actress. We could both end up expelled, and you could end up cancelled."

Mac let out a heavy sigh before angrily stuffing everything back into the plastic bag and standing up. "Well, you've got all semester to figure it out then, don't you?"

"Me? Don't you mean *we*?"

"No, I mean *you*. You're getting paid to take my class. I've provided money, a place to live, the wig, makeup, and I even threw in a new laptop," she said, gesturing to the new MacBook Pro sitting on the desk in the corner of the room. Until that moment I had no idea it was for me. "And that means you get to figure out the logistics of how to do it and not get caught." She stormed out, leaving me staring after her in shock.

She just didn't get how risky me showing up on campus

posing as her truly was – or she didn't care. We were strangers, and she didn't know me enough to know just how badly I could fuck this up. Or maybe she knew and just didn't care what happened to me.

My anxiety was in danger of turning into a full-blown panic attack. Suddenly, I couldn't breathe, like the walls were closing in on me. I felt so stupid for taking her money. For the next couple of minutes, I took slow, deep breaths to calm myself down. I quickly calculated that I'd probably spent about $1,200 of Mac's money getting myself out of debt and buying my books. That meant all I had to do was get my hands on $1,200, put it back in the envelope that she had given me, pack my shit, and leave.

But where was I going to get $1,200 from? I didn't have a stable of expensive purses to sell. In fact, I didn't have a dime to my name because if I did, I wouldn't be in this mess. I'd have to drop out of my classes and move back home with my mother. And that was out of the question. There's something that happens to you when you've been living under someone's thumb for so long and you finally find yourself with some free-dom. You'll do anything not to have to go back to that situation. College had afforded me a way to get away from my mother. Now I was living under the control of some other chick, only this time, I was being paid by her to commit academic fraud. I didn't want to ask myself the question going around my head because I already knew the answer. How would I be able to look myself in the mirror every day knowing that I was helping some spoiled, entitled nepo baby cheat her way through college?

My breathing finally calmed down, but I was still no closer to knowing how to get my hands on $1,200. I needed to get out of this house so I could think. As I passed Mac's room, I heard her talking through the partially closed door. By the tone of her voice, I knew she must be filming something. Downstairs, on my way out, I slammed the front door hard, hoping her camera microphone picked up the sound. I told you I was petty.

I was also hungry. I grabbed a chili cheese dog and a bottle of sweet tea from a food truck on campus and was halfway through my meal before I realized that I'd used Mac's money to buy it. Now I'd owe her $1,210. When I was done, I sat on a bench in the college green and looked up job listings on my phone. There were lots of them, but most were federal work-study jobs for students who'd been awarded financial aid for the semester. The handful of other jobs, such as stocking shelves in the college bookstore, had already been filled by the time I'd called. Even if I had snagged a position from the jobs board, none of them paid much more than minimum wage. I could hardly pay Mac back in installments. It would be like making layaway payments on my integrity. I decided I was going to grab my things and sneak out tonight after she'd gone to sleep. Damn the $1,210. She'd just have to eat it because what else was she going to do? Take me to a small claims court for services not rendered? What would she tell the judge when asked what service I failed to provide? I was so occupied by my thoughts I didn't notice the man walking up to me until he reached out and touched my arm.

"Kendall? You okay?" My now ex, Byron, looked down at me in concern.

He was dressed in a navy suit with a brown leather messenger bag slung across his body. I'd given him that bag when he landed his job at the bank. His baby face, with the ghost of a mustache over his upper lip, and trainers, made him look like a teenager on his way to prom. I'd always loved Byron's boyish good looks and charm. He'd refused to conform to the notion that to be professional you couldn't wear your natural hair and had refused to cut his reddish-brown twists. I'd been proud of him and was proud to be his girl. Now, when I looked at him, all I could see was his sweat glistened naked body pleasuring another woman in the same bed he'd shared with *me*.

"I called over to you, but you must not have heard me," he said when I continued to stare at him.

"What do you want, Byron?" My voice was as dead as my feelings for him.

"Look, I am so sorry for how all that went down the other day. I—"

"What do you *want*, Byron?" I asked again. "Because I've already heard your sorry ass excuses and I'm not interested in hearing them again. It was over between us the minute you started fucking Kayla. I just wish you'd been man enough to tell me instead of letting me find out like that. Unless you have something else to tell my *mousy ass,* like Publishers Clearing House showed up at your place with a check looking for me, there's no reason for us to speak ever again."

Byron's eyes had widened at the word mousy, and I could tell I'd shocked him. He probably thought I would cry and beg him to come back or try to compete with Kayla. But I'd meant what I'd told his new girlfriend. He was tainted. Being with him again would be like eating soup with a dead fly floating in it. He fumbled with the flap of his messenger bag, sticking his hand inside and pulling out an envelope.

"Sorry, here's your mail. I won't bother you again," he mumbled and sat the envelope down on the bench next to me and quickly headed down the street.

"Thank you!" I called out after his retreating form. "And fuck you," I murmured under my breath.

Once he was gone, I sat on the bench for some time and watched wide-eyed freshmen arrive ready to start their college adventures. I'd been one of them not that long ago, with my first taste of freedom from a woman for whom I couldn't do anything right. Sighing, I finally picked up the white envelope. It was a notice from the Bursar's office at Bellbrook informing me that the check for my tuition had bounced. The letter included a number to call if I wanted to set up a payment plan. If I had made no arrangements to pay my tuition by the second week of the semester, I'd be dropped from my classes. Even with what Mac had paid me, it wasn't enough to cover a whole semester. I would need to set up a payment plan, but I couldn't bring myself to pick up the phone to call the number. Instead, I checked my email for the first time that day and noticed Mac had sent me her class schedule. She only had one class this semester, the Psych 101 class I was taking for her. Then I saw who was teaching it. Olivia Bryant, aka Liv. My best friend was teaching the class I'd been hired to take. This could not be happening. It took everything in me not to hurl my phone across the college green as more angry tears filled my eyes.

Then, as if life hadn't laughed at me quite enough for one day, it started to rain. I got up off the bench and hurried toward the nearby library. As it began to pour, I ducked inside the nearest doorway to wait it out, but got pushed inside the building by a laughing group of students on their way in.

I looked around the darkened room and realized I was inside a bar. The room was a large open space with polished wood floors and concrete walls with exposed ductwork in the ceiling. A glass-topped bar occupied one whole end of the room, and at the middle were two-dozen small round tables.

Large black and white photos of Paris, London, Sydney, New York, and Dubai covered the walls and a plasma TV hung in a corner next to a pool table. The sound of laughing, talking people assaulted my ears from every angle. No one seemed to pay much attention to me as I stood awkwardly just inside the entrance in my damp and wrinkled flowered skirt. Kayla was right. Compared to these people, I looked like I was collecting donations for a church can drive.

"There's a seat at the bar, honey," came a voice next to me.

A busty, white woman with short dark hair gestured

toward an empty seat at the bar. The name stitched onto her white uniform shirt read *Gina*. By now, it was raining so hard that it sounded like machine-gun fire on the roof. I was stuck here. So I hurried over and took a seat at the bar. I felt about as comfortable as a fly stuck in honey. I wasn't a big fan of bars or drinking. I'd been a few times with Liv but never had much fun. I told myself I didn't want to be bothered, but if no guys talked to me or asked to buy me a drink, I felt like a loser. The time I'd gotten my purse stolen had been the end of my bar hopping.

"Looks like I'm going to get your name after all, huh?" said a familiar, deep voice.

I found myself face to face with the bartender. To my shock, I realized he was the same hot guy from campus a few days ago. I couldn't believe it. Now he was wearing a tight, white wifebeater that showed off his bronzed, chiseled chest and muscular arms, which had a full sleeve of flame tattoos that ran from his shoulder to his wrist. Damn, this guy was beautiful. And not just beautiful. His smile was so warm and sweet and genuine that it caused an ache in my stomach.

"You... work here?"

"Naw. I'm just back here mixing drinks for the hell of it. Would you like one?" He smiled and winked at me, and I blushed, feeling like an idiot. Of course, he worked here. What a stupid question. Guys this good-looking always made me nervous. I may as well have been sixteen again.

"Hey." He reached out and touched my arm. The sudden heat of his palm on my skin made me jump, and I jerked away like it had scalded me.

"Sorry, what did you say?"

He laughed that wonderful laugh again. It was a deep rich sound that vibrated off the walls and cut through the din in the bar and made me think of dark chocolate and sin.

"What'll you have? I've got bottles full of stuff that will

either put hair on your chest or make you forget your worst problems."

"Really?" I gave him a skeptical look.

He smiled again, melting me like butter in hot maple syrup. "Really."

"What would you suggest for someone whose life has fallen into the toilet?" The words had tumbled out of my mouth before I could stop them, and I could tell by his expression he hadn't been expecting it, but he smiled anyway.

"And would that someone be you?"

"Unfortunately."

"Is that why you'd been crying when we ran into each other?"

"Yeah." I couldn't believe I'd told this stranger about my personal business. But there was something about this man that made me want to tell him everything. And I bet being a bartender he'd heard just about everything.

"Can I get you a drink? It won't solve your problems, but it'll make you feel a little better in the moment."

"Yeah, sure," I said. "But only if you tell me what I should have. I hate beer, and wine gives me a headache."

He took a step back and assessed me with his fingers cupping his chin. He turned his head this way and that like a painter in front of a blank canvas. After a while, he pulled a tall narrow glass from the rack that hung over the bar, and then pulled a lime and some mint leaves from under the counter. He got busy grinding mint, sugar, and lime wedges at the bottom of the tall glass before topping it all off with a rum and sugar water mixture. When he was finished, he sat the clear concoction in front of me on a napkin.

"What's this?" I asked.

"A mojito." He grinned.

"A mo what?"

"It's a Cuban highball. You've seriously never had one?" I

shook my head no, and his eyes widened in surprise. "You don't get out much, do you?"

"Not unless it involves work or studying," I said dryly.

"Well, you look like a mojito girl to me: sweet, salty and a little tart, innocent enough looking but packing a punch."

"You can tell all that about me from a two-minute conversation?"

"I'd be a pretty piss poor bartender if I couldn't."

"You'd make a great psychologist." I picked up the glass and took a small sip. The tart, slightly bitter lime, the sweetness of the sugar, and the freshness of the mint immediately assaulted my mouth, while the effect of the rum hit my bloodstream and made the world look just a little brighter.

He leaned across the bar and whispered in my ear, "Is it good?"

I couldn't tell if it was his warm breath in my ear or the rum that was making me feel so mellow. "Wonderful," I admitted with a smile.

It must have been because of the liquor that I found myself not only wanting to know more about him, but willing to tell him more about myself. Over the course of the next four hours, that's just what I did. At least that's what I assumed I did. I remember little of the evening. Mr. Hottie bartender served me my first mojito, and that's all I remember.

Until I woke up the next morning in his bed.

SEVEN
ADDISON, OHIO

I opened my eyes, not sure where I was, and abruptly sat up. I was alone in a large king-sized bed with black sheets. I heard movement somewhere down below and realized I was on the second level of a loft apartment, with a railing and a set of steps leading to the floor below. I also quickly realized I was only wearing my bra and panties. Where the hell were my clothes and how the hell did I get here? Wherever here was… I had a sour taste in my mouth and felt like jackhammers were going off in my head. I tried to stand, but dizziness forced me back down onto the bed.

Approaching footsteps had me scrambling back into the bed and pulling the sheets up to my chin. Holding a glass of red liquid, the gorgeous bartender from the night before entered the room. This morning, he was dressed in black nylon warm-up pants, trainers, and a tight blue T-shirt. His hair was slicked back like he'd just come from the shower and the water glinting in his hair made his gray eyes glow.

"Well, I see you're finally awake." He held out the glass for me to take. I just stared at him.

"Where are my clothes and how did I get here?" I demanded, ignoring the offered glass.

"You're at my place. Your clothes are in the dryer. I had to wash them because you puked all over yourself and me. And just in case you're wondering, I slept on the couch, so your virtue is intact."

The look on his face told me I amused the hell out of him and that made me feel like a fool. I looked through the railing to the floor below to see that a pillow and blanket were folded neatly on a black leather couch.

"I should apologize." He sat down on the side of the bed. "I should have known you couldn't hold your liquor when you started singing 'Single Ladies' after your fourth drink. You climbed up on the bar and had everyone shouting, *put a ring on it*, and flipping their left hands back and forth. Someone even asked me if you'd be performing again tonight." He laughed that deep-throated laugh again, and I buried myself under the covers and groaned in humiliation.

"I was singing?" He had to be joking. Please let him be joking.

"Like it was karaoke night at a yodeling festival."

I felt him slide closer to me on the bed and tug playfully at the sheets, so I kicked him in the thigh. At least I hoped it was just his thigh. I was still too embarrassed to come out from beneath the covers.

"And what do you mean your customers?" I said, my voice muffled.

"I own the place. The Hub is my bar." I heard a tap and peaked out from behind the covers to see that he'd set the glass down on the bedside table.

"What's that?"

"It's my magic elixir for hangovers, 'cause I know you've got to have a monster hangover."

He pulled the covers off my head. I didn't need a mirror to

know I had bedhead from hell. I didn't bother trying to fix it. I couldn't be bothered to care what this beautiful stranger thought of me when I had much bigger problems.

"What's in it?" I picked up the glass and sniffed at the contents. The smell made my eyes water. Seeing my face, he laughed.

"Tomato juice, Tabasco, raw egg, horseradish, celery, and a splash of vodka."

"Vodka? Doesn't that defeat the entire purpose?" I asked.

"Not at all. Vodka just takes the edge off. If you hold your nose and chug it in one gulp, it goes down much faster."

I wasn't convinced, but since it couldn't make me feel any worse, I went for it. I pinched my nose, put the glass to my lips, and tossed the drink back in one awful gulp. For a horrifying moment, I thought I was going to spew tomato juice all over this guy's sheets, but the feeling passed in a few seconds and warmth spread throughout my body. It didn't make my headache go away, but it made me care a little less about having one.

"Better?" he asked.

"Not too bad," I admitted. Aware that the sheet was slipping, I quickly pulled it back up to my chin. "Could I have my clothes back? I really need to go."

He stared thoughtfully for a few seconds and then headed back down the steps. Five minutes later, he returned with my skirt and blouse neatly folded, still warm from the dryer, and put them on the bed. It hadn't occurred to me until that very moment that he'd undressed me and seen my granny panties. A warm flush of embarrassment burned through me like a forest fire. He must have read my mind.

"Don't worry. I used to be a med student. I can look at the human body in a cold clinical way."

"You were a med student?" The words *Paging Dr. Hottie* flashed through my head. I must have been half-drunk still.

"Uh, that was a joke." The look he gave told me there hadn't been a single clinical thought in his head when he'd stripped me the night before.

What in the world was I thinking? This man could be an axe murderer. He could have drugged me. Why was I lingering in his bed like I was a guest at an inn?

"I need to go. But thanks for everything, uh..."

"Cal." He reached out to shake my hand. "And you'd be?"

"Kendall. Kendall Good." I shook his hand, and he chuckled and mumbled something under his breath.

"What was that?" I asked.

"Nothing," he said, but I could have sworn he'd said, "of course it is" at the mention of my last name.

Back at Mac's place, I rang the doorbell. Within seconds, she appeared in the doorway, eyes downcast and looking contrite. I pushed past her into the house and went straight upstairs, and she trailed behind me to my bedroom.

"I thought you weren't coming back."

"Who says I'm back?" I put my purse down on the bed, purposefully not looking at her. I could feel her staring at me. The silence stretched past uncomfortable and straight to nerve-wracking and awkward.

"I am so sorry, Kendall." She walked into the room and sat down next to me on the bed. She looked like a little girl who knew she'd been bad and was checking to see if Mommy was mad at her. "I'm a bitch. I shouldn't have talked to you like that. You didn't deserve it, and I wouldn't blame you if you left. Please don't leave. I really need you, and of course this isn't just a *you* problem. We've got sixteen weeks to figure this out together."

I knew full well that she was full of shit, but classes started in a week, and I had no plan B for funding my courses this semester. So, for the time being, I was stuck here.

"Fine." I finally looked at her and noticed an expression in her eyes I hadn't seen before. It was fear. It reminded me of the same look in Kayla's eyes after I'd slapped the taste out of her mouth, and I'm ashamed to say it made me feel good. No, not good. Powerful. Mousy Kendall Good was dead. Or at the very least, she was dying. She was standing up for herself. So I pressed on. "And if you want me to stay, this is how it's going to be."

"Oh, so you're calling shots now, huh?" The look on Mac's face was more amused than angry, but she shut up when I flashed her a hard look.

"I will do all your online coursework, papers, essays, online tests. But you will have to be on-screen for any online lectures and show up for the on-campus final."

"But—" began Mac, before I held up a hand, cutting her off.

"I was looking over the syllabus for Psych 101." I pulled up her schedule on my phone, turning the screen to her. "According to this, the final is only thirty percent of your grade. The rest is attendance, tests, quizzes, and a paper, all of which I will do for you. So even if you bomb the final, if you score well enough on everything else, you should pass the class."

"But won't it look suspicious if I do well on everything except the final?"

"Possibly. There are big risks in all of this," I said dismissively. "And here's the next condition I have for sticking around." I sat my phone down.

"What's that?" By now, the apprehension on her face had ramped up a notch, and so did my sense of control.

"You need to switch to another section of Psych 101. I know the GTA who's teaching the one you're registered for, and I'm not doing this to her. You'd better do it right now before the other sections fill up."

I didn't even wait for her response. Instead, I grabbed my robe and shower bucket and headed for the bathroom to take a hot shower. The effects of the magic elixir that Cal had whipped up for me that morning was fading fast. And yet even though my hangover headache was still there, I was feeling better about my circumstances as if, somehow, this plan could actually work.

I should have known that feeling wouldn't last.

EIGHT

PHOENIX, ARIZONA

Enlightened Path Rehab Center
Two Months Earlier

A month after she was admitted, she finally stopped trying to escape. She'd been told by the director that every time she tried to leave the facility, another week would be added to her stay. So far, an extra month had been tacked onto her treatment. There was no point in trying to escape again. Where would she have gone even if she got away? They were in the middle of the desert.

They allowed her to make a phone call at the end of her first week, but she had no one to call. She refused to talk to her mother, the backstabbing bitch. And she couldn't remember the last conversation she had with her father. Most of all, she wanted a drink. She was grateful that her withdrawal hadn't been as bad as her roommate's, who woke up every night screaming, covered in sweat, hallucinating that spiders were crawling all over her. Her own withdrawal just left her with nausea, intense alcohol cravings, insomnia, and awful anxiety that made her want to climb the walls, often sending her out onto the grounds to roam for hours trying to tire herself out. They gave her meds which made her feel like a zombie, and she stopped taking them. It was bad enough being cut off from the outside world; but she'd be damned if she was cut off from her own feelings, even if trying to hide from them had started her drinking.

The TV in the recreation room only had three channels: Classic Movies, Game Shows, and National Geographic. The computer lab computers couldn't connect to any social media sites. She fought hard every day not to lose her sense of time. One day when she was walking the halls, she heard screaming and ran into the rec room to see orderlies attempting to break up a fight over who controlled the TV. She didn't know the names of the two women because she hadn't bothered to ask them or encouraged any attempts at conversation. Even in her group therapy sessions, she didn't pay attention to what the therapist called the other patients. Instead, she knew everyone by their addictions. The white chick with the bleach fried hair was Meth Head #4. They had twelve meth addicts. The older Latina with the rose tattoo on the inside of her right wrist was The Gambler.

Both women were dragged kicking and screaming from the room. They'd be spending the night in a punishment room, a padded room with nothing to sleep on but the floor, where the orderlies took you to the bathroom and fed you when they felt like it. She'd spent enough time herself in the punishment room to know the routine. As she watched the women being taken away, she noticed that one of the orderlies had left his cell phone on the desk. It had yet to revert to its lockscreen.

Quick as a flash, she grabbed the phone and hurried into the women's restroom across the hall, closing herself into a stall. She only had minutes before the orderly would be back. She quickly pulled up her Instagram account and froze as she saw all the brand sponsored posts for jewelry, shoes, and perfume. She opened TikTok and saw exactly the same things.

Anger flooded her body, making her shake like she had delirium tremens. She looked at the name again on both accounts to be sure. Now she knew she had to get out of there, even if it meant playing the game and doing what she was told. Because if she didn't leave soon, that bitch was going to ruin everything.

From the diary of Kendall Good:

December 30, 2011

Dear Diary,

I woke up last night and overheard my mom crying on the phone. I got scared because I thought maybe somebody had died. I was about to burst into her room to see what was going on, but then I heard her say my name. At first, I thought she knew I was up and was calling out to me. But then I heard her say, Kendall can never know. I listened some more, but she must have hung up. Then I just went back to bed but couldn't sleep. What am I not supposed to know?

NINE

ADDISON, OHIO

A week into the fall semester, I found the first red envelope. I was taking books out of my book bag, after a long day of taking my own classes as well as Mac's, when something bright red fluttered to the floor of my bedroom. A few days had passed since I'd unpacked my book bag, so who knows how long it had been in there. I stared in confusion for a few seconds before finally bending to pick it up off the rug. The envelope was bright scarlet with my name written on the front in black calligraphy. Turning it over, I found a gold wax seal on the back with the fleur-de-lis in the center. I didn't think twice before ripping it open, thinking that it was probably a card from Liv wishing me a happy first day of grad school – she did stuff like that – but I knew I was wrong when I pulled out a single sheet of cream-colored card stock with just three words in the center.

I see you.

"*What?*" I mumbled under my breath. I flipped over the card to see if anything was written on the back. There wasn't.

At first, I figured whoever put this in my bag had mistaken

me for someone else. Then another thought came to mind. Could whoever slipped the envelope into my bag also have sent me the photograph of my father and me? If so, why? I'd yet to check the prison my father was serving his time in to see if he'd been released. He crossed my mind so little these days. If he was out, why the secrecy? Why not approach me like an adult? Was he afraid of what I might say to him? Well, he should be. And if I found out he was the one behind the picture and now this weird note, I wouldn't hesitate to call the police.

It occurred to me that Cal could be behind the note, but I highly doubted it. Why would he want to scare me like that? I hadn't been back to The Hub since that night a week ago when I got drunk and ended up in his bed. I'd walked past several times on my way to and from campus and once had almost gone in. But I was still smarting over what happened with Byron and didn't need to open a new can of worms. I may be on my way to the *hoe phase* in my healing process, but I wasn't there yet.

In the meantime, my classes were going well, as was the class I was taking for Mac. She was right when she said that her class should be a piece of cake for me. It was, but that didn't mean what I was doing was without complication. Liv was asking a lot of questions. I obviously couldn't tell her the truth because she'd probably be obligated to report me, since she was technically an employee of the college. So I told her as much as I could without having to outright lie. I was renting a room and paying my rent by tutoring, after setting up a payment plan to pay my tuition. None of it was technically a lie and, for now, at least Liv seemed happy that I hadn't dropped out.

So I gave little thought to the first red envelope and the weird message. I threw it in the trash and went on with my life. Then the second red envelope came. This time I discovered it on top of my textbook when I returned from the restroom at the library. A shiver of apprehension slithered up my spine as I picked it up and glanced around the half-full reading room.

"Did you see who left this here?" I asked a girl a few seats down from me. She was annoyed as she pulled an AirPod from her ear.

"Huh?"

"This." I waved the envelope at her. "Did you see who left it here?"

"No, sorry." The girl shrugged before putting the AirPod back in her ear and turning her attention to her textbook.

I sat back down, looking around the room one last time before I tore the envelope open and pulled another cream square of card stock out. This time there were more words typed on the square of paper.

You're not being very GOOD! You bad girl!

What the hell? I looked around wildly, not sure what I was expecting to see. Everyone's heads were down. Everyone seemed to be studying. Nobody was looking at me, yet someone had left me a note that said they knew what I was doing. At least I assumed that's what they were talking about, because why else would anyone think I wasn't good? Bad girls cheated, and even though I wasn't cheating in my own classes, I was helping someone else to cheat. How did somebody find out? The only two people who knew were me and Mac.

I quickly shoved my things, including the note and envelope, into my backpack and then left. As I walked down the library's wide front steps, I pulled out my cell and called Mac.

"Yeah?" Mac sounded out of breath, and I knew from the sounds in the background that she must be on her treadmill.

"Have you told anyone about our arrangement?"

"Yeah, I made a TikTok about it," she said casually.

"*What*?" I practically screamed into the phone.

"Girl, bye!" she exclaimed with a snort of laughter. "Why would I tell anybody? I'm not crazy."

"Are you sure you haven't told anyone?"

"I just said I didn't. Why are you asking? What's going on?"

I knew I couldn't tell her. If she thought someone was onto our secret, she'd freak out and pull the plug. Once again, I'd be scrambling to try to find a job to cover my tuition on top of having to find a place to live.

"Nothing." I looked around again to see if anyone was watching me. "I was just feeling a little paranoid because I know I'm not supposed to talk about our arrangement. I was wondering if maybe you had told a friend."

"Chill, sis. I may have a quarter of a million followers online, but I got very few real friends and none that I would tell this shit to. That would be like handing someone bullets to shoot me with."

With a silent sigh of relief, I told Mac I'd see her later that night and then hung up. The apprehension and fear didn't go away. Somebody knew what we were doing. But how, and what did they want?

Three days later, I received the third envelope. I was coming out of B&C café with my book bag in one hand and a matcha latte in the other. A kid of about ten years old ran up to me and shoved the envelope into the hand that held my matcha latte.

"That man over there told me to give this to you." The kid pointed across the street toward a figure who ducked around the corner. I was too busy trying not to drop the matcha latte while holding on to the envelope to get a good look, and immediately the boy ran over to join a bunch of other kids getting on a bus.

Impulsively, I darted after the person who'd disappeared around the corner, when my foot hit an uneven spot on the sidewalk. I pitched out onto the street, falling on my hands and knees in front of an SUV that slammed on its brakes to keep from hitting me. My heart hammered so fast that a heart attack almost accomplished what the SUV hadn't.

"Kendall? Oh my God, are you okay?" came an all too familiar voice. I looked up to see Cal, the hottie bartender, staring down at me. He held out a hand and gently pulled me to my feet as a small crowd gathered, and a woman I'd seen inside the café asked if I needed an ambulance as she handed me my keys.

"I'm fine but thanks," I told her, happy when she and the crowd dispersed. My voice was weak and trembling while my heart continued to hammer in my chest. Cal helped me pick up my tote bag and the few things that had spilled out, including the red envelope. There was no hope for my matcha latte which had spilled all over the street.

"You just ran out in front of me. Where were you trying to go?"

"I am so sorry. I feel like the biggest idiot." I examined the scrapes on my palms and tried not to wince. Cal took me by the elbow and guided me over to a table outside the café.

"Don't move. I'll be right back." He hopped into his car and drove it around the corner, parking at the side of the café.

A minute later, he returned carrying a first aid kit from his car and sat down next to me. He cleaned the scrapes on both my palms with a cool, stinging disinfectant wipe, followed by a soothing antiseptic cream. Once the blood was gone, I could tell that the scrapes were superficial, and it had already stopped hurting.

"I am sorry, Cal. Thanks for this. I know you must be on your way someplace because it looks like you're dressed for something important." I hoped it didn't sound like I was trying to get rid of him – which I was – especially when he'd been so kind to me.

While he'd cleaned my palms, I took the time to truly look at the man in front of me. Instead of the jeans and wifebeater from the last time she'd seen him, Cal wore a very stylish black suit that made his bronze skin glow. His curly hair was still doing its own thing, but it seemed he'd gotten a trim since the last time we'd seen each other. On top of all this, he smelled amazing, like clean laundry and sunshine.

"I have a meeting in about twenty minutes, so don't chase me off."

"I wasn't," I insisted, but it was a lie. This man made me nervous, for obvious reasons. But I wasn't rushing him off because I didn't want to be bothered with him. Honestly, I could have looked at him all day long. I was itching to get across the street to follow the figure, even though I knew whoever gave the kid the envelope was long gone now.

"So, where were you off to in such a hurry that you almost became a hood ornament on my car?"

"I thought I saw someone I knew across the street, but I was mistaken. I wasn't thinking."

He gave me a skeptical look, and I could tell he didn't believe a word I was saying. He stood up, giving me his usual amused look.

"Have dinner with me."

"Huh?"

"I'm serious. There's a new soul food restaurant that just opened and the food is amazing. I can pick you up."

Telling him where I live would break Mac's rule about not bringing dudes to her place, but I wanted to spend more time with Cal and there was no use pretending otherwise. *Hoe phase here I come.*

"Are you talking about Cora's?"

"Yep. That be the place."

"How about I meet you there tonight at 6:30?"

"Sounds like a plan. See you tonight."

As I watched him get into his car and drive off, I wondered if I'd just made a mistake. Then I remembered the red envelope.

Checking around me, I pulled the envelope out of my bag, removed the seal, slid out a square of cream-colored card stock, and read the message:

Cheaters never prosper. But you might if you do what I say. Check your email.

I pulled out my phone to check my email, and saw that I had five minutes to get to my next class. My prof marked anyone more than two minutes late as absent, and attendance was a big part of our grade. If I flunked out of grad school, my deal with the devil would have been for nothing. I rushed back to the lecture hall, slipped into my seat and forced myself back into student mode for the next hour and a half.

Two hours later, back at Mac's, I pulled up my personal email. At the top on my inbox was the subject line: *Bad Girl Scavenger Hunt*. Scavenger hunt? What the hell was this about? I stared for a long minute before opening the email. I was expecting a written message. Instead, it was a link to a sound file. I grabbed my AirPods from my book bag and put them in my ears just as Mac sprinted up the stairs, dressed like she'd come back from a run. She glanced into my room as she passed by, tossing up a hand before she disappeared into her room.

I got up and shut the door, returned to the desk and clicked on the sound file. There was no sound for at least thirty seconds. Then a mechanical voice addressed me.

Greetings, Kendall. I won't address you by your last name because we both know you're not being very good right now, are you? How disappointing. I thought you were better than this. I was wrong. But I guess the apple didn't fall far from the tree, huh? Let's play a little game. This first task should be right up your alley.

1. *Tomorrow, steal a tube of Pom Passion lip gloss from Nouveau Boutique. Post a selfie wearing it with #thislipglossisasteal.*
2. *Attend a matinee of* Little Shop of Horrors *at Addison Playhouse and bring home a program. Cut it up and throw it in your trash.*
3. *Go to the dog park next to the Riverwalk and take a pic of a black Frenchie.*
4. *Go to Macy's and try on a pair of black Luciano Silva stiletto pumps and take a pic.*

This all needs to be completed by 5 p.m. tomorrow. Don't be late. I'll be watching. Lastly, you'll need to post the selfies on Instagram over four days. One selfie each day. And if you even think about not doing what I've asked, consider this question: Do you want to end up like Davis Holder?

The message ended. Immediately, I pulled up a browser and googled Davis Holder. There were a bunch of Davis Holders of various ages and races listed all over the world, and nothing about any of them jumped out at me, until I did another search for Davis Holder and Bellbrook College. Then I found it. Davis Holder had been a student at Bellbrook back in 2009. He was the reason Bellbrook had implemented a new code of adding *XF* on the transcripts of any student caught committing academic fraud. Davis, a journalism major, had been caught taking classes for several students for cash and was expelled mere months before he would have graduated with honors. Because of the *XF* on his transcript, he'd been unable to get a job in his chosen field and had sued the college – unsuccessfully – to have it removed. I would have laughed if it weren't so messed up. I groaned as I closed the laptop and laid my head down on top of it.

What in actual fuck? This wasn't a joke or a prank. This was for real. Someone knew my secret and was using it against me to... what? Make me steal makeup? Take stupid photos? Were they hoping I'd get caught and arrested? What was their end goal? Something else caught my attention. I pulled the message back up in my email and listened again to make sure I'd heard it correctly. *I guess the apple didn't fall far from the tree, huh?* I hadn't misheard it. Not only did this asshole know I was committing academic fraud; they also knew about my father. How? I didn't talk about my father to anyone. Not even Liv, who I'd simply told he was out of the picture when she'd asked. It wasn't something I wanted anyone to know about.

When I was twelve, my father was convicted of embezzling a lot of money from the company he worked for. He got twelve years in Lucasville State Penitentiary. My mother divorced him while he was in prison. Now I don't know if he's even still alive, I just know that he should be out by now. My mother never allowed me to visit, let alone visited him herself. She cut him off completely. She refused to talk about him. I'd adored my dad. He was handsome, charismatic, and a lot of fun. When he was sent to prison, it was like he'd died. He cut all contact with me. My mom finally told me the truth when I tried to run away for the second time to see him in Lucasville, Ohio. I still remember that ride home after she caught me trying to get on a Greyhound bus like it was yesterday.

"You'll never see that man again. Do you understand me?" she'd screamed at me.

"You can't keep me from seeing him! He's my father!" I'd screamed back.

"Not after what he did to us!" She had been crying so hard she had to pull over on the side of the road. She had buried her face in the steering wheel and sobbed, but I hadn't felt sorry for her. I hated her.

"You're just jealous because he loves me more than he loves you!"

My mother's head had snapped up from the steering wheel, and she slapped me across the face. I had stared at her in shocked silence while holding my cheek, and then got out of the car and started walking down the highway.

"Kendall! Get back here right now!" She had gotten out of the car and trailed behind me.

"No! I hate you!" I must not have been walking nearly as fast as I had thought I was because she had caught up with me and snatched the back of my shirt. I had tried to twist away from her grasp, but she held on tight.

"Don't you want to know what happened the night you ended up in the hospital? Haven't you ever wondered why you were in a medically induced coma for three days?"

"It was an accident. I fell down the steps." I still wouldn't look at her, but I'd stopped walking, and she released my shirt and turned me around to face her.

"You didn't just fall down the steps, Kendall, you were pushed. By your father."

"You're lying!" I had screamed.

"Why would I lie about something like this? I know you don't remember what happened that night, but you remember how much your father was drinking during his trial, right?"

It was true. While my father was on trial for embezzlement, he was out on bond and spent every moment he wasn't consulting with his lawyers drinking. I'm guessing he knew he'd been caught red-handed. He'd embezzled more than $4 million over the course of five years at the accounting firm where he had worked for fifteen years.

But I was too young to care about what he'd done. He was my father, and I loved him.

"So what? He was just scared of going to prison."

"No, Kendall." My mother had worn a mask of pain that I had ignored because I was hurting too. "He'd been drinking for a while, and he was just able to hide it from you. He was always abusive. I was good at hiding the truth too. Now you need to know what really happened."

"I don't know what you're talking about." I had tried to walk away from her again, but she had grabbed me by the arm and forced me to face her.

"After he'd been found guilty, the day before he had to report to court for sentencing, he'd been drinking all day long. We'd stayed at your aunt Ann's house and had gone home to get some more clothes. We found him passed out on the couch, and I thought we could just grab some things and leave." She had grimaced like the memory physically hurt her. "But then he woke up while we were upstairs and confronted me. Accused me of abandoning him. We got into an argument, and he attacked me. You came out of your room and saw what was going on and rushed over to help me, and he turned around and backhanded you. You were standing at the top of the steps, and you fell down all those steps. He didn't even try to help when he saw you lying there, broken and bleeding at the bottom of the staircase. He just kept attacking me."

I had covered my ears with my hands. It wasn't true. How could it be true? But eventually it had dawned on me that it must be true, because why else had I never heard from my father again? He must have felt guilty for what he'd done to me and my mom. After a while, it didn't matter anymore what he did or didn't do. My life was just fine without him.

At least it was until a few days ago. Now I was committing fraud and being blackmailed by an anonymous freak wanting to see me in stolen lip gloss. The worst part was, I couldn't afford to call this person's bluff and not do what they'd asked of me, because otherwise I risked losing everything. I curled up on my bed, wishing it would all just go away and I could wake up in my old life, until eventually, I drifted off to sleep.

Sometime later, I woke with a start. Glancing at the clock on my nightstand, I saw that it was 6:05. How had I slept for almost three hours? I had less than half an hour before I had to meet Cal at Cora's. I jumped out of bed and looked down at my creased jeans and wrinkled top. It was the same outfit I'd been wearing when I fell into the street in front of his SUV hours ago. I couldn't meet him looking like this.

"Shit!"

There was a knock at the door. "You okay, Kendall?" came Mac's voice.

I let her in, barely acknowledging her as I rifled through my still-unpacked suitcases for something to wear. I didn't own date night clothes. I owned work, class, and studying clothes. My boring wardrobe reflected my boring life. I pushed away the thought that maybe if I'd taken better care of my appearance, Byron wouldn't have cheated and my life would have been a whole lot simpler right now.

"I've got about twenty minutes to pull an outfit together for dinner with a... friend." I refused to call it a date, even though that was exactly what it was. Just like I refused to admit just how much I was looking forward to it.

"And these are your choices?" Mac eyed my pile of T-shirts, flowered skirts, and jeans with a look of disgust.

"Shut up. You're not helping," I moaned.

"Hold up." She left the room and came back a minute later with an armload of clothing which she dumped onto my bed. "Clothes sent to me from brands that I will never wear."

I eyed the pile curiously, seeing a few pieces that could work if I had a body like Mac's, which I didn't.

"Where are you going with this friend? Anywhere fancy?"

"Just dinner at Cora's, that new soul food place."

"Hmm." She shrugged. "A little low-key, but I hear their oxtails are fire. Please tell me this 'friend'," she said, making air quotes, "isn't your cheating ass ex. Because you've got a well-deserved hoe phase coming."

"I was dumb to trust him, but I'm not stupid." I picked up a long black sundress with spaghetti straps.

"Nope." She snatched it out of my hands. "Black is not your color, sis. Try this." She held up a raspberry-colored, fit and flare mini dress with a V neck and 3/4 puffed sleeves. It wasn't anything I'd wear in a million years, mainly because this was the type of dress you wore when you wanted attention. Not the type of dress worn by mousy Kendall Good who sat in the back row.

"Uh… I don't think so. It's too short." I took a step back. She took a step forward, still holding out the dress.

"You are not leaving this house dressed like a nun. We can't do a lot about your hair," she said, gesturing to my head. "But you *will* be leaving this house looking like a snack." The expression on her face told me it wasn't up for discussion.

True to her word, I left Mac's wearing the mini dress and a pair of nude strappy sandals. I'd refused to wear the four-inch black platform pumps she'd picked out. My thick hair was slicked back into a messy bun, held in place by a rose gold clip. Courtesy of Mac, my makeup was minimal and natural, with just a touch of gloss. I had to admit, I looked like a snack – a snack from a vending machine, but still a snack. The color of the dress brightened up my complexion a lot more than the black dress would have. I'm guessing Cal thought so, too, when I finally showed up at Cora's, almost twenty minutes late. He was walking back to his SUV looking grim when he spotted me, and grinned.

"I thought you weren't coming."

"I would have called to let you know I was running late, but we forgot to exchange numbers." His eyes stayed fixed on mine as I walked across the street to join him in front of Cora's. He looked amazing, dressed in jeans and a black button-down shirt. Black may not have been my color, but it was definitely his.

"No worries," he said with a smile. "You're here now. And it was worth the wait." He eyed my look appreciatively and held out his arm for me to take, which I did.

Cora's was a hole in the wall, literally. It was an order window that you both ordered and picked up your food from, located under a covered patio with outdoor seating. The black wrought-iron pillars that held up the patio were wreathed in tiny colored Christmas lights and the patio ceiling was hung with colorful lanterns of various shapes and sizes. Not the fanciest restaurant on earth, but what it lacked in aesthetics, it more than made up for in charm and character. And Mac had been right. The oxtails were fire. As was the fried catfish, mac n cheese, collards, sweet potatoes, corn bread and peach tea.

"I am stuffed." I patted my stomach and pushed my plate away. I probably could have eaten more if the mini dress wasn't so form-fitting.

"Seriously? You've still got food left on that plate. Don't wimp out on me, Good." Cal tucked into his third piece of fish, and I laughed.

"These are bones. I'll weigh a ton trying to keep up with you." Not that the thought wasn't appealing. A hot guy who encouraged me to eat... I might be in love.

"I hope you saved room for dessert." A pretty light-skinned black woman with an afro who looked about fifty, wearing a white T-shirt that said *Cora's*, had walked up to our table holding a giant piece of pineapple upside-down cake covered with whipped cream. She sat it down in the middle of the table.

"Hey, Cora. What's this?" asked Cal. Instead of answering,

Cora stared at me with naked curiosity. I smiled back. Cal wiped his mouth and made the introductions.

"Cora, this is my friend Kendall Good. Kendall, this is my friend and the co-owner of *Cora's*, Cora Daybell."

"Nice meeting you, Kendall. How was everything? Did you enjoy your meal?" Her intense stare told me she was very invested in my answer, and I wasn't about to lie to her.

"It's nice meeting you too, Cora. And, yes, everything was amazing. I'm so glad you guys are here. Addison really needed a place like this."

"Yeah, the last thing we need is another organic microbrewery." Cal shoved his empty plate aside and pulled the cake toward him. Cora slapped his hand away.

"Not so fast, pretty boy. Save some for Kendall, compliments of the chef." She turned to point at a tall, stocky, bald black man wearing a *Cora's* T-shirt standing inside with his back to us. "It's one of our most popular menu items and people say it tastes like home wherever that may be for you. Enjoy." She left to mingle with the other patrons.

"She's nice, and this place is cool. Thanks for recommending it." I reached out and snagged a forkful of cake. The luscious buttery cake melted in my mouth and the pineapple was sweet and tender, but not mushy. It was heaven.

"You okay?"

"What?"

"You're crying." He reached out and brushed away the tear that had slipped down my cheek.

"Oh my God." I wiped my eyes and laughed nervously. Why was I crying over some cake? "Where'd that come from?"

Cal must have sensed my embarrassment because he turned his attention back to the cake, giving me time to pull myself together. I knew exactly where the tears had come from. Pineapple upside-down cake was my father's favorite.

· · ·

"So, where is home for you, Kendall?" asked Cal as we took an after-dinner stroll along the Riverwalk.

The sun was setting, and a gentle breeze blew across the water. I should have been at home studying for a quiz, but I wanted to enjoy my time away from the train wreck of my life for as long as I could. With Cal, I could pretend to be just a regular grad student experiencing the stresses that normal grad students go through.

"Columbus. How about you?"

"Addison born and raised."

"Really? I didn't know you were from here. Is your family still here?"

My question must have struck a nerve because the smile slipped from his face, and he looked away toward the river. "No. I'm an only child and both my parents are dead."

I hadn't been expecting that and replied without thinking. "Yeah, me too."

"You're an orphaned only child too?" He looked surprised, and I quickly corrected myself.

"No! Sorry. I meant I'm an only child. My parents are still alive, I think."

"You think?"

"My parents are divorced. I haven't seen my dad in years, but Mom is alive and well."

"Would you like to see him again one day?"

"Trust me. It's best he's not in my life." I could feel Cal's gaze, as he waited for me to continue, but I didn't.

The topic of parents had knocked the mood down a notch, and we were both quiet for a long minute.

"How'd your meeting go?" I finally asked, hoping to change the subject. Our easy rapport at dinner seemed to have disappeared at the mention of our families.

"About like you expect a meeting with two lawyers and a waste of space to go."

"Ouch. That doesn't sound like it was much fun."

"It wasn't. My mother's estate is being contested by her greedy, idiot husband, and every time I have to be in the same room with the guy, I want to throat-punch him."

It took a while for his words to sink in completely. Mother, contested estate, greedy, husband.

"Oh my God." I stopped walking and whirled around to face him. "Was your mother Lena Bennett?"

"Yeah. Did you know my mom?" He gave me a confused look – which made two of us, because I was confused too.

"No. I didn't know your mom. So, your last name is Bennett?" I suddenly realized Cal had never told me his last name and I hadn't asked.

"Samuel Callum Bennett Jr. Everyone just calls me Cal."

I stared at him, deciding whether I should explain that I was the recipient of the Bennett Fellowship. Better now than later.

"Did you know your mother was funding a fellowship in psychology at Bellbrook?"

"I did." He smiled. "My mom was a therapist here in town for years until she got sick. Endowing that fellowship was important to her because she didn't want another young woman to struggle the way she did when she was in school, having to work multiple jobs. It took her a couple of years longer to grad-uate than it would have done had she gone to school full-time, and she didn't want another woman to have the same experience."

Again, I stared at him, waiting for the other shoe to drop and, after several long seconds, it finally did.

"Don't tell me..."

"Yep. I was supposed to be the first Lena Bennett Fellow until your stepfather contested her will and all her assets were frozen, leaving the fellowship unendowed and me SOL."

"Oh my God, Good. I am so sorry. I've had so much going

on trying to fight this asshole that it never occurred to me it was affecting my mother's charitable donations."

"It's not your fault. We both got screwed over by your stepfather."

"But you probably had everything set up expecting you'd be getting that fellowship money. Is that the real reason you were so upset when I ran into you on campus the other week?"

I merely nodded and followed Cal over to the nearest bench where we sat down. His face had gone red, and he looked truly upset. "How are you paying for your classes?"

"The good old Bellbrook College installment plan. I got a job tutoring and found a room to rent. I'll be fine." I fed him the same line that I fed Liv. And just like Liv, he bought it, which should've made me feel bad for lying. Instead, I was relieved to have a believable cover story. There was no way in hell I could ever tell him the truth.

"Well, I just want you to know that just as soon as this mess is resolved, I will make sure that you get your fellowship money. That's a promise." He grabbed my hand and squeezed it, and it took everything in me not to react to the thrill I felt at his touch.

"Thanks, Cal, I really appreciate that. But I also understand that this is beyond your control."

"I can't help but feel responsible, at least partially, for this mess. My mom and I were estranged for several years, and by the time we reconnected, she had remarried that scumbag. Maybe if I had been in the picture, she wouldn't have fallen so hard for his BS when she was vulnerable and ill."

"There's no way to know whether that would've happened. Beating yourself up about that won't help anyone, especially you."

He looked at me and smiled, squeezing my hand even harder. "Is that your professional opinion as a psychologist?"

"No." I squeezed his hand back. "That's just common sense."

.   .   .

I had Cal drop me off in front of Mac's place, figuring that if he dropped me off across the street, he wasn't exactly at her place, therefore not breaking her rule.

"I had a really great time tonight. Thank you." I went to get out of the car when the doors locked. Alarm bells instantly sounded in my head, and I went rigid with fear. When I gave him a startled look, he put his hand under my chin, tilted my head up, leaned in, and kissed me.

"I had an amazing time too. Thanks for the pep talk. I've been beating myself up over that since my mom died. Probably will for a while. Thank you for officially letting me off the hook."

"Any time," I told him as I leaned in for another kiss.

He was a hell of a kisser, as I knew he would be. After a minute or two, I finally pushed him away. Every bit of common sense I had was telling me not to mount this guy and ride him like he was the last horse out of Dodge. I may be entitled to a hoe phase, but I didn't want to start it like this, where anyone looking out their window could see the SUV rocking.

"I've got to go. I have a big day tomorrow, and I'm sure you do too." Cal unlocked the doors, and I quickly got out of the car before I could change my mind. Cal hopped out too and tried to walk me to the door.

"It's okay. My roommate is weird about me bringing strangers here."

"Not a problem." He held up his hands and took a step back. "Sleep tight, Good."

I waved and then slid the key into the lock, letting myself into the darkened house.

.   .   .

Tuesday was the one weekday that I had no classes. So, of course, it was the perfect day to embark on the *bad girl scavenger hunt*. Besides, I had a time limit in which to complete all the tasks on the list. I had to take selfies after completing each and had to post them over four days and not all at once. I could've wasted a lot of time trying to figure out why, but I just wanted to get it over with and hope that once it was done, whoever this freak was would leave me alone.

There was something else niggling the back of my mind that I couldn't let go of. How had this person come to know personal things about me? It wasn't like the info about my father was a secret. Anyone looking up his name would see that he had been convicted. The bigger mystery was how they knew about my sticky fingers. And then it hit me. The only way someone could know about all the things I'd taken over the years was if they'd read my diaries. But how would that be possible? No matter where I lived, those diaries came with me, all twelve of them, including the one that I was writing in currently.

I kept them all in a box that moved with me from location to location. That box was currently in one of my suitcases, which was under my bed at Mac's. I went straight to retrieve it to check they were all still there. Sitting on the bed, I flipped through them one by one, starting with the most recent. They were all there. No pages appeared to be missing. Nothing seemed wrong until I got to my first diary from 2011 and noticed something that wasn't there before. Several of the pages had dark smears on them. What was that? I held the pages under the desk light to see if I could figure out what the smudges were. Was it chocolate? Had someone flipped through my diary with chocolate-smudged fingers? It wasn't me because I'm allergic to chocolate. Then, as I absently fanned the pages, I caught a whiff of something very familiar. Perfume. Gucci Guilty to be exact. That bitch Kayla had been reading my diary, probably while she was eating candy like it was a damned novel.

Months ago, Byron and I ran into her at a restaurant. I told her how amazing she smelled, and she told me how she layered her perfume with the matching body lotion to get the scent to last all day. Kayla must have had perfumed lotion on her hands when she'd touched my diary. Either that or Byron had gotten her perfume on his hands when he'd touched her, and he was the one who'd read my diary. Somehow, even after what he'd done, I doubted Byron would do that. But Kayla would, which explained why she automatically thought I'd taken her bracelet. She'd read my petty theft confessions. The violation made my stomach clench. Raw and exposed, I got up from the bed and pulled the curtains closed over the window that looked out onto the street.

Was Kayla behind the scavenger hunt? There was only one way to find out.

TEN

ADDISON, OHIO

I met Byron my senior year at Bellbrook. He was fresh off his breakup with Kayla, his high school sweetheart. Should I have been dating a guy who was on the rebound? Probably not. But he was cute and funny and seemed interested in me, and I was too naïve to realize he probably just didn't want to be alone. My relationship with Byron was not a hot, sex-soaked, intense love affair like his time with Kayla. Our relationship was as sweet and comfortable as a pair of UGG boots. Kissing him didn't make me feel the way kissing Cal had made me feel last night, like I had lost all sense of time and space.

I should've known how our relationship was going to end from the beginning. Even though they'd broken up, Kayla was still very much a part of Byron's life. She called him to cry over her boyfriends, family drama, and the crap that was going on at her job. He dropped everything to answer her calls and texts, even with me sitting right next to him, and when I complained, I was told I was insecure and that I had nothing to worry about because they were just "friends". He was coming home to me every night, wasn't he? In retrospect, there'd been no other way that this was going to turn out. When I caught them, I can honestly say I don't know whether I was crying with relief, after finally realizing I wasn't crazy, or anger, because he'd wasted three years of my life, instead of being with the woman he wanted all along. Kayla got what she wanted eventually. But why did she care enough to invade my privacy?

I sat on a park bench across the street from the hospital that Kayla worked at, waiting for her to arrive for her shift. Kayla was a physical therapist. It was almost 9 a.m. before she rolled into the parking lot. I'd intended to confront her before she entered the building, but I'd received a text from my mother wanting to know why I still hadn't sent her my new address. By the time I looked up again from my phone, Kayla was already in the building. *Crap!* I didn't want to talk to her in the hospital. On the other hand, talking to her with the threat of embarrassment in front of her coworkers might work to my advantage. Sounded like a plan to me.

I crossed the street, entering the same doorway Kayla had walked through. Once inside, I realized I wasn't in the hospital proper. I was in the indoor parking space with elevators that went to each level. I headed toward the walkway into the hospital when I heard giggling behind me. I looked around to see Kayla standing next to a Range Rover being felt up by a tall white guy in scrubs who was most definitely not Byron. My mouth fell open. I wasn't so shocked, however, to forget to pull my phone out and take pics of Kayla in a clinch with another man.

It didn't surprise me at all. She'd been working so hard to get Byron back and now that she had gotten what she wanted, she was probably bored and looking for her next conquest. I'd bet my mother that this dude was married or at least in a relationship too. Single guys weren't enough of a challenge for her. I spied on them for a good five minutes before they finally broke apart. Once Range Rover guy had driven away, I walked out into the parking garage and called Kayla's name. She turned to see me standing there and her eyes widened.

"Kendall? What are you... doing...?" Her voice trailed off as I walked up to her holding out my phone and she spotted the pic I'd just taken of her.

"What am *I* doing? The question is, what are you doing, Kayla? I mean, besides getting felt up by some guy in a parking garage. And let me guess," I said, walking up to her. "He's a doctor, right?"

"Are you spying on me?"

"Look, I don't care what or who you're doing. I just need to know one thing."

"And what's that?" She looked around the parking garage, clearly paranoid about whether Byron was lurking nearby.

"Who gave you the right to look through my personal shit?"

"I have no clue what you're talking about?" Her eyes narrowed in confusion.

"I know you were snooping through my diaries. You left chocolate smudges behind and one of them reeked of your shitty perfume. I want to know why you're playing sick games with me." I had expected her to deny it, but she just looked away and refused to meet my eyes or answer my question. "Okay. Fine. I'll just ask Byron if he knows what the hell you're up to with that dude..."

"No! Kendall, don't!" She took a step toward me.

"Then answer me. Why were you looking through my diary?"

"Because I got paid to."

"Paid to?" Who would be so interested in my past that they'd be willing to pay someone to violate my privacy? This was serious and frightening. I glanced around half expecting to see someone lurking behind a parked car watching me. Of course, no one was there.

"I don't know. Byron told me he got a weird email asking for information about you, offering $500 for it. They made it sound like you'd applied for a job, and they wanted to know what kind of person you were."

"If they sent it to Byron, why were you the one doing the looking? Were you two looking through my diaries together?"

"Byron thought it was a joke, and he trashed the email. When he wasn't looking, I forwarded it to me. Sorry, sis, but $500 is $500."

"Did you reply to them in person or by email?"

"Email." She sighed like she was bored and kept looking at the elevator doors.

"I know you've never liked me, but why would you give someone my private information, not knowing who you were dealing with? What the hell were you thinking?"

"What's the big fucking deal?" Her voice was so full of attitude, but I noticed she still wouldn't look me in the eye.

"The big fucking deal is that this person is threatening me. You can't be that hard up for $500."

Her eyes got big, and I could tell I had finally gotten through to her.

"Seriously? I didn't know they were going to be doing all that."

"No, you just saw dollar signs and threw me under the bus so you could buy yourself a pair of expensive shoes." I nodded toward what looked like a pair of Golden Goose tennis shoes with a glittering pink star on them.

"You're not going to tell Byron, are you?"

"About you selling my personal information, or about you grinding against a married doctor in the hospital parking lot?"

"Any of it." There was actual fear in Kayla's eyes, which baffled me. The future psychologist in me knew there was most likely some kind of hole in her she was trying to fill with her affairs, and Byron was merely collateral damage. I was suddenly so relieved that this wasn't my problem anymore.

"Not if you give me that email address."

"And if I do, will you promise you won't tell him?"

I was silent for a few seconds, enjoying watching her twist in the wind. Finally, I said, "I don't give a damn about you or Byron. I had to find out the hard way about him, just like he's going to have to find out the hard way about you. And trust me, he *will* find out. But not from me."

I was headed back to campus when my mother called, and I finally told her Byron and I had broken up.

"Byron's a spineless idiot, and if you'd have listened to me years ago, I could have told you he wasn't right for you," insisted my mother.

"Why have you always hated Byron?"

It was true my mother had loathed Byron almost from their first meeting. She had nothing good to say about him, and it confused me, since Byron came from an excellent family, was educated, and had a great job.

"Do you remember that first time I came to dinner and met him?"

"Yeah, I remember. Why?"

"You'd left the room to go check on the roast, and I asked him what it was he loved the most about you. And do you know what he said?"

"What?" I asked, not sure I wanted to know.

"He said he loved your cooking and how you took such good care of him. Nothing about your intelligence, sense of humor, your looks, your passion, or your drive. It was all about what you did for him and how sweet and caring you are. He could have been describing his mother. If you'd married him, he'd have insisted you stay home and take care of a house full of kids, including him."

Mom launched into a full-blown rant about narcissistic men and all the red flags to look for in the future. I had to hold the phone away from my ear because once she got started, she wouldn't stop until she was satisfied I'd gotten the point, which she drove into me like a stake through a vampire's heart. It felt like forever before I could get her off the phone.

Five minutes later, I sat in B&C café composing a message to the email address that Kayla had given me. The email was: employeeinfoservices@thenet.com. I knew Kayla was the one who'd given this person the info about my father and my stealing, but how did this person know I was taking Mac's classes? How had they gotten ahold of that photo of me and my dad? I took a deep breath and fired off an email:

Who is this? And why are you blackmailing me?

I got a response less than five minutes later that said:

Don't you have a scavenger hunt to complete? Get moving. Because I'm watching and the clock's ticking.

What do you want from me?

I emailed back.

Tick Tock, bitch.

My blood ran cold.

I had until 5 p.m. to complete all the items on the list. I wanted to get it over with as quickly as possible. Nouveau

Boutique was a five-minute walk from the college. I got there and found the section in the back where they sold the makeup. Quickly looking around, I snagged the last Pom Passion lip gloss and the one right next to it called Raspberry Rain. With the practiced swiftness that I'd perfected over years of petty theft, I slipped the Pom Passion lip gloss up my sleeve and carried the Raspberry Rain to the counter.

"I love this place. I've never been here before," I told the cashier, who brightened up at the compliment.

"Thanks, we've only been open for about six months, but the response from the community and college students has been great."

"And I'll take this too," I told her, grabbing a pack of spearmint gum from a rack next to the register. She rang me up, none the wiser that I had something extra up my sleeve, and I hurried out the door. In the alley around the corner, I removed the Pom Passion and spread a thin coat over my lips. I pulled up my phone and took a quick selfie and then posted it on my Instagram with the #thislipglossisasteal. I checked but could see no one who looked like they were following me or watching me. Everyone was minding their own business and going about their day. Lucky them.

Next on the list was attending a matinee of *Little Shop of Horrors* at the Addison Playhouse, which was four blocks away. For the next hour, I sat in an audience of about two dozen people watching a production of a musical where only a handful of the cast could sing. The plant monster, Audrey II, was made from papier mâché. I left during intermission and snagged a program on my way out the door. The instructions said that I had to attend but said nothing about staying for the whole thing.

Back at Mac's place, I was happy to be home alone. As I was told to, I took a pair of scissors and cut up the program and dumped it in the trash, wondering how in the hell the freak who was blackmailing me would know that I had done it.

I was about to leave for the Riverwalk dog park when Mac came storming in. She did not look happy.

"We need to have a talk," she told me.

"It will have to be quick because I'm on my way someplace and I'm already late."

She pulled something up on her phone and then held it out to me. It looked like the screen for her online class, and I briefly glanced at it before looking at her in annoyance, impatient to get out the door.

"What am I looking at, Mac?"

"The grade for my quiz. I got an A+ on that quiz you took for me the other day. An A+?"

"And?" Her pissy attitude, coupled with my need to get going, made me pissy too. Why wasn't she thanking me?

"I just need to pass this class, Kendall. I'm not trying to get on the dean's list. I thought we talked about how this needed to be believable. I am not an A+ student, and no one is going to believe that I suddenly have become one."

She had a point. But asking me to get an average grade in a class was like asking me to gouge my own eyes out with toothpicks.

"I'm not about to apologize for getting you an A+. I will promise from now on your grades will be average AF. Okay?" I didn't wait for her response and left her standing there staring after me.

There were only five people in the dog park when I got there. And of the dogs that were there, I could see a beagle, a husky, a German Shepherd, and a black lab. But no black Frenchie. I sat on a bench and pulled a bottle of water from my bag. Five minutes later, an older white woman showed up with an adorable black French bulldog.

"Hey, are you new here?" asked the owner of a beagle

whose bone-shaped name tag identified him as Odie. His owner, a white guy about my age, dressed in running clothes, plopped down on the bench next to me right as I was about to pull my phone out to snap a pic of the Frenchie. It took a few seconds for me to realize that he was talking to me. Although his tone was friendly, his eyes narrowed, and I realized he was probably wondering why I was there without a dog. I should have borrowed Spanky from Liv.

"Oh, yeah. I love dogs," I stammered, earning me an even more suspicious look. "I can't have one because my roommate is allergic. I like to come here occasionally and watch the dogs play. I haven't seen you before here either."

"Well, we're not here every day. I work long hours, so I try to take this guy out and spend as much time with him as I can on my days off."

"I guess that's why I haven't seen you guys before. I'm Kathy, by the way." I wasn't about to give him my real name. I held my hand out for him to shake, and he gave it a quick pump.

"I'm Dave, and sorry for the third degree. About a month ago, a lady with a Frenchie who was a regular here got her dog stolen. Frenchies are expensive and get stolen a lot."

You saw a black woman sitting here alone without a dog and automatically thought she was a thief? I had wanted to say but didn't. And besides, I am a thief.

"I read about that in the news. But I didn't hear anything else about it. Did she ever get her dog back?"

"No. And it was a real shame because she adored that dog." He shook his head.

While we were chatting, the black Frenchie played ten feet away with a dachshund while its owner talked to another woman holding a puppy. Now would be the perfect time to snap a pic and make my escape, but Odie's daddy wouldn't shut up and I had to listen to him drone on about the benefits of a raw diet for Odie. After what seemed like forever, a pretty young woman arrived with her Corgi, Dave rushed to join her, and I was able to quickly snap the pic of the Frenchie and leave.

So far, everything on the scavenger hunt list I'd been able to do with ease but without understanding. Why in the world was I doing this crap? What did this person really want from me? I was going to be seriously pissed if I found out that this was all a joke by someone I knew. Until then, I couldn't take the chance that this person was going to run snitching to the dean. All I had to do was complete the last item on the list, which was to try on a pair of Luciano Silva stilettos at Macy's. But there was a big problem. When I arrived at the store, they didn't have a pair of black Luciano Silva stilettos in my size. The only pair they had was size eight. Would my blackmailer know? I spied a pair of identical Nine West black stilettos and quickly put them on behind the clearance rack. I carried the Luciano Silva box with the other shoes with me out onto the sales floor and made a show of preening in them in front of a mirror, before snapping a pic of my feet, happy that I wasn't being asked to buy them because the price tag made me wince. I walked around the shoe department, still holding the Luciano Silva box in case this person was watching.

When I was done, I left the store and headed back to Mac's, checking on the way that I had the shoe and dog pics saved to my camera roll to post over the next three days. I sent an email to the address that read:

I've done everything you've asked. Now please leave me alone.

I waited for a response that never came. But I couldn't shake the feeling that whoever I was emailing wasn't done with me yet.

ELEVEN

PHOENIX, ARIZONA

Enlightened Path Rehab Center
Five Days Earlier

They sent a black SUV to pick her up. Her mother had the
good sense not to be there when she was released. Instead, she
sent her PA, Alayna, the latest in a long string of put-upon
young women her mother hired, then chewed up and spit out.
She could never figure out exactly why her mother needed a
PA, other than just wanting to flex. None of them lasted longer
than six months, usually. Alayna was heading into month seven,
so maybe there was hope for her.

"You look good," said Alayna, lying through her pretty
capped teeth.

She glared at Alayna without speaking, noticing the shopping bags she'd brought with her, knowing she wouldn't like a
single thing that was in them.

"Your mom sends these and her love. She says the two of
you can talk once you get home."

"And who says I'm going back home after what she did
to me?"

"I hope these fit." Alayna ignored her comment. "You look like you've lost weight."

Instead of answering her, she grabbed one of the shopping bags and pulled the contents out. Sure enough, her mom had picked out clothes for a middle-aged Disney princess. Lots of pastel dresses, skirts, and flowy tops. Her mother knew she hated stuff like this. She was being punished for refusing her visits and phone calls for the last three months. It didn't really matter because Alayna had been right. She had lost weight. So, none of this ugly shit was going to fit anyway.

"Our flight leaves this evening, so you have plenty of time to rest and get ready. I booked you a spa treatment and a mani/pedi." Alayna looked her up and down, her expression clearly conveying that she found her current appearance lacking.

But she didn't care. All she wanted to do was get home and undo the damage that was being done and hope to hell that it wasn't too late to fix it.

TWELVE
ADDISON, OHIO

Two days passed and still no response from my stalker. I was feeling hopeful that it would be the last I heard of them. When I sent a second message, it came back as undeliverable, advising me that email address no longer existed. I had no choice but to move on with my life. I posted the selfies at the times I had been instructed to, just in case this person was still watching, which I was sure they would be.

In the meantime, I decided I needed a distraction, and what better distraction than a hot guy named Cal? I grabbed another cute mini dress from the pile of clothes Mac had dumped in my room the night of my date with Cal at Cora's. This one was eggplant-colored with a deep V neck and batwing sleeves. I left my hair loose. I had gotten it cut that morning into a blunt cut bob that fell to my chin. Mac wasn't home to do my makeup, so I opted for tinted moisturizer and a little lip gloss. Then I headed to Cal's bar, The Hub, and parked myself at the bar and drank virgin peach margaritas for an hour before he showed up.

To say he didn't exactly look thrilled to see me was an understatement, and I instantly felt stung and stupid. That I hadn't heard from him since our date a few nights ago should've been my first clue that he wasn't interested. It was too late to get up and leave because he'd already seen me.

He finally came down to my end of the bar. "What do I owe the pleasure of this visit, Good?"

"Just needed to get out. A woman can't live on studying alone." I should have just called up Liv to come over for a pizza. "How are you?" I asked when he began polishing shot glasses, still looking distracted. I realized whatever was going on with him probably had nothing to do with me. At least I hoped it didn't.

"Same shit with my mother's husband. Different day."

"Do you want to talk about it?" I reached out and touched his forearm. And he looked up and gave me a smile.

"Sure, why not? Have you eaten?"

"No. What did you have in mind?" Cal gave me a wicked look that made blood rush to my face, and he laughed.

"Well, I'm not much of a cook. But I can order Door Dash with the best of them."

I laughed and allowed him to lead me out of the bar and up to his loft, where he ordered takeout from a local Mexican restaurant.

"What happened with your stepfather?"

He gave me a grim look. "Do me a favor and don't ever call him that again."

"Sorry," I said with a nervous laugh. "What's his name?"

"Nick. Nick Palmer, a forty-year-old con man who I don't think has ever had a job in his miserable life."

"How'd he meet your mom?"

"He approached her about investing in a gym he was trying to open here in town. She turned him down, and he asked her out. Then he laid the charm on thick, and she fell hard because ever since my dad died six years ago, she'd been lonely and vulnerable."

"You said she was ill?"

"Brain cancer. It was her second bout with it. She knew she'd made a mistake marrying Nick, but by the time she decided to divorce him, she was sick and no longer had the energy. Instead, she changed her will, leaving everything to me and he's contesting it."

"I'm sorry you're having to go through this."

"And I'm sorry you got caught up in this whole mess. Endowing the Bennett Fellowship was my mother's legacy, and he's tainted it. I've blocked him from accessing her bank accounts and using her credit cards. But since her house is his legal residence, I can't evict him, and I know for a fact that he's selling off everything in the house because he's broke and giving my mother's jewelry to his side chicks."

"Can he do that when the estate hasn't been settled yet? Isn't that against the law?"

"It is. But since I don't know about everything my mom owned, it's easy to put it up on eBay or a private auction site and ship it off."

His anger and frustration were palpable, and the silence was so awkward I didn't know what to say to him.

"Sorry I'm such shitty company, Kendall. That's why I haven't called. I've been dealing with this asshole's bullshit for two days. Every time something I know belonged to my mom pops up for sale on eBay, I get an alert. Of course, I can't prove it belonged to her, let alone do anything about the sale. It's driving me crazy."

"Cal," I said, softly inching closer to him on the couch. He turned to look at me. "Your mom is not her stuff. You have no control over what her husband is doing with her things. If it means that much to you, you can always keep track of everything that's been sold and try to buy it back when her estate's been settled." I inched even closer and laid my hand on his arm. "I didn't have the pleasure of knowing her, but do you really think she'd want you angry and hurting over replaceable things?" I thought I'd gone too far when anger flashed across his face, but it was gone in an instant and he was silent, his expression unreadable, as he thought about what I'd just said. So I pressed on. "Is this really about her stuff or about your guilt over not being around to protect her?"

I felt the tension instantly leave his body as he squeezed my hand. "Damn, Good. That was some deep shit," he said with a warm smile. "I guess that's why you're the Bennett Fellow."

We looked at each other, each of us leaning in for a kiss, when both his cell phone and the doorbell went off, making us jump apart before bursting into laughter.

"I bet that's our food. I'll get the door. You get your phone." I got up from the couch and slipped back into my sandals.

After retrieving our food from the delivery woman, I was on my way back up to Cal's loft when I heard a noise that sounded like a woman crying. It came from the direction of an open door that led out to the alley behind the bar. I sat the bag of food down on the step and went to investigate. A short, stocky white guy pinned a blonde woman against the opposite wall. I recognized her as a server from my first visit to The Hub.

"You wanna get mouthy with me? Then this is what you're gonna get." He slugged the blonde in the stomach so hard she doubled over in pain, clutching her middle. Then he grabbed her by her hair and jerked her back up, and slapped her face so hard you could have heard the crack down the street.

"Don't you ever talk to me like that again! You hear me?"

"Yes... Phil. Please... stop. I'm... so sorry. I won't do it again," gasped the blonde. Her face was bright red from where Phil had slapped her.

"Hey!" I shouted before I could stop myself. "You let her go!"

"Mind your own business, you nosy black bitch," snarled Phil.

I'm not sure where I got the nerve or the courage, and I

certainly didn't want to make things even worse for the poor woman, but I'd had enough of people, especially men, talking smack about me. I must have still had some pent-up anger over what I'd overheard Byron saying about me.

"The only ugly I see in this alley is a runty motherfucker who beats on women to make up for having a little dick!"

Phil shoved the woman against the wall and came charging at me.

"What did you say, bitch?"

Oh, shit. Me and my big mouth. Phil was short but had muscular forearms and could probably wipe up the alley with me. Unfortunately, I hadn't thought beyond insulting him.

"I don't know what she said," came Cal's voice from the door to the alley. "But if you don't get your sorry ass out of here, being short and stupid is going to be the least of your problems."

Phil froze in his tracks and weighed his options. Then he gave Cal and me an evil look before turning to leave.

"Just have your ass home on time tonight or you won't sit down for a week," he told the blonde as he left. She wiped her face and hurried back inside, practically knocking Cal down.

"Oh, and Bennett," said Phil, turning to face Cal. "You may be hot shit because your mommy bought you a bar, but don't be acting like you're better than me, 'cause it ain't been that long since your ass was putting on a khaki uniform one leg at a time just like I did."

I stared at Cal in confusion. Cal's eyes, which up until that moment had never left Phil's smirking face, slid away from him. His expression was suddenly tight and angry. How in the world did Cal know this lowlife?

"What's he talking about? What uniform did you both wear?" I looked from one man to the other. Phil saw my confused expression and burst out laughing.

"What? You didn't tell your girlfriend that you went ham on your daddy with a fireplace poker? Well, that should be one hell of a conversation." With that, Phil was gone. Cal leaned against the doorjamb with an unreadable expression on his face as all the color drained from it.

"Cal? What is he talking about?" I needed for him to tell me I'd misheard because I couldn't have heard him correctly. Was this a joke?

He hesitated and then took a deep breath. "We both served time in the same prison," he said, unable to look at me. "I'm a convicted felon, Kendall."

As I fled the alley, the sound of Cal's voice calling my name echoed in my ears. A convicted felon who'd assaulted his father with a fireplace poker? And I'd almost slept with this man? I'd showed up at his bar tonight with the sole intention of actually sleeping with him. Now my hoe phase had officially ended before it had even started.

"Wow, Kendall," I mumbled to myself as I unlocked the front door of Mac's place and stepped inside. "You have the *worst* taste in men."

It was dark inside the house, which was strange because usually the porch light was on. I flipped the switch in the foyer, but no light came on.

"Hey, Mac!" I called out while my eyes adjusted to the darkness. "You home? Did you forget to pay the light bill?" I took a few steps into the living room and called out again. "Mac?" My foot slid out from under me, and I fell hard on my ass. I tried in vain to stand up but slipped again. There was something wet and sticky all over the floor, and now it was all over me. "What the fuck? Mac! Where are you? Are you home?" I yelled.

I rolled onto my hands and knees. Using the nearest wall, I inched my way up into a standing position and flipped the living room light switch on. And that's when I found out why Mac hadn't been answering me.

She was lying spread-eagle on the living room floor. Her eyes were wide open and unblinking.

"Mac?" I took a step toward her and almost slipped again. But Mac didn't answer, and she never would again. She was dead, lying in a pool of her own blood, with the heel of a black stiletto pump jammed into the side of her neck.

From the diary of Kendall Good:

December 15, 2011

Dear Diary,

I know what really happened that night. My dad tried to kill me. I wish he had.

THIRTEEN
ADDISON, OHIO

Instead of ditching Alayna at the airport when they landed in Columbus and taking a bus to Addison, she should have just gone home. What Alayna didn't realize was that when she'd been released from rehab, and her belongings were returned, her credit card was still in her purse. For four days, she'd been holed up in a hotel room, watching and waiting and biding her time, and now it had all gone horribly wrong.

She ran from the house as fast as she could and didn't stop running until she reached the Riverwalk three blocks away. Everything was so screwed up. She'd just wanted to talk to her, that's all, to ask why she'd been impersonating her online, but she never had the chance, and now she never would. Thinking about all that blood made her stomach roil, and she had to rush over to a clump of bushes to vomit. She was dizzy when she was done. She should have sat down, but she wanted to get out of there and as far away from the horror she'd just experienced as possible.

Worst of all, Kendall was now involved. When she fled the house and watched her arrive across the street and let herself in, she thought she was seeing things. What was she doing there? How had she gotten mixed up in this mess?

She hurried down the path, trying to catch her breath, and zipped up her hoodie to cover her bloodstained T-shirt. She worried a couple walking toward her might notice it, but they never even looked at her. Sweat ran down her back. There was only one thing left to do, and she was dreading it. She pulled out her cell phone and pressed a name in her contacts list. She'd had it for years but never dared call. It rang several times before a low melodic voice finally answered.

"Yes?"

"Jackie Good?" she said tentatively. Over the years, she'd imagined making this phone call so many times. She couldn't believe she was finally making it, and under these circumstances.

"Speaking."

Once she heard Jackie's voice, all her nerve left her, and she hung up not sure what she'd been about to say to this woman. The phone rang in her hand, and she almost dropped it. It was the number she'd just called. Jackie's number. She let it ring for what seemed like forever before finally answering it.

"Hello?"

"Who is this and why did you just call me?" Jackie Good sounded highly annoyed and she almost hung up again. But it was now or never. She gathered her courage and went for it.

"I need to meet with you. It's important. It's about Kendall."

FOURTEEN

ADDISON, OHIO

The police had questions for me. Lots of questions. I called Liv to pick me up at the ER and bring me some clean clothes. Mine were covered with blood. Mac's blood. The memory of what I walked into tonight kept flashing in my mind when I least expected it, causing me to freeze and relive the horror.

"Kendall? Are you okay?" Liv rubbed my back.

"Yeah, I'm okay." But I wasn't. How could I be okay after finding a dead body? And not someone who'd died of natural causes. Mac was murdered.

We were waiting for me to be released when two police detectives from the Addison PD showed up.

"Ms. Good?" asked a middle-aged balding white guy. A much younger and shorter black man with a goatee and glasses accompanied him.

"Yes," I said, looking from one man to the other.

"I'm Detective Peter Delaney and this is my partner, Detective Terrell Wallace. We just need to ask you some questions about what happened tonight if you're up to it."

"Does she have to do this right now?" asked Liv. "Can't she come down to the station later? She's had a big shock."

"And you'd be?" asked Detective Wallace, giving Liv the once over.

"I'm Olivia Bryant, her best friend. And I'm not sure we saw your badges." Good old Liv was in mama bear mode, and I couldn't have been more grateful not to have to deal with these detectives alone.

The detectives looked slightly embarrassed as they pulled their badges out and showed them to us, even though I wouldn't have known whether they were real or fake.

"Ms. Bryant," said detective Delaney gently. "We'd like to speak to Ms. Good while her recollection is still fresh. We'd appreciate it if you could step outside."

Liv protested, but I cut her off. "It's okay." I put a hand on her arm. "I'm the one who found her, so I am the one who gets to answer the questions."

"I'll be right outside if you need me." She side-eyed the detectives before heading out into the hallway. When she was gone, the detectives turned their attention back to me.

"Can you please go over how you came to find the deceased?" asked Delaney.

I recounted my evening to the detectives, leaving out the part about finding out my date was a convicted felon, and concluded with entering the dark house and slipping in Mac's blood before finding her body.

"And what is your relationship to the deceased?" asked Wallace.

"Roommates. I was renting a room from her."

"Were you friends?" asked Delaney.

"No," I said honestly. "I needed a place to stay, and she had a spare bedroom she offered to rent me." There was no way I could tell them the actual nature of my relationship with Mac and how I came to be living with her.

"It was just the two of you living in the residence?" asked Wallace.

"Yes."

"And when was the last time you saw Ms. McCoy?"

McCoy? Who were they talking about?

"I'm sorry who?" The look of confusion on my face caused Delaney and Wallace to look at each other before Wallace responded.

"The deceased? Savannah McCoy?"

"No." I looked from one man to the other. "I have no idea who that person is. Are we talking about the same murder? Because the woman I found was Mackenzie Burk."

"Ms. Good, the woman you found deceased at 1222 Riley Avenue Apt C was a twenty-four-year-old theater grad student from Columbus named Savannah McCoy." Wallace pulled up something on his phone and took a step closer to the hospital bed and handed it to me.

On the screen was a smiling young black woman with curly dark hair that fell to her shoulders. It looked like the headshot actors used in their portfolios. She looked slightly different from the woman I'd been sharing a home with for the past week and a half, but if you put a pink pixie cut wig on her and made her makeup heavier and put a gold stud in her nose... this was the woman I'd known as Mackenzie Burk. And then I remembered what the woman who called herself Mac told me when she brought me the bag of makeup and wig after I'd moved in.

"Makeup is magic, and I can make you look like anyone."

Clearly, she had done that by turning herself into the socialite and influencer, Mackenzie Burk. I'd been living with an imposter all this time and didn't even realize it. I couldn't even tell the detectives the true nature of our association because I could still get in a lot of trouble for what fake Mac had hired me to do. Was I even taking her class? And why in the world would this woman hire me to take someone else's class?

I needed to tell these men something. They were looking at me expectantly.

"I'm not sure exactly what's going on here," I told them. "But this woman approached me after she overheard me telling Liv at a café on campus about my breakup and that I had no place to stay. She said she had a room I could rent, and I moved in the next day."

"She introduced herself as Mackenzie Burk, daughter of Marcus Burk?" asked Wallace, clearly doubtful about what I had just told them.

"Yes. She looks so much like her, I never questioned it." *Why hadn't I questioned it?*

Was it because she looked and acted just like Mackenzie? If I was being truthful, something had bugged me about her all along. Before we met, I'd briefly followed Mackenzie Burk on Instagram and TikTok, until my studies, library job, and Byron started taking up all of my time. It must have been a good five years since I looked at her socials. Back when I viewed her content regularly, her posts and videos always fascinated me. Her life was so unlike mine, so carefree and adventurous. Meeting her had been somewhat of a letdown. In fact, my fascination with her had quickly disappeared, which, I thought, was because of how spoiled and entitled she was in real life. Now I knew it was because she was an imposter. She talked the talk and walked the walk and made herself look like Mackenzie Burk, but she didn't have the natural charm and charisma that made the real Mackenzie so watchable. I'd been so desperate and in need of a refuge that I'd bought her act completely.

"But what about the apartment? She told me her father owned the building."

"The building is owned by a woman named Grace Russell. She lives in one of the units. She said Ms. McCoy moved in a year ago. She was an actress and studied theater at Bellbrook," said Delaney, consulting a notebook he'd pulled from inside his suit jacket.

"She also worked as a makeup artist for the Addison Playhouse," continued Wallace, and all the hairs on my forearms stood up.

That's when everything clicked. The scavenger hunt. Making me go to the playhouse. The trip to Macy's trying on the shoes. *The shoes*. One of which I bet was now sticking out of fake Mac's neck.

"You're sure this woman's name is Savannah McCoy?"

"It is according to her landlord and all of her neighbors and her identification," said Delaney.

"Her dog sitter even showed up with her dog Biscuit this morning," said Wallace.

"Her dog? I never saw a dog the entire time I lived there."

"The dog had been with the sitter for two weeks. She said she hadn't heard from Ms. McCoy and showed up to return the dog and get paid."

"Was it a black French bulldog?" I asked, already knowing the answer.

"Yeah, why?" asks Wallace, shooting his partner a look.

"I thought I saw a picture on her cell phone wallpaper," I lied. What the hell was going on? Clearly whoever had killed the woman I'd been living with was trying to set me up to take the fall.

"Are you okay, Ms. Good?" asked Delaney.

"Can I please have a glass of water? This is just so surreal." Wallace was the one who poured me a cup of water and handed it to me.

"Would you have any idea if Ms. McCoy had any enemies? Did you witness any confrontations between her and anyone?"

"No," I said, happy to be telling the truth about something. "We rarely saw each other, and I didn't see her at all today, well, you know, not until I found her, that is."

"Do you know if she was dating anyone or in a relationship?" asked Wallace.

"If she was, I never met this person. She even told me I

couldn't bring men to the apartment." I'd thought it was an odd rule about not bringing men to the house. Now that I thought about it, of course she didn't want me to bring anyone to the house because she was playing a game. She was impersonating Mackenzie Burk, and only wanted a few people exposed to that lie.

"Is there anything you know about this young woman that could help shed light on who did this to her?" asked Delaney.

I made a show of thinking about it. I couldn't tell them the truth about why I was really living with her or about the scavenger hunt. They needed to know, but I couldn't tell them one thing without revealing another truth which would ruin my life. Instead, I asked a question of my own.

"Do you have any idea why she would impersonate Mackenzie Burk? Do you think this is some kind of identity theft?"

The detectives look at each other. Wallace answered, "It certainly happens. Mackenzie Burk has a large social media following, and we've seen our share of influencers who've had their identity stolen by people who impersonate them online for gain. But they usually give themselves away to anyone paying attention."

"Meaning?" I replied, realizing this was some kind of dig at me.

"Meaning, why would Mackenzie Burk, who comes from a wealthy family and has a large online following, need to have a roommate?" He said it in a way that felt like an insult. Like, was I stupid enough to think someone like her would need someone like me? It couldn't have been anything except a scam.

"I never even gave it a second thought because I was desperate and needed a place to stay." I didn't mean for it to sound so defensive, and Delaney's face softened.

"No one is accusing you of anything, Ms. Good," he said, shooting Wallace a look. "We're just trying to get a clear picture of the victim and since you were living with her, we thought you might provide that."

"But it sounds like you may have been a victim too, right?" Wallace was staring at me so intensely it felt like his gaze was piercing my soul.

What was his problem? Were they playing good cop/bad cop, and it was his turn to be bad cop, or was he just an asshole? I didn't want to continue this conversation and needed to change the subject quickly.

"Was that really a high-heeled shoe sticking out of the side of her neck? I only caught a glimpse before I ran out of the house, but I could've sworn that's what I saw."

Wallace was still staring at me, eyes narrowed, and it was Delaney who finally answered me.

"I can confirm that it was a shoe you saw, a black Luciano Silva stiletto platform pump size eight. Did you recognize that shoe? Is it something you'd seen the victim wearing?"

"I've never seen that shoe before," I lied. "But have you seen her bedroom? It's literally a walk-in closet, and she has probably four or five dozen pairs of shoes. It could have easily been one of her shoes."

"A forensics team is going through the entire house, and we've yet to find a mate to that shoe, either in her closet or anywhere else."

If they were searching the house, then that meant they probably searched through my room as well. I tried hard to think about anything in my room that would incriminate me or show that I'd been committing academic fraud.

"Since the house is now a crime scene, will I be able to get back in there and get my things?"

"Once we're finished processing the scene, we can have an officer escort you over to get your things in the next day or so," said Wallace. "And we'll need for you to come down to the station to go over your statement and give us your fingerprints."

"Fingerprints?" I said in alarm. "Why do you need my fingerprints?"

"It's standard procedure to eliminate your prints from any other prints found at the scene," said Delaney.

"Oh," I said, taking a breath, very aware that Wallace was still watching me closely. "I guess that makes sense."

"If there's anything you remember that might be helpful, anything at all, please call us." Delaney handed me his card, and he and Wallace left.

Once they were gone, the situation hit me like a ton of bricks. I was back in the same place I was before I met fake Mac. Although I still had a little over half of the money she had given me now safely in my bank account, I was once again homeless and wondering about my next move. I guess things could have been worse. I could have a stiletto pump in my neck.

Cal had been blowing up my phone for two days when Liv finally had enough.

"Are you going to call him back or not? It doesn't sound like he's going to stop trying to get in contact with you. Can't you at least listen to what he has to say and tell him you don't want to see him again to his face?"

"I went out on one date with this guy. I don't owe him shit."

"True," she conceded. "Technically, it was a date and a half. How do you know whatever happened between him and his father wasn't self-defense? All you heard was what some asshole in an alley said. You never gave him a chance to tell his side of the story."

Liv was right. Besides, if anyone knew about being attacked by their father, it would be me. I didn't know why I was being so judgmental when I had my own demons. I let out a sigh because she was right. I should at least have a conversation with him.

"Fine. I'll talk to him the next time he calls." That next call came less than a minute later. Only this time I answered it.

"Hello?"

"Kendall?"

"Hi, Cal." I didn't know what else to say. This was awkward AF.

"I read about what happened in the paper. Are you all right?"

"It was a shock, but I'll live."

"Can we please get together and talk? I know you probably have questions, and I just want to tell my side of the story."

"Why is it so important to you? We barely know each other."

"I know, but what you heard in the alley was only part of the story. If even after you hear my side, you never want to see me again, I'll respect that and leave you alone."

I was silent for a while before finally agreeing. "Okay. How about tonight at Cora's?"

"Sounds great. How about six?"

"I'll see you then," I said and hung up.

"Now see," Liv said, grinning at me. "That wasn't so hard, was it?"

"Shut up."

Later that morning, I met the police at Savannah McCoy's apartment. An officer escorted me inside, guiding me straight up to the guest bedroom so I could pack my things. I glanced into the living room on my way up the steps. There was still a large blood stain staining the hardwood floor where the body had lain. My stomach turned, and I tried to block out the image of her body. When I got to my temporary room, it was obvious they had searched everything. The mattress was askew; the bedding was stripped from the bed; the drawers had been opened and even my suitcases had been gone through.

I got busy packing my things back into my suitcases. I was surprised to find the MacBook Pro Savannah had given me was still there and hadn't been confiscated. On a whim, I took it, reasoning that it had been a gift, and my laptop was on its last legs. I also packed the pile of clothes fake Mac had said she'd never wear. While I packed, I thought about everything that this woman had told me about the Burk family and about her own life. Had everything been lies? She was playing a role. Why had she hired me to take her class? Was it because she was too busy being an imposter? What about Mackenzie Burk's social media accounts? Was Savannah posting on her socials? If so, how did she get access to her accounts? I pulled my phone out to check, when I heard voices coming from Savannah McCoy's room. I stepped into the hallway to listen.

"All of it? You mean everything in this room is fake?" said a disembodied male voice. I walked toward the bedroom, stopping just outside the door, and peeked around the corner. Two officers, a man and a woman were standing in the middle of the bedroom I thought belonged to Mackenzie Burk.

"Yep," replied the female officer. "I used to work for the Consumer Product Safety Commission, and we were constantly investigating counterfeit designer bag rings."

"How can you tell?" The male officer was holding up the Birkin by the handle and staring at it in confusion.

"Stitching and hardware. The real stuff doesn't have coarse-looking stitching or hardware that's discolored or the wrong color metal. The Made in China labels really give it away. I'm betting collectively these bags cost less than a grand.

"Clothing too?"

"Most of it is either fake designer crap or came from thrift stores." She pulled a dress from one of the racks and held it up. "See, still has the thrift store tags on it."

I backed away from the bedroom door before they spotted me eavesdropping. I felt like the biggest fool. I was standing in front of the Burk family portrait. Was this even real? I took a step closer and touched it, realizing for the first time that it wasn't a painting. It was a poster of a painting. Damn. Even the painting was fake. Disgusted with myself for being so stupid and naïve, I turned to go, and found the officer who'd escorted me inside standing behind me giving me a suspicious look.

"Ma'am, are you finished getting your things?"

"Uh, yeah. I'm done." The officer was nice enough to help me get my suitcases down the stairs and outside. Once I was on the sidewalk, I gave the building one last look, and the officer closed the apartment door.

A few hours later, I left Liv's place, where I was staying, to meet Cal at Cora's. I was wearing the long black sundress Mac had told me not to wear. She'd been right; the color and long loose style did nothing for me. But I didn't want to give Cal the wrong impression. I made it only half a block when an unmarked Crown Victoria pulled up alongside the curb next to me and Detective Wallace got out of the passenger side and stepped in front of me. Delaney remained behind the wheel.

"Ms. Good, could you please come with us?"

My heart raced, and blood rushed to my face. "What for? What's wrong?"

"We just need you to come to the station to clear up a few things." He held open the back door on the passenger side, and I realized I had no choice but to get in. Why did they need to see me again? What had they found out?

FIFTEEN
ADDISON, OHIO

They left me sitting in an interview room for over twenty minutes. During that time, I tried hard not to freak out. Had they found out that Savannah wasn't the only fraud? When the door finally opened, detectives Delaney and Wallace walked in, and each took a seat at the table.

"Am I under arrest?" I looked from one man to the other.

"No," replied Delaney. "You are not under arrest, Ms. Good. And you can leave at any time."

"We just needed to clear up some information that we discovered at the scene, and hope you can help us out," continued Wallace.

"What information?" I clasped my hands in front of me on the table, and it took everything in me to control the trembling.

Wallace sat a laptop on the table, propping it up and scanning through a screen full of images until he found what he was looking for and then turned to face me.

"For example, can you please tell us why we found this in the trashcan of the room you were renting from Savannah McCoy?"

Looking at the screen, I saw the program I'd gotten from the

Addison Playhouse, the one I had torn up per the instructions of
the scavenger hunt. I had thrown it into the kitchen trashcan.
How did it get into the trashcan in the guest bedroom?

"It's a program for *Little Shop of Horrors*. It's playing at the
Addison Playhouse, and I went and saw the matinee." I figured
it was best to stick as close to the truth as humanly possible
without revealing why I'd really been at the Addison Playhouse.

"You had no idea that Savannah McCoy worked at the
Addison Playhouse as makeup artist?"

"I had no idea her name was even Savannah McCoy. So,
how would I know if she worked at the Addison Playhouse?"

"In your statement yesterday, you also said you didn't know
Ms. McCoy had a dog. Is that correct?" asked Delaney.

"That's right." It was hot and stuffy in the room. I opened
the water bottle I'd been given and took a couple of quick swigs
before recapping it and turning my attention back to the detectives. It was a distraction so that I could pull myself together.
I'm sure they probably knew it. Wallace took the laptop and
pulled something else up and turned it to face me. My stomach
clinched involuntarily.

"If that's true, why do you have a picture of Savannah
McCoy's dog on your Instagram?"

Now probably would've been a good time to fess up about
the scavenger hunt, but there were so many questions about it
that I could not answer, so I kept my mouth shut.

"My best friend, Liv, who you met at the hospital, also has a
French bulldog, named Spanky. I was passing by the Riverwalk
dog park and saw a dog that looked like Spanky, and so I took a
picture and posted it. How was I supposed to know that it was
the same dog belonging to a woman I was living with? A woman
who lied to me about her identity."

"And how about this?" Wallace pointed to a photograph of
me wearing the Pom Passion lip gloss with the #thislipglos-
sisasteal. He then pulled up Savannah McCoy's Instagram

page, showing a picture of her posing outside Nouveau Boutique, also wearing the same Pom Passion lip gloss, also with the #thislipglossisasteal. The post talked about how long-lasting the lip gloss was, and how it was on sale at Nouveau Boutique. I guess now I knew why there had only been one left.

It finally hit me that this has been the plan all along. Whoever was behind the scavenger hunt had killed Savannah McCoy and framed me. I was feeling trapped and desperate, but I couldn't show it.

"And?" I replied with bravado that I was not truly feeling. "If you tap on the hashtag, you'll see how many other people have used it. I'm sure me and Savannah McCoy are not the only ones."

Wallace did as I suggested and tapped on the hashtag. Over one hundred other people had used the same hashtag. I breathed a silent sigh of relief.

"You still maintain that you don't own a pair of Luciano Silva stiletto pumps in size eight?" asked Wallace.

"If I could afford a pair of Luciano Silva's, I wouldn't be having to rent a room in a stranger's apartment. The price of those shoes equals almost a month's rent. I don't have that kind of money."

"We're guessing that's why you went and tried on a pair and then posted the pic also on your Instagram page?" asked Wallace.

"If that's a crime, then this police station would be filled up with every woman in town."

I was getting angry now. Angry that I was in this situation. Angry for trusting a stranger at face value without doing my due diligence. Angry that Byron had fucked Kayla and ruined our relationship, even though I should've seen it coming a mile away. And angry that I was now having to defend myself in a murder investigation.

"Then why did we find a Luciano Silva stiletto in the room that you were renting from Savannah McCoy?" asked Delaney.

"What?" I sat up straighter in my seat. "I don't own a pair of Luciano Silva's."

Delaney got up from the table and knocked on the room's door. Seconds later, it open and a uniformed officer handed him something enclosed in a clear plastic bag. Delaney shut the door and carried the bag back to the table and set it down. Inside was a single black Luciano Silva stiletto pump.

"We found this hidden at the bottom of the laundry basket in the room you were renting from Savannah McCoy."

"That is not my shoe. And I don't know how it got in the laundry basket."

"Yet it's a match for the one used to murder Savannah McCoy," said Wallace, glancing over at his partner before continuing. "How do you explain that?"

They must have found the shoe when they searched my room while I was still in the hospital. Then something else occurred to me. The shoe used to kill Savannah McCoy was a Luciano Silva, but the shoe that I had tried on in Macy's was a Nine West pump that looked almost identical to this shoe. Macy's hadn't had my size. Someone had either bought or stolen the pair they thought I'd tried on. They used one of them to kill Savannah and frame me.

"I can't explain it because I don't know what's going on. Someone is obviously trying to frame me."

"And who would that be, Ms. Good?" said Delaney, looking genuinely interested in my answer.

"Well, have you checked to see whose prints are on the shoe? They couldn't be my prints. I've never touched it. It's not even my size. I wear a six."

Both men looked at each other, and that's when I realized they already knew my prints weren't on that shoe. They'd brought me in for questioning over some Instagram posts, which were circumstantial evidence. They had no smoking gun, or they would've arrested me already. I stood up.

"We're done, right? I have nothing more to tell you and I have to go." Both men abruptly got up and Wallace opened the door for me.

"This is still an active murder investigation. You are required to make yourself available for further questioning," said Delaney.

"I will." I nodded. "But next time, I'll bring my lawyer." I left without looking back as I added *murder suspect* to *homeless*, *broke*, and *no luck with men* to my current reality.

It was after seven o'clock when I left the police station. I didn't head for any destination. Instead, I walked for the sake of walking. I sent Cal a quick text to let him know I wouldn't be able to make our dinner tonight and told him I'd be in touch. I walked through downtown Addison to the riverfront where I found a bench, sat down and pulled up Mackenzie Burk's Instagram page. I looked through all her recent posts. Quickly I realized it hadn't been Mackenzie posting for several weeks. It was Savannah. Mac's usual content was full of fun, and her charm and charisma were palpable. Whether she shared her morning run to get coffee, or reels of her getting ready, or videos of her unboxing clothing hauls, Mackenzie was always fun to watch. For the past two weeks, however, not only had she been posting very sporadically, but the content was completely different. The newer posts were mostly still photographs or carousels, rather than reels, and she never fully faced the camera. Most were sponsored posts that showed off earrings, nail polish, shoes, and anything that meant she didn't have to show her face or speak to the camera.

I wasn't the only one to notice. There were hundreds of comments about the changed direction of her content, asking if she was okay. How in the world had Savannah gotten access? Did she hack her account? Did the real Mackenzie know what was going on? Speaking of Mackenzie Burk, where the hell was she? Had the police been in contact with her family about the woman who'd been murdered while posing as her? How angry would the real Mackenzie Burk be if she discovered someone had been impersonating her? Angry enough to kill? None of these questions shed light on the scavenger hunt. Who was behind that? And why was somebody trying to frame me?

I sat there for a long time before I finally got up. Somehow, instead of walking back to Liv's, I found myself in front of The Hub. I saw Cal inside, with about half a dozen patrons tending the bar. My hand was out ready to open the door and go inside, when I noticed that one patron had Cal's sole attention, a pretty redhead. She must have been a comedian by the way Cal was laughing at whatever she was saying. I quickly ducked out of sight before he saw me, annoyed at the jealousy that flared at the sight of him talking to another woman. I had much bigger problems to worry about.

When I turned to leave, I saw an older black man leaning against the passenger side door of a beat-up gray pickup truck parked at the curb. He looked familiar, and was wearing a Cora's restaurant T-shirt, and I realized he was the chef I'd had seen when Cal and I had dinner there.

"If you're looking for Cal, he's inside," I told the man and started on my way down the street.

"Have I changed that much, Kendall?"

His words stopped me in my tracks. He took a step closer to me, standing directly under the streetlight so I could get a better look at him. My heart pounded and I felt lightheaded as if I might faint.

The last time I'd seen Raymond Good was before he'd been sentenced to twelve years in prison for embezzlement. I hadn't seen him the day of his sentencing because I was in a coma in the hospital after he'd shoved me down the steps for trying to stop him from attacking my mother. The Raymond Good I remembered was taller and slim and handsome with a killer smile and drip for days. I had never seen my father in jeans or sweats. He lived in suits and ties and dress shoes and always smelled like a million bucks. The man before me now was heavier and shorter than I remembered, with muscular arms, a thick neck, and bald head, and was dressed in a T-shirt, faded jeans, and trainers. His face was also much fuller, and he had a gap between his front teeth where there hadn't been one before. But when he gave a tentative smile, revealing familiar deep dimples, I knew exactly who he was.

"Dad?" It came out barely a whisper, and I took an involuntary step backward.

"I'm not going to hurt you, baby girl." He threw up his hands and took a step back. "I saw you walking and figured it was time you knew I was in town."

"What do you want? Have you been following me?" I looked around wildly and realized we were the only two people on the street.

"I just want to talk. That's all, just talk."

"Why the hell would I want to talk to you? You almost killed me?"

He let out a sigh and leaned back against his truck again. Tense seconds passed while I tried to decide if I should run into the bar or call the police.

"I am so sorry, baby. This is a conversation that we should've had a long time ago. But you were a kid, and your mother would never bring you to see me or let me even talk to you on the phone."

"What's there to talk about? I was in a coma for three days."

"I understand how you feel, Kendall. If you just let me—"

"Stay away from me!" I spat out at him. "Or I'm calling the police and having you arrested for harassment." I walked away, until something I hadn't heard since I was twelve stopped me dead in my tracks.

"Kendall Clarice Good!" My dad's booming voice still had the same effect on me after all these years.

I turned and stared daggers at him. "How dare you use my full name after what you did! You have no right to even have my name in your mouth."

"Let me ask you just one question. Then I'll leave you alone." He walked closer to me and looked me in the eye.

"What?" I snapped, itching to be gone.

"Do you remember what happened that night or were you told by your mother what happened?"

I couldn't speak and looked away from him. I didn't remember what happened that night. My memory of that entire year was patchy. I had snatches of memory here and there, and my mother had filled in the gaps that eluded me.

"She told me my father shoved me down the steps. Why would she lie about that?"

He let out a breath, clenching and unclenching his fists that were hanging by his side, his face a mask of indecision over something he apparently did not want to say.

"Your mother told you the truth. Your father shoved you down those stairs." He stared at me, waiting for the implication of what he just said to sink in. Finally, understanding dawned on me.

"What are you saying?" Tears welled up in my eyes.

"Kendall." He sighed, putting a hand on my shoulder. "You were six months old when I met your mother and fell in love with her. You were fourteen months old when we got married. You are and always will be the daughter of my heart, but you are not my daughter by blood. I'm not the one who pushed you down those stairs."

. . .

Twenty minutes later, we were at Cora's, sitting at a table inside the kitchen. The restaurant had been closed for about an hour. Cora, who turned out to be my dad's wife, was sweeping up when we walked in. As soon as she spotted me, she broke out into a big smile and pulled me into a hug. They'd met last year when she'd participated in a prison outreach program to teach a cooking class to inmates who were about to be released. Although he may have lost his looks, apparently my father was still a charmer and Cora had quickly fallen under his spell. He was also a natural at cooking. While she'd supplied the capital to start the restaurant, it was his dishes that kept people coming back.

"I couldn't believe it the other day when Cora told me Cal was here. I looked out into the courtyard and saw him at a table with you. You have no idea how hard it was for me not to run out here and pick you up and swing you around like I used to when you were little." He looked down at the table, embarrassed. It took everything in me not to admit that I had wanted that too, a long time ago. Now I was just confused, and all I wanted now was answers.

Cora left the room to give us some privacy, and the awkwardness seemed to stretch on forever. "Were you ever going to tell me?"

"I wanted to tell you when you were old enough to understand, only your mother didn't let me."

"Why?" I wasn't really surprised; my mother wanted to control everything about my life, including my access to any kind of information about her past that she didn't want to talk about.

He shrugged and looked down at the table. "I don't think she wanted to answer questions about who your real father is."

"Do you know who he is?"

"No. I swear, Kendall, I don't know who he is. Jackie would never talk about him. Anytime I tried to ask her questions, she would cut me off and not speak to me for days. I learned quickly to stop asking. But I know one thing."

"What?"

"Whoever this man is, he broke your mother. I don't think she was ever the same because of what happened with him."

"She never talked about what happened between them and why they split up?"

"The only thing she ever told me about your father was that he stole something from her she could never get back."

That could've been anything, I thought as I sat across from the man I'd thought was my father my whole life. I should have felt relieved that what I had believed about him all these years was a lie. But now I felt like the one who'd lost something I would never get back – the twelve years I spent hating a man who had nothing but love for me. Why had my mother lied to me all this time? Who was this man sitting across from me now? What should I even call him? He must've read my mind because he reached out and took my hand.

"I would love for us to get to know each other again, Kendall. But I won't push it. It's up to you. You don't even have to call me dad if you don't want to. I would love it if you would because I still consider myself your dad and I've missed you every day for twelve years."

"I want to believe you. But how do I know if any of this is true?"

His face fell, and for a moment, I thought he might cry. "If you go to the Bureau of Prisons' website," he said softly, "you can look me up, either by name or my inmate number, which I'm happy to give you. It'll show that when you had your accident, I was already serving my sentence. I was already in prison when you got shoved down those stairs."

My mind was reeling, and I was still lightheaded. "Then why didn't I ever hear from you? Not a card, a letter, a phone call, nothing. Mom said you didn't want to see me. Is that true?"

"I wrote to you almost every day when I first got there and sent you a card on your birthday. I knew Jackie was probably throwing all my letters and cards away. But I kept sending them until they released me, hoping that one of those letters would slip through and get to you. The last letter I sent you was to let you know I was being released and what my new address was. It came back as undeliverable."

He reached inside his back pocket and pulled out an envelope, set it on the table and slid it across to me. Sure enough it was a 4 x 6 envelope addressed to Ms. Kendall Good at my mom's address. That was why my mother had gotten a PO Box not long after my father went to prison. She said she needed one after a bill went missing and ended up being late, and that I was to blame. That was just an excuse to have the mail forwarded to a post office box, so I wouldn't see what was coming in from my father. What the hell was wrong with her? With trembling fingers, I opened it and read:

Dear Kendall,

It's been so long since I've seen you and so long since we talked. I'm not even sure you're getting my letters, but I wanted to reach out one last time to let you know that I'm being released from prison next week and I would love to see you. I know how much I disappointed you when I did what I did, and I wanted to apologize to you again, and I hope that one day you can forgive me, and I can be your dad again. I am including my address in this letter, and I hope to hear from you when you're ready.
I love you,

Dad

It was too much. The tears that had been swimming in my eyes finally slipped down my cheeks, and I buried my face in my hands and sobbed. Dad instantly got up and came to my side of the table. I hugged him, burying my face against his shirt, crying for all the lost time that was stolen from us.

"Try not to be too angry with your mother, Kendall. She was just trying to protect you." He tilted my tear-streaked face up. He was crying too.

"She was just trying to protect herself and the man who hurt us. She gave me a father when she married you. She knew you weren't the one who pushed me, so why was she trying to keep us apart? Was she still involved with my father?" I asked, wiping my eyes with the back of my hand.

"Only she can answer that. I'm sure she must have had her reasons."

"I'm afraid to ask her because I know she's just going to lie again. She's been lying for twelve years. Why tell the truth now?"

We were silent again, but this time, it wasn't awkward. Both of us were trying to figure out what to talk about next. There was twelve years' worth of stuff to talk about.

"Can I ask you something else?"

"Anything."

"Why did you do it? Why did you steal that money?" I could tell that wasn't what he was expecting, but he gave me a small smile and nodded.

"There are so many things that I could say. So many excuses I could make. But honestly, I did it because I could. I was put in a position of trust that I abused. The first time was a small amount, just $1,000. But then I got away with it and did it again. Each time for larger sums of money. Each time I got away with it, my ego skyrocketed. I loved being the big shot and show-ering the people I loved with gifts, trips, and all the finer things in life. It made me feel good about myself. I paid for that mistake with twelve years of my life and having to pay restitu-tion probably for the rest of my life to pay off the money I stole."

It was true. Before my father went to prison, we had family trips to Disney and the Grand Canyon. There were cruises and trips to Paris and the Caribbean that my father would take my mother on. Expensive jewelry on Mom's birthdays and Christmas. They both had new cars every year before he got caught. After they caught him, everything had to be sold, including our home. I remember how humiliated my mother was when we left that house and moved to a rental during my father's trial. I left my private school and my friends who I never saw again. But the man sitting before me now bore little resemblance to the man I last saw twelve years ago.

"Cora seems really nice." I said, making him smile.

"Cora is my home now. She's the shining star that makes everything in my life so much better, so much bigger, and so much brighter. She's damn sure more than I deserve."

We both looked up to see Cora carrying a cake pan with some plates.

"I figured it's about time I got out here with some medicine." She sat a pineapple upside-down cake in the middle on the table.

"You made this, didn't you?" I asked my father. His only response was to beam with pride.

"She had already passed away before I met your mom, but your grandma Good made the best pineapple upside-down cake. This is her recipe. It's my way to honor her and let her know that her baby boy is back on the straight and narrow and trying to make it right."

The three of us ate in companionable silence for about a minute. Cora was the one who broke the silence.

"Are you and Cal getting married?"

My fork froze halfway to my mouth, causing my dad to burst out laughing and my face to burn with embarrassment.

"Don't mind my wife, Kendall. She's never been one to beat around the bush."

"That's his polite way of saying I'm nosy." Cora gave my father a playful punch on his arm. "You don't have to answer that."

"No. It's okay. To answer your question, Cal and I have only been on one and a half dates." I would have mentioned that convicted felons weren't my type, but I didn't want her to think I was being judgmental about her being married to one herself.

"Sorry. You two just looked so great together the other night that I thought you guys were a thing."

"No worries." I smiled at her to show that I wasn't offended.

"I guess you must've found out about his past, huh?" asked my father.

"How did you—" I began, but he held up his hand and cut me off.

"Cora wasn't the only one here that noticed the vibe between you two the other night. When she just mentioned his name, you grimaced. Plus, I saw you tonight, staring into The Hub like you were trying to decide whether you should go in."

"Yeah, you got me. I was just really shocked when I found out. Now I don't know what to think."

"I know Cal, and normally I wouldn't be asking my daughter to have an open mind because I spent twelve years with some of the worst scum humanity has to offer. But Cal is a good guy."

"How do you know that? Did you two serve time in the same prison?"

"No, but we did both attend the same small business semi-nar, an outreach program for ex-offenders, and became good friends. If being in prison taught me anything, it's how to read people. He told me his story, and I believe him."

"Which is?" I asked, looking from him to Cora as they exchanged glances.

"Sorry," he said, shaking his head. "It's not my story to tell. Just give Cal a chance to tell you himself."

I nodded in agreement, though I wasn't sure I had the bandwidth for Cal or whatever his story might be. Someone tried to frame me for murder, and that was all I could think about. Cal would have to wait until I got my life back under control.

"Did you ever see Mimi again?" asked Dad around a mouthful of cake.

"Who?" Was he talking about a relative?

"Mimi? Your best friend from middle school. You two were thick as thieves."

Back before my father had been arrested, and our lives turned to shit, I'd attended one year of Calvary Academy, a private Christian School, which had always surprised me since neither of my parents were churchgoers. I loved that school, from what I remembered of it. My memories of what had happened the night I was pushed down the stairs were gone, but not only that, I had patchy memories of the entire year. I vaguely remembered being friends with a girl whose big smile and loud laughter still lingered in my brain, but her face eluded me.

"That entire year is kind of a blur. I don't really remember much about it."

"I'm so sorry." Dad glanced at Cora and shook his head. "You lost so much because of what I did. I may not have shoved you down those stairs, but my conviction set it all in motion. I—"

"Don't." I grabbed his hand. "Please. Let's move on. Haven't we both been in prison long enough?"

He smiled, nodded, and slid a second piece of cake onto my plate.

. . .

Much later, after I'd said my goodnights, Cora insisted on driving me back to Liv's.

"Can I ask you a favor?" she said once she'd pulled up in front of Liv's building.

"Sure. What's up?" Cora was looking so serious that I almost didn't want to know what she was about to say.

"I know this is none of my business. But please, don't hurt him."

"Hurt him? You mean Dad?"

She nodded her head. "We only moved here because he found out this is where you were going to college. He's been too afraid to approach you. He even found out where you lived and sent you an old picture of the two of you that he kept with him in prison. I can understand if you decide you don't want a relationship with him. But don't get his hopes up and then change your mind. It'll kill him. Seeing you again is what kept him going in prison."

I felt the hot prick of tears and was in no mood to cry again. Instead, I grabbed her by the hand. "Now that you guys have found me, good luck trying to get rid of me." I got out of the truck and shot my new stepmother a smile and a wave before disappearing inside.

SIXTEEN

COLUMBUS, OHIO

Despite what my father told me about not being too hard on my mother, she owed me a lifetime of answers, and this wasn't a conversation I wanted to have over the phone. The next day, I borrowed Liv's car and drove to Columbus. My mother still lived in the house she'd bought after my accident. A brick two-story colonial four blocks from Capital University in a suburb of Columbus called Bexley. My mother worked two jobs to keep our house. Once she'd established her psychology practice, she could finally pay it off.

I let myself into the house with my key. My mother wasn't home, which shouldn't have surprised me. She worked for a major insurance company headquartered in Columbus, as well as running her own private practice, and worked long days. It was four o'clock, and I knew she wouldn't be home until at least six. That gave me time to do what I came to do before our conversation.

I started in her bedroom. I searched through all the drawers and her jewelry box, then looked under the bed and finally checked the closet. Her clothes were as neat and organized as she was. Her suits were arranged in primary colors. No pastels for my mother. They hung neatly in a color-coordinated line like a paint sample strip you get from the hardware store. Her shoes, seven pairs of low-heeled pumps, sat on a rack underneath. The shelves above held neatly stacked boxes. I pulled a chair from her vanity table and stood on it so I could reach the boxes and went through them one by one.

The last box I looked through was an old hatbox that was empty except for a photo album. I got down off the chair and flipped through the album. There were old family pictures, starting with my mother as a child and her parents, my grandparents. There were pictures of her sister who died in a car crash when Mom was sixteen. From there, the pictures changed. Everybody looked sadder and older. My grandparents no longer smiled.

Next came pictures of my mother with my father. My mother looked so young, pretty, and carefree. I vaguely remembered her being like this when I was growing up before my dad went to prison. I finally came to the pictures of the three of us at Christmas, and Dad showing me how to ride a bike. I must have been about five. Until last night, I'd forgotten how nice my dad's smile was.

I put the album back on the shelf and inadvertently nudged a shoebox, which slid out and fell to the closet floor, spilling its contents. A pile of letters addressed to me with a return address of Lucasville Correctional in Lucasville, Ohio. There were dozens of cards dated on or around my birthday. None of them had been opened.

I sat and stared at them, and before I realized it, fat sloppy tears dripped on the letters in my lap from my wet face. I heard a gasp and looked up to see Mom standing in the doorway, staring at me in shock. I wiped my face with the back of my hand and stood up.

"What in the world are you doing? How dare you invade my privacy like this!"

"How dare you keep these letters from me! They were mine! How could you keep them from me?" I shouted at her.

"As long as you were living under my roof and I was your legal guardian, I had every right to keep those letters from you," she seethed.

She crossed the room in three steps and tried to snatch the letters from my hands. I stepped back and held them out of her reach.

"Who is my real father? And don't say Raymond Good because I know that's a lie! You've been lying to me my entire life!" Mom stopped instantly, her face reddening, her mouth opening and shutting. This was the only time I'd ever caught my mother completely surprised and at a loss for words.

"Kendall, I was only trying to protect you! Why can't you see that?"

"Protect me from whom? Dad never pushed me down the stairs. You lied and made me hate him for years. Why would you do that to me? Why punish me like that?"

"You? I wasn't trying to punish you! It was him. He was the one who tore our family apart, not me! I didn't want him poisoning you with his lies and empty promises. Now give me those letters!"

My mother lunged at me, grabbing for the letters, and I backed away but didn't see the ottoman behind me and fell over it, cracking my head hard against the dresser. Pain shot through my head, and I fell onto my side, too stunned to move or make a sound.

"Kendall!" screamed my mother.

She rushed to where I lay. I feebly struggled to my feet until a wave of dizziness hit me so hard I had to lie back down. Something warm and wet trickled down the side of my face. I touched it and looked at the blood smeared on my fingers. I was getting blood on my mom's perfectly pristine white rug and the thought made me giggle.

"Don't move, sweetheart," was the last thing I heard my mother say before I passed out.

I woke up in the emergency room with a doctor stitching along my hairline. The gash took five stitches to close. I didn't have a concussion, but because of my previous head injury, they told Mom to watch me closely during the night and to bring me back if I became confused or started vomiting.

The drive back to my mom's was silent and awkward. I felt too tired mentally and physically to talk, and Mom's face was pale and tight with unreadable emotions. I couldn't tell if she was furious with me or with herself, or with Dad, probably all the above. She wordlessly tucked me into my old bed, and I closed my eyes and fell into a dreamless sleep, only to wake a few hours later. I turned onto my side, saw my mother asleep in the rocking chair by the window, then heard and felt a crunch of paper. I pushed the covers back to find the thick stack of my father's letters bound by a rubber band. Mom had tucked them into bed with me.

"How are you feeling?" she asked late the next morning when I came down to the kitchen.

She wore a pair of tan slacks and a white wrinkled shirt, and she looked older and tired. This was the worst I'd seen her look in twelve years.

"I'm okay. I have a monster headache, but other than that, I'm fine."

"I'm so sorry," she said in a trembling voice.

"About what? Lying to me about who my father is, lying about who really pushed me down the stairs, or not giving me the letters and cards that belong to me?"

"All of it. I thought I was doing the right thing. I just didn't want to see you hurt."

I'd never seen my mother this vulnerable and upset. Even during my father's trial and the humiliating aftermath, I'd never seen her cry. But her tears didn't move me.

"But I *was* hurt. So that didn't work out so well now, did it?"

"Kendall I—"

"Are you going to tell me who my father is?"

We stared each other down. Mom looked away first and went to the sink to fill her teapot. "It's best you don't know."

I watched her make tea, incredulous, my eyes filling with tears of anger and frustration. "Well, until you tell me, I have nothing to say to you. If you change your mind, you know where to find me." I left and once outside the door, heard her break down and start sobbing. Should I have gone back to comfort her? Maybe. But when had she ever comforted me?

I had the letters, and that was all that mattered to me now.

SEVENTEEN

BEXLEY, OHIO

She'd been told to get home in the best way she could. So she was uncertain of what kind of reception she would get when she finally arrived at her parents' stone and stucco Tudor-style mansion in Bexley, Ohio, an affluent suburb of Columbus. She had a suspended driver's license and a credit card in her purse and used that to get a Greyhound bus home. Then a city bus took her to her parents' home. Alayna was the one who opened the door, giving her a foul look instead of a greeting.

"Where's my mom?" she asked, not even bothering to look at her mother's assistant, as she pushed past her into the house.

"In her studio, and she's not to be disturbed."

She almost laughed. Her mom had spent every spare moment in the studio for the past five years and had yet to produce another album. Of the five subsequent albums she had released, none compared to her first Grammy winning album *For the Grace of God*, which swept the Grammys in the gospel category back in 1998, the year before her daughter had been born. Her mother never came out and said so, but she'd always got the impression her mother thought her birth had been a curse and hadn't brought anything good to her life. As a result, she grew up in a household with a resentful mother and an absent father. There was always a reason her father was never at home and always on business trips, which were code for hanging out with his hoes, but he was home now and would be for the foreseeable future.

She went to her room and shoved her bag with the bloody clothes—and the thing she'd taken—on a shelf in her closet. After that, she showered, changed into jeans and a hoodie and then went down to the kitchen for something to eat. She was starving. After what she'd seen in that house last night, she thought she'd never want to eat again. But she was wrong. She opened the fridge, pulled out peanut butter and jelly, and grabbed some crackers. She spread some peanut butter on a Ritz and shoved it into her mouth when a voice made her jump.

"So the prodigal has returned, huh?"

Blessing Burk was standing behind her daughter, giving her a placid smile that hid the rage within. Had she been just a few years younger, her mom wouldn't have hesitated to slap her across the face for causing her so much trouble. But she was an adult now, and she was angry too, and returned her mother's expression in kind. She licked peanut butter from her lips before responding.

"Wow. And not even the hero's welcome?"

Her mother always wore black. It was her signature color. Today's ensemble was a black silk sleeveless cowl neck shirt tucked into black jeans with black leather mules. Her long bone straight weave was pulled from her face into a ponytail that hung down her back. She wore no makeup and no jewelry except for her wedding set. A four-carat, pear-shaped diamond with a platinum diamond band. And her mood, despite her smile, was as black as her clothing.

"Heroes don't get busted for DUI and have to be forcibly placed in rehab for their own good."

"My own good? I did not consent to that three months of bullshit."

"Watch your mouth," her mother warned, taking a step toward her. "It was rehab, or jail. I did not give you a choice because you've proven that you can't make adult decisions. So I made it for you. Now wipe your mouth and go up and say hi to your father."

"Does he know I'm back?"

"Girl, he didn't even know you were gone. Never asked about you once." She watched her mother leave the kitchen, her mocking laughter setting her teeth on edge.

A minute later, she walked into a room on the second floor occupied by a hospital bed and IV poles. The last time she'd seen her father, he'd lost a lot of weight, but now he was almost skeletal and barely recognizable as Marcus Burk, former outfielder for the Reds turned successful businessman. He had pancreatic cancer at the end stage. No one outside the Burk family knew he was sick, let alone dying. That was her mother's doing. He was so doped up because of the pain that he slept most of the time. She kissed him on his stubbled cheek and left the room, encountering Alayna just outside the door.

"What have you done now?"

"What are you talking about?" She tried to get around her, but Alayna blocked her path.

"Two Addison police detectives just showed up looking for you."

"How the hell should I know what they want?" She knew exactly what they wanted, and her stomach turned as she remembered the horror of the night before. Despite this, she wasn't about to let this stuck-up bitch get to her.

Alayna gave her a look of disgust. "You are so ungrateful. Do you know how many women would love to have Blessing as a mother and grow up in a house that looks like this? You've been given so much, and you've given back so little. The least you could do is make your parents proud."

She took a step closer, but Alayna didn't flinch, holding her ground. "You need to be very careful. You don't know who you're dealing with. But I'll let you in on a little secret. My mom has had a bunch of girls just like you work for her for years. All of you trying to be just like her, trailing behind her in your all-black outfits like her spooky little clones. One of them was named Savannah. She was the one whose job you got after she flew a little too close to the sun and got burned. Trust me, you don't want to end up like her." She left Alayna standing there staring after her. She had probably made a big mistake, but the look of horror on her face was worth it. Downstairs in the living room, two men, a balding middle-aged white man and a short black guy with glasses, were talking to her mother.

"Here she is. Detectives, this is my daughter Mackenzie."

Her mother patted the seat on the couch next to her. Mackenzie dutifully sat next to her and smiled inquisitively at the men.

"Detectives? What's going on?"

"Ms. Burk, I'm Detective Peter Delaney and this is Detective Terrell Wallace. We were hoping you could help us with our inquiries into a recent homicide in Addison, Ohio," said the white guy.

"Homicide?" said Blessing in alarm, turning toward her daughter. "Why would my daughter be questioned about homicide?"

"Ms. Burk," said Detective Wallace. "Do you know a woman named Savannah McCoy?"

"Yes. Why?" She looked from one detective to the other. "Is she in some kind of trouble?"

"I'm sorry to inform you that Savannah McCoy was found deceased in her home last night. Homicide."

"Oh my God!" exclaimed Blessing, her hands flying to her mouth. Mackenzie thought her mother had missed her calling as an actress. She was so much better at making people think she cared than she was at singing.

"What was the nature of your relationship with Ms. McCoy?" asked Wallace.

"She was my social media manager. I hired her to run my Instagram and TikTok accounts."

"And why would you do that?" asked Delaney.

"My daughter had been away in a treatment facility for the past three months and didn't want her social media presence to be put on hold," interjected Blessing, and Mackenzie could have kicked her. She wasn't ashamed of having been in rehab, but it wasn't her mother's place to share her personal business.

"You hired her to impersonate you online?" asked Wallace. "Why not just take a break and get back to it when you get out of treatment?" asked Delaney, causing her to roll her eyes.

"I didn't hire Savannah to be me online. I hired her to edit and post content that I'd already created. Most of the big-name influencers have a social media manager. Besides, my personal life is my own. I don't do GRWM for rehab content."

"GRWM?" Delaney looked confused and looked at his partner.

"Get Ready With Me," said Mackenzie and Detective Wallace in unison. She could tell Wallace was embarrassed that he knew this by his sheepish grin. It made him a little more likable, but not by much.

"My sister is an influencer," he admitted.

"Look." She was itching for this conversation to be over. "I'm booked for brand deals and product placements into the spring of next year. They have already paid me for those contracts, and they needed to be fulfilled. I hired Savannah to take care of all that for me. But she was just supposed to be posting content and recycling my old posts that did well. I had already made a lot of the videos. They just needed to be edited and scheduled. She wasn't supposed to be pretending to be me."

"When did you find out that she was, in fact, posting, pretending to be you?" asked Delaney.

"Not until after I got out of the treatment facility a few days ago and finally checked my social media."

"You didn't check your social media accounts for three months?" The look Wallace gave her showed he clearly didn't believe her.

"They took my phone when I got checked in and the computers they had couldn't access social media. It's part of their treatment philosophy."

"How long did she work for you?" asked Delaney.

"I hired her the month before I entered treatment." That was true. Savannah had worked for *her* for just a few months. She'd been her mom's assistant for almost five months. She was silent, waiting for her mother to speak up. But she never did.

"And where were you last night between 9 p.m. and midnight?" Wallace leaned forward in his chair, waiting for her response.

"My daughter was here," insisted Blessing rather dramatically. The detectives ignored her and turned their attention to Mac.

"We need to hear that from your daughter, ma'am."

"I was here. I got out of treatment a few days ago and have been lying low. I've barely left the house."

"But you just said you were trying to get ahold of Ms. McCoy. Are you sure you didn't go to Addison to confront her? After all, she was impersonating you, and possibly even ruining your... what is it they call it?" Delaney turned to look at Wallace.

"Brand," replied Wallace, pushing up his glasses.

"It's very important that my daughter avoid stressful situations to avoid a relapse." Blessing put her arm around her. It took everything in Mackenzie not to shake her arm off. She'd never been affectionate, and to have her displaying affection now was both extremely disingenuous and disturbing.

"My mom is right. I needed to be in a better frame of mind before I confronted her. I've worked too hard on my sobriety to have a confrontation send me over the edge."

"What about your classes? Aren't you still a student at Bellbrook?" Delaney stood up and was rocking back on his heels and absently rubbing the fingertips of his right hand together. She knew a nicotine addict when she saw one, plus she got a whiff of cigarette smoke when he stood up. He was fiending for a cigarette.

"I withdrew. I won't go back to Bellbrook again until next semester."

"Have you ever seen this before, Ms. Burk?" Wallace pulled up a picture on his phone and showed it to her. It was a black stiletto-heeled pump. Mackenzie looked at it and shook her head.

"This looks like a Luciano Silva. I've never owned a pair of Luciano Silva's. I'm more of a Manolo girly."

"A what?" Delaney looked confused.

"Manolo Blahnik. It's a designer brand of shoes. Those and Louboutin's are the only pumps I wear," she replied.

"How about you, ma'am?" Wallace held the phone out to Blessing, who looked and shook her head.

"No. It doesn't look familiar. Did it belong to Savannah?"

Instead of answering, the detectives got up. "We'd like to thank you both for your time. We may need to ask you some more questions during this investigation."

"Of course." Her mother nodded.

She stayed behind while her mother walked them to the door and gave them a genial goodbye. Once the door was closed, her mother was back in the living room in an instant, grabbing Mackenzie by the arm and dragging her to her feet.

"What the fuck have you done?" She was so close Mac could smell the expensive bourbon she kept hidden in her studio on her breath.

"Probably just saved your ass. I told you to stay away from her. I told you I'd handle it."

"But you didn't, did you? I'm always having to clean up behind you," Blessing spat out at her.

She jerked out of her mother's grasp and ran back up the steps to her room and slammed the door.

She was unaware of Alayna standing just around the corner.

EIGHTEEN

ADDISON, OHIO

I spent the next day reading all my father's letters and cards. I spread them out in chronological order and started with the first one, which arrived on my twelfth birthday. In it, he wished me happy birthday and said he hoped I was being a good girl for my mother. He also apologized for not being there and for getting into trouble and making Mom and me sad. He'd drawn little doodles around the edges of the letter, of smiley faces and trees and flowers. He promised to call me soon and ended the brief letter by telling me he missed me and not to worry about him and how he hoped I'd come see him soon.

The other letters were much the same, but the level of sadness and frustration over Mom divorcing him and at my non-responses and not visiting him came through loud and clear. Even so, he never blamed me. He had to know it was Mom keeping us apart. I also learned a bit about his life in prison. He'd taken culinary classes and joined a Bible study group. He also worked out a lot. The last letter was dated a year ago, about three months before the letter he'd given me two nights ago. By the time I'd finished reading them all, my eyes were swollen from crying, and I had a raging headache. Probably not the best idea since I'd hit my head, but I'd been waiting twelve years for these letters and didn't want to wait another minute. When I was done, I gathered all the letters together and put them in the same box I kept my diaries in.

I was still staying with Liv. My air mattress was less than ten feet from Spike the boa constrictor's tank, and I had a hard time sleeping at night because of Spanky's snoring and farting. I had to find a new place to stay. I was scrolling through the listings for campus housing looking for a new room to rent when Liv came home looking uncharacteristically annoyed and grumpy.

"What's wrong with you?"

"I hate fucking technology." She plopped onto the futon next to me and propped her flowered Doc Martin encased feet up on the coffee table.

"What happened? You love technology."

"The first paper of the semester and half of them used AI, which means half the class are going to get Fs, meaning I'm going to get phone calls from freaked-out parents yelling at me for failing their little geniuses and ruining their perfect GPAs."

Unease spread through my veins like adrenaline. Liv's face wore a mask of disgust and my pulse quickened. She couldn't possibly know about my stint of academic fraud. But I felt lumped in with the AI paper writers all the same. "Damn. That's messed up. How could you tell they used AI?"

"The college implemented new AI content detectors this semester. They can't catch everything, but they have a high level of accuracy."

"Are you really going to fail half the class?"

She sighed and ran her hands through her hair in frustration. "No. I'll give a very long lecture on academic dishonesty and give the ones who used AI a chance to redo the papers to get a passing grade with twenty points taken off the top so there's no way they can get an A. But they won't get Fs either.

And I'll still get calls from pissed-off parents ready to kill me."

"Won't you get those calls, regardless? Remember that student you told me about whose mom screamed at you for twenty minutes for giving her son an A- instead of an A+ on a pop quiz? And these are college students, not middle-schoolers."

"I know," she said, slumping down further onto the futon. "But it just kills me to have to explain to adults why AI isn't allowed. I mean, seriously? Why don't they get it? I'm not getting paid enough for this shit."

I was about to unload another encouraging platitude on her while figuring out how to change the subject when my phone beeped with a text. It was Cal. Saved by the felon.

> I've got a bargain you can't refuse. Can you meet me at the HUB at 7?

The question wasn't, could I meet him? The real question was, did I want to? Then I remembered what my dad had told me about Cal the other night and got up from the futon.

"Where are you going?" She looked so dejected I almost didn't leave.

"I've got to make a quick run. I promise I'll be back soon with comfort food. In the meantime, find us a good K-Drama to watch.

When I got to The Hub, Cal was waiting for me, and I followed him up to his loft. "Thanks for coming."

"I can't stay long." I sat down on his couch and Cal sat across from me on the loveseat.

"Then I'll make this quick. I can't give you the cash you need, but I can still help you."

"How?" I eyed him skeptically.

"I need help at The Hub. I can pay you a salary and let you stay here in the loft." Was he serious? He was offering me a job as a barmaid?

"I can't move in with you, and I don't know the first thing about serving drinks," I said primly. He laughed his deep-throated laugh, making me irrationally annoyed.

"First of all, you wouldn't be moving in with me because I don't live here. I'm living in the apartment above the garage at my mom's house until her estate is settled. I only stay here sometimes when I work late. And secondly, I wouldn't be hiring you to serve drinks. My office and files are a mess, and I need someone to get me organized."

I considered this for a moment. Staying in the loft would certainly solve my housing problem, and getting paid would help take care of my living expenses and keep me in school. It should have been an easy decision, but my last offer of help had been from an imposter whose murder I was now a suspect in. Just like this situation, there were so many ways this could go wrong. My next tuition installment payment was due in two weeks, however, and I'd be damned if I'd ask my mother for help or drop out of classes I was doing well in just to have to start over again in the spring semester. Nope. I would use this opportunity to make lemonade out of lemons. But there was still the matter of the elephant in the room, which was his conviction for assault, and not any old assault. He'd assaulted his own father.

"It's the best I can do until my mother's estate is resolved," he said when I didn't reply right away.

"It's not that." The look on my face told him what I was thinking.

"Yeah, about that." His face flushed, and he ran a hand through his curly hair. "All I can say for now is that I'm no danger to you, Kendall. That shit stain Phil doesn't know me, and he was running his mouth about something he knows nothing about. I know I have a lot of nerve asking you to trust me when you don't know me. One reason I need you to help me in my office is because I need your help to find something I really need, and once I find it, it will explain everything and help me out of a huge bind."

"What's going on?" I was both intrigued and instantly on guard since Savannah had also needed my help, and look where that had gotten me.

"I've lost my liquor license." Cal's voice was flat, and his look of dejection was palpable.

"What happened?"

"Until my mom died, she was the owner of The Hub. She let me run it, but she was the actual owner, so the liquor license was in her name. When she died, the ownership of the bar passed to me, meaning the liquor license needed to be in my name and that's not allowed for a convicted felon. If it was a minor felony, maybe, but not for someone like me who's been convicted of felonious assault with a deadly weapon."

"There's nothing you can do?"

"I am working on it, but these things take time to go through the court system. Until this gets resolved, The Hub will be a bar that can't serve alcohol."

Neither of us had to say that a bar serving no alcohol would probably not be in business for very long. I couldn't imagine how Cal must be feeling, having built up a clientele and a reputation in the community, only to see it destroyed.

"I am so sorry."

"I know, Good. I know."

"How does me helping you clean your office help you with that?"

"My mom wrote a letter about what happened the night my dad got hurt, and my lawyer thinks it could get my conviction overturned. I'm thinking it's in a box I took from my mom's house. Wherever it is, I need to find it quick or I'm going to lose my business."

Why was I such a sucker for people with problems? Was it because misery loved company or because I had a savior complex? Probably both. That was why I was studying psychology, wasn't it? Or was it because it was nice seeing people with bigger problems than me? I wanted to think it was the former. Some days I couldn't tell.

"I'll take it."

"You will?" He looked more than surprised; he was stunned.

"I will. Thanks, Cal."

"Then it's a deal." He stuck out his hand. I shook it, wondering if I was making a big mistake.

"Why don't we celebrate? Let me take you to dinner." He gave a hopeful look, and I almost said yes, then remembered Liv's face. Sad and frustrated wasn't a good look on her.

"Sorry. I've got a bestie to console tonight. Rain check?"

"Absolutely."

I walked out of The Hub and crossed the street. When I looked back, Cal was still watching me.

NINETEEN
ADDISON, OHIO

I arrived at the Addison police station with the lawyer my dad recommended. I'd called him at Cora's after Detective Wallace contacted me that morning, saying they needed to urgently see me again. If I didn't come in right away, they'd send a squad car after me. The lawyer was a young woman named Rachel Weathers who worked for Addison's Legal Aid Society. She was the lawyer you got when you had no money to pay for a more experienced one, and yet she looked nice enough and certainly seemed capable when I talked to her on the phone. In her tan skirt, cream blouse, and black ballet flats, however, she looked like she should be shelving books in a library. When Detectives Delaney and Wallace entered the room, I noticed Wallace was carrying an iPad that he propped up in the middle of the table.

"We would like to thank you for coming in, Ms. Good," said Delaney, as he sat next to his partner.

"It didn't sound like I had much of a choice," I said to no one in particular.

"We just need to clear up some confusion over your original statement. We'd appreciate your cooperation," said Wallace.

"What confusion?"

"You said in your earlier statement that you did not know Savannah McCoy before you moved in with her. Is that correct?" asked Delaney.

"That's right." I looked from Wallace to Delaney as a nagging feeling clawed its way from my stomach into my throat.

"Were you recently in a relationship with a man by the name of Byron James?" Wallace watched me closely.

"Byron? Yes, we dated for three years and broke up three weeks ago. What does he have to do with all of this?"

"So, you never saw this post?" Wallace then turned the iPad in my direction to show Savannah McCoy's Instagram page.

After I found out who she really was, I'd scrolled through her feed, but I'd only gone back a few months because, frankly, her posts were boring as fuck. The post that Wallace confronted me with was from eight months ago. In it, Savannah was standing with a shirtless man whose back was to the camera. Savannah's arm was wrapped around his neck and her tongue grazed his ear. The caption read: *He looks like a snack, and he tastes like one too.* The post had the hashtag #lookinglikeasnack. The snack's face may not have been facing the camera, but I'd know those reddish-brown twists anywhere. Aside from the twists, there was also a mole on his left shoulder. It was my ex, Byron.

I shouldn't have been surprised that Kayla wasn't the only one, but I was. I wondered how many others he'd been with that I didn't know about. More than anything, I wondered again how I could've been so wrong about a man I spent three years of my life with.

"No." I slowly let out a breath. "I had never seen this, and if I did, we would've broken up a lot sooner."

"What does this have to do with my client? Women find out every day that they've been cheated on. How is this relevant to

Ms. McCoy's murder?" asked Rachel, speaking up for the first time.

"We're getting to that," said Delaney, putting his elbows on the table and leaning forward.

"Ms. Good. Do you remember this incident?" Wallace turned the iPad toward me again. This time, they showed black and white CCTV footage from the hallway outside of Byron's apartment. In the brief clip a woman slapped the snot out of another woman. There was no sound, but there didn't need to be. The video showed me getting right in Kayla's face and saying something that sent her heading off down the hall, clearly in fear of me as she yelled out something to me before disappearing into the elevator.

"She provoked me. Where's the sound?" I insisted, looking between the detectives, whose expressions were neutral.

Even I knew how bad this looked. I'd smacked Kayla when I found out about her and Byron. The detectives thought I'd taken it further with Savannah and killed her when I found out about her and Byron. Combined with all the other things they'd found, like the Playhouse program, the picture of her dog, and the other things that I was made to do in the scavenger hunt, I may as well have a big, red cartoon arrow pointed at my head.

"Really? All I see is you attacking that woman without provocation," said Wallace with a sneer.

"As my client has already pointed out, Detective Wallace, there's no sound on this video. We don't know what was said or even in what context this confrontation took place."

"You are correct, counselor," said Delaney calmly. "When you take this video into consideration with the other evidence such as Ms. Good living with the victim, her going to her place of employment, her having a picture of her dog, trying on a pair of shoes like the one found to have killed Ms. McCoy, and the lip gloss post. I'd say we have obvious reasons for wanting to talk to your client."

"That makes for a lovely story, but do you have any concrete physical evidence that connects my client to the death of Ms. McCoy? DNA? Fingerprints? You know... What constitutes as real physical evidence?"

I looked over at Rachel in awe. She may look like a mouse, but she was sitting straight up in her chair staring the detectives down and giving off boss bitch energy. I certainly felt much more confident when I saw that Wallace and Delaney were at a loss for words.

"I'm assuming you have my client's fingerprints and DNA?" she asked the detectives.

"Yes, we do. But..." Wallace began before Rachel cut him off.

"Then when you get some concrete evidence, my client will be happy to answer any further questions you have. Until then, we're done with this fishing expedition. Let's go, Kendall."

She got up, and I trailed after, looking back to see that Delaney was slightly red-faced and looked exasperated. Meanwhile, Wallace glared after us and said nothing.

"Wow," I told her as we walked out of the doors of the Addison police department. "Being asked to come down here was worth it since I got to see that."

"I love when people underestimate me," she said, looking straight ahead.

"Why?"

"I am very aware that I look like I should be reading picture books to little kids in the library. People usually only think that about me one time before they realize I'm unfuckwithable. You have my number if you need me again."

I watched her go, feeling completely put in my place for my earlier assessment of her, realizing that it was the same kind of thing that people had been doing to me my whole life. I should've known better.

Questions swirled around in my brain as I walked home.

None of it made any sense. As I searched my purse for bus fare, a question hit me. How could Savannah McCoy afford to pay me ten grand? She wasn't the real Mackenzie Burk, and as I'd learned from the police officers, everything in her closet bedroom was fake. Why go to such lengths to fool me? Who had put her up to it? There was one person I could ask. I doubted he'd tell me the truth, but I called him anyway.

Byron agreed to meet me that afternoon at the B&C café. He was anything but friendly on the phone, so I was surprised when he showed up. He was dressed as if for a date, and I wondered if he was meeting Kayla afterward, or some other chick, or if this was some kind of misguided attempt to impress me.

"I thought you said there was no reason for us to speak again."

"Turns out there's a reason after all, Mr. #looking-likeasnack."

He sighed and rolled his eyes. I pulled up the Instagram photo of him and Savannah McCoy and showed it to him. He sat back in his chair, glaring with his arms crossed at his chest.

"We're not together anymore, Kendall. Why do you care if I was seeing someone else?"

"I could point out that when this picture was taken, we were still very much together. I won't because I no longer give a fuck. But since the woman in this picture with you was brutally murdered, I was wondering what you knew about her."

It was clear by his neutral expression Savannah's death wasn't news to him. "How did you know her?"

"As much as I hate to speak ill of the dead, she was as big a liar as you are and sucked me into her orbit. I was renting a room from her. I was the one who found her body and I've now been questioned twice by the police."

"Yeah, they talked to me too," he said, looking down at his lap.

"They did? Did they mention me?" When he didn't respond, it took everything in me not to leap across the table at him. "And you didn't think to warn me because...?"

He shrugged, looking like a sulky little boy being questioned about why he'd shoved a Lego up his nose. Why hadn't I noticed what an idiot this man was? "You told me you didn't want to talk to me again. So, why should I have warned you about anything?" He wouldn't look at me and kept glancing around. There was only another couple in the café besides the staff. Why was he being so weird?

"Oh my God," I said as clarity finally caught up with me. "You believe the police? You think I killed her because I was jealous you were screwing her behind my back? You think Kayla was the last straw, and when I found out about Savannah, I snapped." He didn't need to respond. The look on his face as I burst out laughing said it all.

"Shut up!" he snapped, but it took me a full minute to get it together.

"You are so pathetic." I wiped my streaming eyes with the napkin my matcha latte was sitting on. "And any decent human being would have warned someone they had claimed to care about that they were in the police's crosshairs. Obviously, I was expecting too much."

"What was I supposed to think?" he whispered. "Kayla had a bruise on her cheek for days after you hit her. I didn't know you were capable of violence."

"Kayla's mouth wrote a check her ass couldn't cash. That slap was for the both of you."

We were both silent while I sipped my latte and stared at him. Finally, he swore under his breath and gave me what I'd come here for.

"I didn't know much about Savannah other than she was

trying to break into acting. We only hooked up a few times. I didn't even realize she'd posted that picture of us on her Instagram until the police showed it to me."

"How'd they know it was you?"

"That wasn't the only picture she'd taken of me. There were others on her phone of my face, and they did a reverse image search and found me on the bank's website."

I knew the picture he was referring to. It was his employee picture listing him as Byron James, investment advisor, showing him looking every bit the young, approachable professional you could trust to guide you through achieving your financial goals. Admittedly, he was great at his job; it was being a faithful boyfriend that eluded him. I wondered how many others there'd been.

"How'd you meet her?"

"She came to the bank to apply for a loan. She was pretty, flirty, and fun," he replied pointedly, apparently still stung because I'd laughed at him. The implication that by comparison I wasn't any of those things wasn't lost on me.

"How much did she apply for? Don't tell me it's confidential because she's dead and you owe me."

"Five grand."

Was that money she'd planned on paying me? "Was she approved?"

"She called two days later and withdrew her application."

"Why?"

"She said she got a new acting gig that was paying her a lot and she no longer needed the loan. And no, she didn't tell me what it was. Are we done?"

"Well done steak couldn't be any doner than we are. But I have one more question."

He sighed heavily and rolled his eyes.

"You said it was just a hookup. Did Savannah think it was

more? Did she threaten to tell me, or Kayla, and you had to stop her?" His eyes got so big I thought they'd pop out of their sockets. I wasn't the only one sitting at our table with means, motive, and an opportunity to kill Savannah McCoy. And if I got dragged back down to the police station, I was going to tell Delaney and Wallace that.

"I don't know what that chick thought, and I hadn't even seen her in months until I saw her face all over the news and that's the truth."

"Have a nice life, Byron. Tell your girlfriend I didn't take her bracelet." That I was getting so good at lying was worrying me a bit. But once you fell down the lying rabbit hole, it became easier to keep doing it.

"She found her bracelet, but do you blame her for thinking you took it?"

I shot him a look and his gaze slid off my face to look somewhere beyond me. His evasiveness told me that Kayla must have told him what was in my diaries. *Assholes*! Did I blame her for thinking I'd stolen her bracelet when she read I was a petty thief in my diaries? No. I blame myself for making them accessible for anybody who wanted to read them. While I lived with Byron, I'd kept them in a box under the bed. As I looked at Byron for what I hoped was the last time, I realized what he'd said. Kayla had found her bracelet. But how? I still had the bracelet. It was in my jewelry box. So if it wasn't her bracelet that I had found, whose was it?

I got up to go, but he stopped me.

"Hey, you won't tell Kayla about Savannah, will you?" He looked so scared. I laughed again.

"Let me guess. You were seeing all three of us, weren't you?" He wouldn't respond. "Look." I took a big slurp of my latte. "I'll tell you the same thing I told your girlfriend. I had to find out the hard way about you, just like you'll have to find out the hard way about her. But she won't hear anything from me." I was already headed out the door before he got the gist of what I'd just said.

"Wait! What? Why did you tell her that?"

But I was already gone.

The next morning, after my class, I turned up at The Hub, took one look at Cal's office, and wanted to run. He'd lied when he said it was a mess. It was beyond a mere mess. It was like a bomb had gone off in the tiny back office. Every surface was covered in piles of paper, file folders, and unopened mail. The long metal desk – or rather what I could see of it – was covered with invoices and receipts and an old Apple computer that wasn't plugged in. The one metal filing cabinet in the room had drawers that wouldn't close because they were so full of crap. Then there were the boxes stacked almost ceiling high along the back wall.

"Most of this stuff was here when my mom bought the place," came Cal's voice from behind me. He held a box of heavy-duty trash bags in one hand and a broom and dustpan in the other.

"Oh, I'm going to need a lot more than that to cut through all of this junk." I gestured around the room. "Has this office ever been cleaned?"

"Are you kidding? I only come in here long enough to go

through the mail. I'll let you get to work," he said, giving me a look of pity before leaving me with this colossal mess.

Most of Cal's belongings from his mother's house had ended up in the office. Did these things hold too many sad memories for him to keep at his place or was there just not space for them? I started going through boxes and found trophies for baseball and wrestling and cross-country all the way from elementary school through college. There were boxes of old textbooks and comic books and baseball cards. From everything I found, it seemed like Cal was a pretty typical teenager.

It was a box of old photographs that interested me the most. There were pictures of Cal as a baby and a toddler through to his high school graduation, some with people who must have been friends or relatives, others photographs of sports teams. One picture in particular jumped out at me. It was of a tall, handsome white man with thick brown hair and a mustache. His arm was around a smiling brown-skinned woman who wore her straightened hair to her shoulders with bangs. They looked young, maybe early thirties. The man wore an ill-fitting suit while the woman wore a floral print dress. It was the woman's wrist that caught my attention. She wore a gold bangle bracelet with a heart at the center. It looked the same as the bracelet I'd found under Byron's bed. What in the flip? How would Lena Bennett's bracelet have come to be under Byron's bed?

"How's it going?" Cal's voice nearly made me jump out of my skin. "Sorry. I thought you might need this." He handed me a cup of coffee.

"Thanks. Are these your parents?" I held out the photograph for him to look at. He stared at it with a sad smile.

"Yep. This is them. They'd probably only been married a few years when this picture was taken. Much happier times."

"That's a pretty bracelet she's wearing." I tried to make my voice sound as casual as possible, even though all I wanted to do was tell him everything.

"My dad gave that bracelet to her for their very first Valentine's Day. She never took it off. At least she didn't until he told her he was leaving her for another woman. Then I never saw her wear it again afterward."

"Did he leave her?"

Cal merely stared at the photo for a few minutes before setting it face down on the desk. His expression was unreadable.

"I'm sorry," I blurted. "That was too personal."

"No, it's okay. It's just hard seeing pictures of them when they were so young and in love, not realizing what was going to happen to them. To answer your question, no, he didn't end up leaving my mother. They stayed together until the bitter end. And it was hella bitter."

"Sorry."

"I get the impression that you have a similar story about your parents."

"Not the infidelity part but definitely the bitter part. The sad thing is, I think my mom is still in love with my dad."

"Why do you think that?"

"She has a piece of a pineapple upside-down cake, his favorite, every year on his birthday. She doesn't think that I know about it, but I do."

"Do you think she knew he was stealing from his workplace?"

This is a question that I had turned over in my mind for the last twelve years. Did my mom know what my dad was doing? The answer that I didn't want to admit to myself was, yes, I think she knew. How could she not have known? My father in his former pre-prison life had been an accountant at a large accounting firm, a job with decent pay but not enough to shower my mother with everything he'd given her. She had to wonder where the money came from. I suspect that she just didn't care because she enjoyed the gifts and the trips and the cars. So she turned a blind eye and enjoyed the ride until it came to an abrupt stop, and she got thrown through the windshield.

My mom was different when I was younger, happy, carefree and fun, with lots of hugs and cuddles for me. Sadness lurked inside her, and as a kid, I sometimes caught her crying. Then I had my accident and Dad was in prison, and nothing was the same anymore, including my mother. She became a sad shell of the woman she was before. The carefree, fun-loving woman of my childhood became rigid and rule-driven with a high moral code that no one, least of all me, could live up to. She became obsessed with my success. If I got an A, it should've been an A+. If my GPA was a 4.3, it should be at 4.5. I had to be the top of everything before I even got minimal praise from her. I made the dean's list my sophomore year at Bellbrook, and she barely batted an eye. It was then I asked her why she hated me so much.

"Hate you?" She'd stared at me in disbelief. "Everything I do, every criticism, every suggestion is to make you a stronger person, so you never have to rely on a man, ever! Don't you dare think I don't care about you because everything I do is for you and for your benefit."

I watched her leave the room after that conversation and broke down in tears. She just didn't get it. What in the world had happened to her? Was it just my father going to prison? Was it the humiliation she'd experienced while having to sell everything we owned and scramble to find a new place to live to cover my father's legal bills? Or had something else happened to her that I didn't know about? I desperately wanted to know, but I also resigned myself to the fact that I probably never would. After my father's conviction, trying to be close to my mother was like trying to cuddle an iceberg. She shoved me away at every turn while driving me toward success.

"I think she had to have known. I also think she's convinced herself that she knew nothing about it. My mom likes nice things, not as much as she used to, but the things that she has are expensive and high-quality."

"Does she know your dad is in Addison?"

"No. I'm not sure she needs to know. She burned that bridge when she divorced him. I'm not judging her for that. I have no idea what I would've done in her shoes with a child to take care of. She was still in school when all this was going on and hadn't established her practice yet. She must have been terrified. It doesn't change that she lied to me for years about what really happened that night. I see no point in letting her know that he's here, let alone that he's remarried and moved on with his life."

"Meeting Cora has probably been the best thing that's happened to your father in years."

"I hope he doesn't mess it up."

"Me too," he replied before leaving me to get to work.

Two hours later, I'd made a big dent in the office. I still had a long way to go, but at least you could see the top of the desk now. I headed out from the office to the bar area to get a bottle of water when Gina, the busty brunette who was Cal's head server, stopped me.

"Hey, it's Kendall, right?"

"Yeah," I replied slowly as I looked around the bar, surprised to see it full.

"I'm in a bind, and I need some help. Cal left for a meeting and said you might pitch in if I asked you nicely."

She wanted me to help her serve. The horrified expression on my face made her snort with laughter.

"Don't worry. It's easy and you'll even get some tips." She seemed desperate, and even though I really didn't want to, I couldn't leave her swamped.

"Fine. What do I have to do?"

"Great, 'cause Donna called off again and we're booked for a college trivia luncheon. They don't care if they can't drink alcohol, but I can't take care of them all by myself."

"What's Donna's deal? Her husband didn't beat her up again, did he?"

"Who knows? You ask me, she's smelling herself. She keeps telling me she doesn't need this job 'cause she's making good money at her second job. She won't quit working here, though."

"That's weird. Why would she keep both jobs?"

"Tips?" Gina handed me a uniform shirt like the one she wore, only this one had no name stitched onto it.

"Tips?" I repeated, confused.

"Yeah, Donna works as a stripper on the side over at the Honeypot on Grand. Phil doesn't work and depends on her tips to feed his beer and gambling habit. I guess she didn't bring home what he was expecting the other night, and he can't figure out why since she came home so late."

"Is that why she didn't show up for work?"

"Who knows. If I had to guess, I'd say Donna's got something going on on the side with one of her regular Honeypot customers. But you didn't hear that from me?"

"Got it," I said, though I had no one to tell.

By 2:30, the bar was finally clearing out. The trivia luncheon had been a big hit. My feet were aching from running back and forth from the bar, and I still had to work in the office until five. Luckily, Donna finally showed up, and I could get back to my original job. When I passed by her on my way back to the office, I saw she had a black eye and bruises on her face that her thick makeup barely concealed.

"Are you okay?" I asked her retreating form as she breezed right past me without speaking.

She whirled around and glared at me. "Do me a favor and stay the hell out of my business," she seethed.

"Was I supposed to just watch him beat the crap out of you?" I wasn't expecting a thank you, but if anyone deserved her anger, it should have been her lunatic husband.

"You just made things worse, and besides," she cut me a look, "I can handle Phil."

"Oh really? Because from where I was standing, it looked like you were doing your best impersonation of a punching bag."

"I got it all under control. Trust me, Phil's in for a big surprise soon. I won't be anybody's punching bag for much longer."

I watched her go, eager to get back to the office to sit down and wonder what she'd meant as I unpacked the rest of Cal's boxes from his mother's house. My first job was to help him find that letter his mother claimed she wrote him. I hoped, for both our sakes, she was telling the truth. I opened another box when my phone beeped with a notification. I glanced at the screen and did a double take. I'd started following Mac's account again, and Mackenzie Burk – the real Mackenzie Burk – had just uploaded a new reel.

TWENTY-ONE
BEXLEY, OHIO

"What do you think you're doing?"

Mackenzie had just come home from her court-mandated therapy session, feeling like she'd been dragged through the mud, and was in no mood to be around people. Entering her bedroom, she found Alayna standing in front of the full-length mirror wearing her black mini dress with her black Dior saddle bag slung over her shoulder. She didn't even seem to realize Mac was in the room because she was too busy staring at herself.

Mac could feel anger rise like mercury in a thermometer on a 100-degree day, not because Alayna was wearing her things, but because she had violated her space. Anyone who knew Mac knew they didn't enter her room without an invitation. She'd had the room designed to be her own private sanctuary. It was the one place where she could be totally alone and unburdened by the pressures put on her by her parents. When Alayna finally turned around, her expression was anything but contrite.

"What do you think? I need an outfit for my date tonight. Do you like it?"

"You must be trying to get fired."

Alayna laughed and turned back to admire herself some more. "You aren't using these things. They're just hanging here collecting dust because you insist on looking like you just rolled out of the gutter. You may not appreciate everything that your lifestyle has provided for you, but I do."

"Did you hit your head or something? Take off my shit and get the fuck out of my room."

"Yeah, I don't think so."

Alayna tried to walk past, but Mac reached out and snatched the Dior bag off her shoulder and threw it to the floor. Next, she grabbed the neckline of the black mini and yanked it so hard it ripped down the front, and gold buttons flew everywhere. Alayna's mouth fell open, and she instinctively shoved Mackenzie away from her.

"You can have it now." Mac admired her handiwork as a smirk lifted one side of her mouth.

"You just ruined a $1,200 dress!"

"I just ruined *my* $1,200 dress. I'd rather take scissors to all this shit than see it draped on some raggedy bitch's ass. Now get the fuck out of my room."

Mac turned her back on Alayna. When she glanced back toward the door, she was surprised to see the other girl still standing there wearing the ripped dress. Alayna bent down to pick up the Dior bag and slung it over her shoulder. She took a step closer to Mac.

"You need to watch how you talk to me."

"And why is that?"

"I know that both you and your mother lied to the police yesterday. Only people who have something to hide lie to the police."

"What—?"

"Don't even try it." Alayna held up her hand. "Why didn't you tell the police that Savannah used to be your mom's PA? I was here that night the police questioned you. Neither one of your asses was home. You haven't been here since I went to Arizona to get you. Your mom wasn't here that night either. So I'm gonna go out on a limb and say that neither one of you wants the police to know that. But my silence is not free."

Mac just stared at her, realizing Alayna had her by the throat. There was no way the police could find out she'd been in Savannah's apartment that night. Considering the reason her mom had fired Savannah, the thought that her mother could have killed her former PA lurked in the back of her mind like a phantom.

"What do you want?"

"For starters, this." She held up the Dior bag. "I'll let you know about the rest."

Alayna turned on her heel and left the room, and Mackenzie realized the one thing she hated more than her mother's foot on her neck was an arrogant nosy bitch with her foot on her neck. It was time she got out from under this mess and finally contacted the person she'd purposefully stayed away from for twelve years.

She'd paid the rent on her Addison apartment to the end of the year. The only reason she wasn't staying there in the days after she'd run away from Alayna was that she knew her mother would come looking for her there first. As soon as she let herself into the apartment, the musty air hit her in the face. It was the first time she'd been there since before her forced stay in rehab. Dust motes floated through the air and made her sneeze. The first thing she did was go into the kitchen to throw away all the food in the refrigerator. Then she bagged up the trash and took it out back to the dumpster.

The rest of the apartment wasn't in bad shape. Even though she'd grown up in a house with maids, she was pretty neat and organized, especially in her bedroom where she had done most of her filming for her channels. It had been converted into a small boutique dressing room, with shelves of purses and shoes lining either side of the walls. She looked at the camera equipment, tripod and ring lights stored at the opposite end of her bedroom and felt overwhelmed at the thought of filming again. Since her socials had been taken over, her channels no longer felt like her own. What had possessed Savannah to pretend to be her online? It made so little sense. She was being paid a good salary to be her social media manager. Why had she overstepped her bounds? And how in the world had Kendall gotten involved in this mess?

Mackenzie stripped out of her clothes and stood in front of the full-length mirror in her bedroom. It was the first time she'd had the courage to look at herself since they had admitted her to rehab. She already knew she'd lost weight, but her skin looked dull, and her hair was dry and brittle. Dark circles were under her eyes. She didn't recognize herself, or at least the woman she was to her 250,000 followers. The persona she'd crafted online wouldn't be caught dead looking so bad. She took a long hot shower, conditioned her hair and put a moisturizing sheet mask on. Afterward, she set up her camera equipment and filmed a *get ready with me* video to reclaim her spotlight. When she was done, she surveyed her work, with the new auburn curly wig and a freshly beat face. She wasn't back to one hundred percent, but it was way better than she'd looked in months. She threw on some jeans with some purple hi tops and a black peplum halter top, grabbed her Louis tote, and headed out the door.

She had no clue how to find Kendall. As a freshman at Bellbrook, she'd spotted her at freshman orientation and was desperate to approach her, but she'd held back, remembering what had happened the last time she'd seen her. Instead, she'd stared until Kendall finally glanced her way and looked right through her. She hadn't recognized her at all, and Mac's disappointment physically ached in her chest. Then again, why would she have recognized her, after all those years?

Mackenzie thought about all of this when she headed to the library. She knew at one time Kendall worked there but wasn't sure if she still did or what she would say to her if she did. How did you tell someone who didn't remember you that you used to be best friends when you were twelve? How would she explain that she hadn't approached her in the five years they'd both attended Bellbrook? Mackenzie had sat out entire semesters at a time for various reasons including alcohol abuse and depression. She took great lengths to make sure nobody saw that side of her life. Social media was one big diary where people bared their souls and struggles to strangers. Mackenzie had never been one of them. Even if she wanted to, her parents would have lost their shit.

Mac made her way to the reference department where Kendall used to work, only to be told she no longer worked there. As she headed down the library's front steps, her phone beeped, and she opened an Instagram DM.

Hi Mackenzie,

You don't know me, but my name is Kendall Good. I need to speak with you about a woman named Savannah McCoy. I know you must be busy, but can you meet with me? It's very important. Kendall Good.

A phone number followed. Mac stared at the message so long spots appeared on the screen. She hurried to a bench on the college green and composed her reply, feeling like a huge weight had been lifted off her chest.

TWENTY-TWO
ADDISON, OHIO

When I arrived at Avenue Vee, Addison's only vegan restaurant, Mackenzie was seated at a table in the back. She had her back to me, but I knew it was her because she was the only black person in the place besides the guy running the register. I was halfway to the table when she turned and spotted me. She stood and smiled. *This* was the Mackenzie Burk I remembered from back in the day. Not the Savannah McCoy version who I still couldn't believe I'd fallen for. Looking back, I could see all the ways in which I'd been fooled, from her Cincinnati Reds jersey to the hat and sunglasses she often wore, to the fact she never looked me directly in the eye.

Her big smile slipped a bit. "Kendall?"

"Hi." It was all I could manage to get out as I took the seat opposite her. "Sorry I'm late." Why was I feeling so nervous? Judging by the smile on her face and her relaxed demeanor Mackenzie seemed very much at ease. Why was I being so weird?

"No worries. I just got here myself." The waitress suddenly appeared next to the table, interrupting the awkward silence.

"I'll have the fried avocado wrap with extra chili oil and sweet potato fries."

"I'll have the same and some water with lemon." I told the waitress who smiled at us and left to put in our orders.

"Are you plant-based too?" Mackenzie took a sip of what looked like raspberry tea.

"No," I admitted, feeling stupid. "But it sounded good."

"It is. Even my meat-loving friends like it, so I think you will too."

Mackenzie seemed laser-focused on me, taking in every inch of my face, my messy topknot, my long khaki skirt, my T-shirt, and my makeup free face. What she was thinking I'll never know because her expression remained neutral as she sipped her iced tea.

"Sorry," she said finally. "This is just really awkward, isn't it?"

"You think?" I replied dryly, causing her to burst out laughing. She had a loud, contagious laugh that made me want to laugh too. Something about it tugged at my memory. I figured it was probably from when I used to watch her online, even though I didn't remember her laughing like this. I realize she probably only shared part of herself on her socials and wisely saved the rest for people she knew and loved. Something about hearing her laugh like that hit differently, but I couldn't put a finger on what it was.

"So, how did you meet Savannah?" she asked me, finally addressing the elephant in the room.

"I was at the B&C. I'd just finished telling a friend of mine about a bad breakup I'd recently been through and that I had no place to live. When my friend left, she approached me and introduced herself as you. To be honest, she really did look like you. Or maybe I was just desperate when she offered me a room to rent in her apartment."

I could have mentioned that the first time I'd spotted

Savannah impersonating her, she was outside Dean Brogan's office, but I didn't want to go into all that. Now I thought of it, when I searched my memory of that day, I couldn't remember seeing her go into Brogan's office. I just assumed she had. If she hadn't had an appointment, then why the hell was she there? Had she been following me?

"She did kind of look like me," admitted Mackenzie, interrupting my thoughts. "I mean she would to someone who didn't know me well. And she was a talented makeup artist. So I get why you could've mistaken her for me."

"How well did you know her? How did you guys meet?"

"She was referred to me by an acquaintance who knew I was looking for a social media manager. I was getting burned out doing everything myself. We only met once before I offered her the job. I never got to know her because..." Her voice trailed off and she shook her head.

"Can I ask you something?" I was aware that my next question could ruin our rapport and make her want to leave. I went for it anyway.

"Sure." She looked uncertain, and that's when I realized there were probably things about this whole situation she didn't want me to know. I got it because I was hiding shit, too, but I still had to ask.

"Where have you been? Why did you let Savannah impersonate you online? Did you think no one would notice?"

"Is that what you think I did?"

She looked genuinely taken aback. That's when I realized I had gotten it all wrong. "Well, yeah, because why else would she be impersonating you online?"

"I get why you would think that. Sorry. This is just so unreal." She took another sip of her iced tea. "To answer your question," she said, hesitating for just a few seconds. "I was in rehab." She lowered her voice and glanced around. "I've had a drinking problem since high school, and it spiraled out of control about a year or so ago. I've been in Arizona at a rehab facility for the past three months and just got back a few days ago. I hired Savannah to be my social media manager not realizing that she would start impersonating me on my socials the minute I got put into rehab."

"Put into rehab? You didn't go willingly?"

"Not exactly. My mom tricked me and told me to meet her there for a tour of the facilities. Only she didn't show up, and after the tour, they wouldn't let me leave."

"Is that even legal? It sounds like kidnapping?" I was incredulous that in this day and age you could be forced into a rehab facility against your will.

"Not when my mom had a court order stating that I could be put in a rehab facility instead of serving jail time, for a substance use disorder and DUI. I guess by that point she was so sick of my shit she was willing to try anything to save me."

Mackenzie looked away from me, and I got the feeling that last part, and the robotic way she said it, wasn't true. Why did I get the impression she had mommy issues just like me? Maybe we could start our own club.

"That's fucked up."

"Beyond fucked up," she deadpanned, and we both burst out laughing, releasing our stress more than finding humor in the situation.

As we finally calmed down, our food arrived. I promptly dug in because it kept me from having to make any more conversation or ask more questions I didn't have a right to ask. True to Mackenzie's word, the wrap was delicious, as were the crispy sweet potato fries. As amazing as it was, all I had to do is think about my dad's oxtails to realize I could never ever be vegan. I thought about eating Thai food with Savannah the night she offered me money to take her class. I should have known then she was a fraud when I'd watched her eat her chicken Pad Thai. The real Mac had always been plant-based. I'd blown it off thinking she'd been through a lifestyle change.

"If you were involuntarily admitted, did she know? Something must've happened to make her think it was okay to impersonate you online and in real life."

Mackenzie put a fry in her mouth and was thoughtful for several long seconds. "I'm assuming my mother told her. She handled my affairs while I was in rehab, including paying my bills. She must have been paying Savannah. I'm sure she contacted my mom and asked where I was when she couldn't get in touch with me."

"Could your mom have asked her to impersonate you online? If she's anything like my mom, she wouldn't want anyone to know I was in rehab. That would be admitting I wasn't the perfect daughter that she wanted me to be."

Mackenzie's raised eyebrow told me that I'd said too much. Instead of apologizing for TMI, I took another bite of my veggie wrap.

"Damn. Are you sure our moms aren't sisters?"

Before I could respond, two giggling white girls showed up at the table. Mackenzie instantly turned up the charm a notch as they gushed over her videos, told her they were big fans. Once she'd taken a few selfies and the girls were gone, she turned her attention back to me.

"I sell a lifestyle online that's curated and aesthetic. It's not my real life. I don't film my struggles with alcohol, being hungover, or not getting out of bed for days because of my depression. Anyone on the outside looking in would think I have a perfect life because that's the way I've presented it online. There are the brand deals and collaborations that bring in cash and freebies. A lot of chicks want my life. I think Savannah got a taste of what it was like to be me and didn't want to give it up."

It made perfect sense, but I didn't buy it. Someone had paid

Savannah McCoy to impersonate Mackenzie Burk and ensnare me in a trap, I was sure of it. So far, I hadn't been able to confide the real reason she'd hired me to anyone. I was tired of carrying this secret around and needed to confess. Mackenzie was as good a person as any to confide in because I couldn't tell Liv.

I took a big gulp of my water and went for it. "I've got something to tell you."

"What?" she said in alarm at the seriousness of my tone.

I looked around. We were the only two people in our section of the restaurant. I quickly unburdened myself to her, explaining how I'd been hired to take her class and the story Savannah had spun and how even her apartment was made to look like her walk-in closet, complete with fake designer clothes and purses. When I was done, my throat was dry and Mac just stared as a whole range of emotions flitted across her face, starting with confusion, then fascination, and finally, disbelief. The waitress came back to clear our plates and Mac absently ordered us two pieces of carrot cake. It was as if she hadn't just been told that someone was trying to frame me for the murder of a woman impersonating her. I'd also revealed that I'd been impersonating her as well, by taking her class. I was too afraid to look at her and stared at my napkin instead. When I finally looked up, she shook her head.

"That's what this is really about? You got caught up in some bullshit because you were being shady your damned self and it blew up in your face? Did I get that right?"

"Pretty much." I wanted the floor to open and swallow me. Why did I tell her? Now she must think I'm a horrible person. She probably even thought I wanted the rest of the money Savannah had promised me.

"Welp." She dug into her slice of carrot cake that the server had just brought us. "I'm not sure whose class you were taking, but it damned sure wasn't mine."

"What do you mean?"

"My mom cancelled my fall classes because my release date from rehab was after the semester started and would put me too far behind to be able to catch up. I'll have to reschedule them for spring semester."

Then whose class had I been taking? Were the tests I'd taken and the paper I'd written for Savannah? That didn't make sense. She was a theatre grad student and the class I'd taken was an undergraduate psychology class. She could have told me anything, and I never would have known the truth.

"I'm so sorry. I've messed everything up." I could feel the prick of tears welling up in my eyes. Mac kicked me under the table. "Ouch!" I reached down and rubbed my shin.

"Stop it." She pushed her plate of half-finished cake to the side. "Savannah was as much of a victim as you are," she said, and then made a face. "Well, maybe more of a victim since she's dead. Anyway, whoever is behind this picked you because you were desperate, in a bind, and therefore vulnerable. A lot of people would have done the exact same thing in your shoes."

"So, you're not mad?"

"Oh, I'm hella mad at this whole messed-up situation. My point is that I know how you got from point A to point F."

"F? Don't you mean B?"

"No. I meant F. As in F for fraud, you shady bitch." Mac burst out laughing, and my face burned with shame.

"Oh my God! I'm sorry for everything. I knew I shouldn't have told you." I grabbed my purse and got up to leave. Mac grabbed me and pulled me down into the booth next to her. Then she laid a photograph on the table.

It was a photo of two smiling black girls aged around twelve, mugging for the camera, trying to look grown up in their summer halter tops and jean shorts, their lips thickly coated with shiny pink lip gloss. Their hair, usually worn in ponytails with barrettes, was loose around their shoulders. I recognized myself right away, though I couldn't remember posing for the picture let alone the girl who was in it with me. There was no mistaking the slight cleft in the chin and the big smile now. The other girl was Mac.

"But... how?" I stammered. "I... I don't remember this at all." The scar along my hairline started to throb, and I grabbed my water and took a sip.

"I know," she said softly. "It was taken at the Ohio State Fair twelve years ago. We lied and both told our moms we were meeting up with a big group of friends from school, but it was just the two of us. We had so much fun. I got my first kiss from Timmy Ryan on the giant Ferris wheel, and we ended up having to go home early because you got your first period and..."

"Wait," I said. "Hold up. This is... just." I searched for a word to describe what I was feeling but, "wild" was all I could come up with.

"Yeah." Mac gave me a tentative look and must have realized she'd completely blindsided me. "Sorry. I've been wanting to approach you for a while now and didn't know how you'd take it. I shouldn't have sprung it on you like that. You probably think I'm crazy."

I was so confused. Then I remembered my dad asking me about my best friend from back then and whether I was still in touch with her.

"Are you...?" I began, and watched as Mac's face lit up.

"Yes," she said, nodding her head. "I'm Mimi."

TWENTY-THREE
ADDISON, OHIO

By the time Mackenzie Burk was enrolled in Calvary Academy, a private Christian school outside of Columbus, aged twelve, she'd already been to two other private Christian schools. She'd attended her first school, Trinity Christian, from kindergarten to third grade and had to leave when they closed due to low enrollment. Her mother abruptly pulled her from her second school, Anointed Grace, before the start of sixth grade without explanation. She didn't find out until a few years later – when she was in high school – that her mother had caught her father having an affair with her pretty young fifth grade music teacher.

Whichever school she attended, the story was always the same. Everyone expected her to be like her parents, to sing like her Grammy Award-winning Mama or be an elite athlete like her former pro baseball-playing Daddy. Mackenzie was neither of those things. It never took people long to label her as nothing special and speculate that she must be a disappointment to her parents, which Mac had always believed she was. By sixth grade, Mac decided things at Calvary would be different. She went by the name Mimi, a cool fun-loving persona she'd created to prove to people that she was more than the unremarkable daughter of famous parents.

Mimi took crazy dares, broke the rules, and kept everybody laughing. It worked. Kids flocked to be crazy cool Mimi's friend, everyone except the other new kid, a shy, quiet loner named Kendall Good who everyone thought was stuck-up. She avoided Mimi like the plague, which made Mimi try even harder to be her friend. On a day when Mimi was cornered in the restroom at lunchtime by a bunch of seventh grade girls, because haters will always hate, and Mimi had her fair share of them, surprisingly it was Kendall who saved her from a beatdown. Kendall was in a stall when the confrontation began to escalate, and had pulled up explosive diarrhea sounds on her phone, turning up the volume and moaning and groaning for effect. She even poured the remains of her leftover vegetable soup on the floor from her thermos. The girls, including Mimi, left in a hurry, disgusted and retching. When Kendall finally emerged from the restroom, and the other girls were gone, Mimi came back, and they laughed until they cried.

They were inseparable after that. At least they were until Kendall's dad was arrested and she had to leave school. By the time she graduated from high school, Mackenzie was done being Mimi. Mimi had become a hard-partying juvenile delinquent well on her way to being a full-blown alcoholic. It was time to reclaim her birth name and leave Mimi in the rearview. Although she'd left the name behind, Mimi's vices had stuck with her like toilet paper on the bottom of her shoe.

"I'm sorry." Kendall stared at Mac like she was seeing her for the first time. "I barely remember you at all."

"I know. I heard you'd had a bad accident and lost your memory. That's why I stayed away. For better or worse, fate seems to have brought us back together."

Fate had brought them back together before, after Kendall had left Calvary, but it made Mac too sad, angry, and guilty to think about that time. She'd spent twelve years burying the memory under recreational drugs, alcohol, and casual hookups. That was the day everything changed for the worse. Now Kendall was back in her life. Did that mean things were going to get better? What would Kendall think if she knew the truth?

Mackenzie and Kendall parted ways half an hour later, with promises to call and keep each other up to date on the investigation into Savannah's murder. Mac would have offered Kendall a ride, but her license had been suspended because of her DUI and her mom had Alayna put her car in a storage facility while she was in rehab. She took the bus back to her place, and already regretted meeting up with Kendall. She thought about the bloody shirt hidden in the closet of her bedroom back home, and knew she was going to disappoint Kendall. She always ended up disappointing everyone.

I spent the rest of the night trying to study while thinking about my dinner with Mackenzie. How was it possible that we'd been friends from my life BTA? That's how I categorized my life. Before the accident and after the accident. The more I thought about it, the more I thought I must have some small fragments of memory of my friendship with Mac. Why else had I been so drawn to her? I'd devoured all of Mac's content my first semester at Bellbrook. I was utterly fascinated with her life. She was a shining light, and I was a moth. Could that have been my subconscious remembering her? I didn't have any other explanation for it.

But something was bothering me. If she knew me back in the day, Mac would have known about my father. Could she be behind the scavenger hunt? Maybe she was angry about Savannah impersonating her online, and angry at me for not remembering her. It sounded beyond sad and petty but not impossible. People had killed for less. I only had her word that she was in Bexley the night Savannah was killed. As of now, I had no reason not to believe her. And yet I didn't believe her. The psychologist in me sensed she wasn't telling me everything.

Around ten, I finally gave up on studying and headed back down to Cal's office to get some more work done since the bar was closed – and to continue searching for the letter. Each day fewer and fewer people were coming to The Hub. The trivia luncheon had been a hit, and Cal had added more food and coffee to the menu, hoping to boost the before work and lunch clientele. But having no liquor license, for a bar that thrived between 9 and 2 a.m., was going to kill this place. Even if I found the letter, would it be enough to overturn his conviction in time to save The Hub? What if his mother's husband had already found the letter and destroyed it? Then what would he do?

It was going on midnight, and I was about to pack it in, when I overheard muffled voices. I closed Cal's office and walked toward the alley. The door was slightly ajar, and when I pulled on it, it opened easily. Duct tape had been placed over the lock so that it wouldn't close all the way. I heard voices again and poked my head outside. Turning to the left, I saw two figures partially concealed by the dumpster. One I recognized right away. It was Donna, the server. She was against the alley wall, kissing a man I'd never seen before. He was as tall and muscular as her husband, Phil, was short and stocky. I couldn't see his face but could tell he was white with dark close-cropped hair. Donna was a grown ass woman, but she had no business using the alley behind Cal's bar as a place to cheat on her husband. The guy already had enough problems. I quickly pulled the tape off the lock, quietly closed the door and walked back to the loft. When a shadowy figure stepped out in front of me, I shrieked.

"Easy, Good. It's only me." I recognized Cal's voice before I saw his handsome face smiling down at me.

"You scared me shitless!" I pressed both hands over my

chest to still my rapidly beating heart as I glared at him. "What are you doing here?"

"Sorry." He gave me a contrite smile. "I came back to try to get through the rest of those boxes, but I see you beat me to it. Find anything?"

I didn't really want to admit that I still hadn't found the mythical confession letter that his mother had supposedly written, but that's exactly what I did because there was no use in sugarcoating it.

"No," I said, still breathless. "There's still a lot of stuff to go through and the letter could be anywhere."

"Shit." He sank down on the bottom step leading up to the loft, and I sat down next to him.

"We'll find it." But would we? What were his options if we didn't? He didn't respond. Instead, he stared out into the darkened bar looking like his world was ending.

"I finally thought things were turning around for me and now this." He buried his head in his hands.

I felt for him and was willing to help him any way I could. Holding his hand and patting him on the back wasn't going to help if we couldn't find that letter, and neither was him feeling sorry for himself. I nudged him and he looked over at me.

"What's your plan B?"

"Plan B?"

"Yeah, plan B. What will you do if we can't find the letter, or we do find it and it doesn't help you get your conviction overturned? What happens if you can't get your liquor license back?"

"Close... I guess," he said, like it should be obvious.

"Close? Are you really going out like that?"

"What else can I do?"

"There's a lot you could do with this space that doesn't include serving alcohol. Your mom left this place to you, Cal.

You can't just close shop and walk away. Sometimes, our dreams are forced to evolve and change shape and end up as something even better."

He sighed and grinned at me. "I hear you, Good. And I get it. But... it's just hard right now. I'll figure it out," he said, standing up.

"Promise?" I stood up too.

"Promise." He looked down at me with those sexy half-lidded eyes and without hesitating, he bent to kiss me.

I kissed him back. Soon his warm hands roamed all over me as I locked my arms around his neck. He lifted me so my legs could wrap around his waist. How he managed to walk up the steps to the loft with me wrapped around him like a koala bear on bamboo I didn't know – or care. Hoe phase had finally begun.

I was wrapped in a terry cloth robe the next morning, about to fix my lover some breakfast, when I heard a knock at the door. No one I knew besides Liv and Dad knew where I was staying, so I figured it was someone from the bar looking for Cal and I flung the door open.

Only it wasn't anyone from The Hub. It was my mother.

"Mom!" I gasped and involuntarily stepped aside as she waltzed right in uninvited.

My mother was dressed, like always, in a suit with a double strand of pearls around her neck. She had seven suits all the same style but in different colors. They were expensive suits, tailored just for her, and well taken care of, but she'd been wearing them since I was a senior in high school. She'd also worn the same hairstyle since I was in high school. Her hair was pulled back in a chignon at the nape of her neck. When my mother walked down the street, people got out of the way. She wasn't a woman you messed with. I hadn't spoken to her since I'd left her house with Dad's letters, when I told her I didn't want to talk to her unless she told me who my real father was. How had she found me? Then it hit me, and I grabbed my cell phone from the counter.

"Are you tracking my location again? You promised me you'd stop." I quickly pulled up the settings on my phone to discover I'd been right. My location was shared with her. She'd had access to my phone since the night I hit my head during our confrontation over the letters. I turned off location sharing and glared at her.

"I am not a child! You had no right to do that!"

"I had every right! What are you doing here? What happened to your fellowship? I called the graduate student's office and was told the Bennett Fellowship wasn't awarded this semester."

Cal chose that exact moment to come sauntering into the kitchen wearing nothing but tats and a smile.

"Who the hell is this?" Mom spat out, looking horrified from me to Cal like she'd just caught us hooking up on the floor.

Cal jumped behind the kitchen island and grabbed his jeans from the back of a barstool. My mother averted her eyes as he struggled into his pants and mouthed, "Who is she?" at me.

"Cal, this is my mother, Jackie Good. Mom, this is my uh, ah…"

"I'm Cal Bennett, ma'am. Nice to meet you." Cal stuck out his hand for Mom to shake, but she just stared at it like it was a snake about to bite her.

"Explain yourself, Kendall, right now!"

"Uh, that's my fault, ma'am," said Cal, and before I could stop him, he launched into the explanation for why I was no longer the Bennett Fellow. Her mouth was set in such a hard line her lips disappeared and I thought she might be sick.

"Mr. Bennett," she finally said, leaning against the island for support. "If you don't mind, I'd like to speak to my daughter alone."

"Sure." Cal grabbed his shoes and shirt from the floor on his way out the door. He'd left his briefs behind on the floor in his haste to leave, and Mom rolled her eyes in disgust. I wasn't the only Good woman who could benefit from some sexy time.

"I was going to tell you."

"When? When you got pregnant or got a sexually transmitted disease from that tattooed thug?"

"He's not a thug!" I blurted, wondering how hard she'd hit the roof if she found out about his criminal record. "Since we're on the subject of explanations, can I assume you're here to tell me who my real father is?"

She slammed her purse down on the kitchen island. "He's not important! Why do you even want to know? He's never been interested in having a relationship with you! He refused to even sign your birth certificate."

"I still have a right to know who he is. And if you won't tell me, you can leave." I turned to go, but Mom wasn't done making me feel like shit.

"Are you sleeping with that man to pay the rent?"

I whirled around, my face flaming and my fists curled by my side. "What did you just say to me?"

"Well, are you?" Mom crossed her arms and waited, and it took everything in me not to scream at her.

"What is wrong with you?" I could barely get the words out as tears welled up in my eyes. "I'm not even going to answer that."

Mom got busy picking invisible lint from the sleeve of her suit jacket, unable to meet my tear-filled gaze. She knew she'd gone too far, and yet she'd rather drink gasoline than admit it, or apologize for implying I was pimping myself out for rent money.

"If you needed money, why didn't you come to me?"

"Come to you?" I laughed, incredulous. "Why would I

come to you? You made it perfectly clear that you paid for my undergrad degree, so grad school was on me, remember?"

"I wasn't talking about *giving* you the money." She looked like I'd just suggested she lick a toilet seat. "I was talking about a loan."

"Didn't you hear Cal when he said this is only a temporary situation until his mother's estate is resolved?"

"My God. Are you an idiot? Of course, he'd tell you that! What else would he say to someone wanting a chunk of his mother's estate? He has no intention of giving you a dime. He's going to string you along until he's gotten what he wants, then he'll leave you high and dry. Men!" she spat out. "They're all the same!"

We stared at each other in silence for a long time before I finally spoke.

"Cal's not Dad. And I'm not seriously involved with him."

"You say that now. You probably even believe it. But I know you, Kendall. You're not the casual sex type. You'll get attached the way we women always do, and you're going to get hurt. That tattooed... man hardly looks like the settling down type. Once he gets his hands on his mother's money, he'll be gone."

"You don't know that," I protested.

"I do know that and so do you."

"Well, don't worry," I told her, heading for the stairs. "If he does, I won't bother you. I have a shiny new diary all ready."

"Kendall! Come back here! I'm not finished talking to you!" she called out after me.

"Bye, Mom." I called over the railing.

When I got out of the shower, she was gone.

From the diary of Kendall Good:

September 5, 2022

Dear Diary,

The Good News: I got laid last night. Best. Sex. Ever. The Bad News: My mom has lost her damned mind. More later. Too pissed off to write.

TWENTY-FIVE
ADDISON, OHIO

Blessing refused to accompany her daughter to the Addison police station to sign their statements. Mac hadn't wanted to go, either, but she had no choice. She knew if they didn't show up, the detectives would just come back. So she arrived without her mother, who texted her that morning to let her know that she wasn't feeling well and not to expect her. Translation: she was hungover.

Her mother drank a lot at the best of times, even more so when she was stressed. If anyone needed to go to rehab, it was her. Not that Mac didn't have her own issues with alcohol. She was an alcoholic. As much as she was still mad at her mother for tricking her into rehab, it was the right thing to do. She just wished she'd had a choice in the matter. She was on the receiving end of something she'd often dished out when she was drinking – unreliability. You couldn't rely on an alcoholic to keep any of their promises. Just like you couldn't rely on them to act in their own best interest. Mac knew that all too well. When she was growing up, her mother's drinking disgusted her, and she swore she would never be like her. Now here she was almost twenty-five years old and a recovering alcoholic herself.

Instead of feeling sympathy and kinship with her mother, she still felt disgusted. The woman could see everyone else's faults but her own, and she had a huge blind spot for her husband's flaws.

When Mac arrived at the Addison police station, she hoped all she had to do was go over the statement she'd given herself, sign it and leave. But once Detectives Delaney and Wallace heard that she was in the building, they took her into a room and explained they wanted to go over her statement again. Shit!

"Thank you for coming in, Ms. Burk. Do you have some time to go over the statement with us?" said Delaney after she'd been waiting about ten minutes.

She knew damn well she didn't dare say no or it would look like she was hiding something. So Mac shrugged and tried to look as nonchalant as possible.

"Sure. I have no problem with that." She forced a smile. The coffee and blueberry croissant she'd eaten that morning turned to lead in her stomach. That's when she spotted a folder lying on the table next to Detective Wallace. She could tell by how thick the folder was that it didn't contain just her statement, which couldn't be longer than a page and a half.

"Good," said Wallace. "We're hoping you can clear up one more question we had regarding these."

He opened the folder and pulled out several pictures before spreading them out on the table. She realized at once they were all from her Instagram account. There was a picture of her at an influencer event in LA a year ago. A makeup brand had flown her and twenty-five other influencers out for the launch. The company's packaging was black and white, and everyone invited to the official launch party was required to wear only those colors. Mac had worn a one shoulder white jumpsuit with a pair of black stiletto pumps, a pair of Luciano Silva stiletto pumps. She'd tagged every designer item she'd been wearing that evening: Jumpsuit: #aliceandolivia, Platinum Cuff Bracelet & Earrings: #davidyurman, Shoes: #lucianosilva.

Of all the things they could have shown her, this was barely incriminating. She instantly felt better, although she couldn't let them see how relieved she was.

"I'm assuming you're referring to my shoes in these pics?" She looked from Delaney to Wallace, who'd clearly been expecting a different response from her.

"According to your statement," began Delaney before his partner cut him off, earning him an irritated glare. "You stated that you didn't own a pair of Luciano Silva pumps. You claimed you only wore Manolo's and Louboutin's. Yet here you are pictured wearing a pair of Silva's."

Mac leaned back in her chair and let out a sigh. "Look, detectives. I can tell you don't know how the influencer world works, although I'm surprised you don't, Detective Wallace, since you claim your sister's an influencer. If you did, you'd know that Luciano Silva was one of the sponsors of that party and gifted every influencer who attended a pair of stilettos."

"You wore them even though you claim not to like the brand? Isn't that hypocritical?" Delaney was looking at Mac with barely concealed disapproval.

"Firstly, I may not be a fan of their shoes because they run too narrow for my feet, but I love their clothing and other accessories. Secondly, I'm not in the habit of alienating brands who might want to work with me in the future. So I stuffed my feet into those shoes for the red carpet walk and then changed into sandals once I got inside." True enough, the only pics of her wearing the shoes were pics of her posing on the red carpet.

"Where are those shoes now?" asked Wallace, who seemed determined to catch her lying about something.

Mac pulled her phone from her purse and pulled up her YouTube account. She showed him the vlog she'd posted about the launch party letting viewers know that, as a thank you for her channel reaching 100K subscribers, she was giving away the pair of Luciano Silva stilettos, that she'd worn for five minutes, to a random commentator. A woman named Leah Smythe, a subscriber from Baltimore, had won the shoes.

"Are we done or is there anything else you wanted to ask me about?"

"Your mother was supposed to come in today as well. Will she be stopping in at some point today to go over her statement?" Delaney asked as he shoved the pictures back into the folder.

"She's sick and I wouldn't expect her today. I'm sure she'll be here tomorrow." Mac doubted her mother would be in any day that week and that wasn't a good thing. She needed to cooperate with the police, or it could blow up in both their faces.

TWENTY-SIX

ADDISON, OHIO

I was in a shitty mood for the rest of the morning. After my shower, I got dressed and left the bar in a hurry, not wanting to face Cal again and have to apologize for my mom's behavior. I needed to talk to somebody, but Liv was teaching a class and I'm not sure she would have understood, since she was so close to her own mother. Instead, I called Mac, but she didn't answer, and when it came time to leave a message, I chickened out and hung up. Even though we'd been besties back in the day when we were kids, it didn't mean she wanted to hear my grown-up problems. So I headed to class and took my quiz, which I felt pretty sure I'd gotten an A on. At least one thing in my life was going well.

I was still worried the college would find out I'd committed fraud. If I had committed fraud at all because whose classes had I taken? When I tried to log back into the online portal using the login Savannah had given me, nothing came up. I checked in the catalog for the course numbers and found there wasn't a match. I'd even called the registrar and been told the same thing. The classes I'd taken didn't exist. I felt better but even more confused. I half expected that any day now I was going to be dragged into Dean Brogan's office, expelled, and the infamous XF would be put on my transcript. Then there was the bracelet I'd found under Byron's bed. It wasn't Kayla's bracelet, and it looked identical to the one Cal's dad had given his mom. Was Byron sleeping with whoever had lost that bracelet? It wouldn't surprise me since Grand Central Station was running through his bedroom.

When I got to the bar later that afternoon, Gina told me Cal was in Columbus, meeting with his new lawyer. I took one look around the empty bar, and Gina and I exchanged a look that said it all. If the boss didn't get his liquor license back soon, The Hub was done. I got to work on the office. All the boxes had been unpacked, and I'd filled two large dumpsters full of trash and still found no letter. I'd have gotten a lot more done if I wasn't still thinking about the argument with my mom.

Every argument we'd ever had, I'd caved first and apologized, even when it wasn't my fault. I pulled out my phone and was about to press her name in my contacts list before I stopped myself. What was I thinking? I'm a grown ass woman and she showed up at my place unannounced and got her panties in a bunch when she found out I had a sex life. Okay, maybe not a sex life per se. But she found out I had the sexual urges of a grown ass woman. Just because she'd encased herself in ice after Dad went to prison didn't mean I had to. What she'd accused me of made me not want to talk to her again for a very long time. Unless, of course, she was ready to explain who my real father was. That was the only conversation I was open to having with her right now.

I took a dinner break around five and went out to grab a sandwich. When I got back, a white guy sat at the desk in Cal's office flipping through a stack of mail like it belonged to him.

"May I help you?"

The man turned and gave me a lazy half smile that didn't reach his eyes. He stood up slowly like he was going out of his way to show me he wasn't at all pressed about being someplace he had no business being. He wasn't as tall as Cal, probably six feet with broad shoulders and muscular arms. He wore a black warm-up suit and black trainers. I caught a whiff of sweat clashing with cologne, and the cologne was losing, badly. I was reminded of a boy I knew from high school who opted for cologne over showering after gym class and always smelled feral. Whoever this was had probably just come from working out. He reluctantly tossed the mail back onto the desk with a bored look, but still hadn't answered me.

"Are you looking for Donna?"

That got his attention. His head whipped around. I could almost see his thoughts tripping over themselves to figure out how I knew about him and Donna, as a blush crept up his neck. I knew that while Phil was a good foot shorter than this guy, he'd wipe the floor with him. I knew a lot of guys like him. The guys who were only nice to girls they thought they could get something from, whether it be money or sex. My resting bitch face usually protected me from men like this because they knew they'd have to put in more work than it was worth to try and make me smile.

"I'm looking for Cal. He around?" His lazy half smile turned into a sneering grin that showed off very straight and unnaturally white teeth.

"No. He's out for the rest of the day. Can I give him a message?"

"Nope." He walked past me, and I held my breath ready for him to be gone. I couldn't resist twisting the knife.

"Can I give Donna a message?"

He paused for just an instant and turned. "I don't know anyone named Donna." He mumbled something else that I could have sworn sounded like bitch and then he was gone.

I looked around the office to see if anything was missing. Had he been in here two days ago, I wouldn't have been able to tell if anything was missing, but I'd made a lot of headway and everything that had been at Cal's mom's house was neatly arranged in piles along the back wall behind the desk. From what I could tell, none of the piles had been disturbed. The only thing it seemed Mr. Funky had touched was the stack of mail he'd been flipping through when I'd arrived. What was he looking for? Gina walked past the office on her way to the bar and I called out after her.

"Hey. Did you see that guy who was in here about five minutes ago?"

"What guy?" She looked confused.

"White guy about six feet. Really short, dark hair, black and blue warm-up suit." Gina's eyes went wide.

"I thought I smelled him. Funky attitude and body odor?"

"Yeah, him! Do you know him?"

"Unfortunately. That's Nick Palmer. He was married to Cal's mom. If he was here in the bar, he was violating a restraining order."

"Oh my God," I breathed. "He told me he was looking for Cal, but I caught him going through the mail on his desk."

"Great." Gina's shoulders slumped. "With everything that's going on with the liquor license, all we need is for Cal to find out he was here and go ballistic. The last time they were in a room together, Cal almost ended up back in prison."

"Is that why Cal filed a restraining order?"

Gina snorted with laughter. "Cal didn't file the restraining order on him. Nick filed the restraining order on Cal."

"Should I call the police?"

"Naw. Just tell Cal when he gets back. Let him deal with it." She started to walk away when I remembered what I'd seen in the alley the other night.

"He could have also been here to see Donna."

"Excuse me?" Gina abruptly stopped, and I explained how I'd seen Donna in the alley with a man who looked very much like Nick Palmer. "He must have met her at the Honeypot because she sure as hell didn't meet him here when he's not allowed within fifty feet of the place."

"You said you thought she had something going on with one of her regulars there. Could it be with him?"

"Wouldn't surprise me. According to the boss he's been running through his mom's money. It's a good thing Donna quit before Cal found out and fired her."

"She finally quit?"

"Found her uniform shirts and name badge in a plastic bag on the alley door when I came in this morning. No note or letter of resignation. I'm gonna assume she won't be back. At least let's hope not. She was about as reliable as an Ohio weather report."

The bell next to the register in the bar surprised us both, and Gina rushed off hoping it was a customer. All I could think about was what Nick Palmer was looking for in Cal's office?

Turns out Gina was wrong. Donna did come back. I'd just finished taking a long hot bubble bath when I heard someone walking around downstairs in the bar. It was after 10 p.m. and the bar was closed. Was it Cal? I heard the back door to the alley close, realizing that whoever had been downstairs must have left. I ran to the bedroom window overlooking the alley. Below, somebody crossed the street before getting into the passenger side of a waiting black SUV. It was Donna with Nick Palmer sitting behind the wheel. What was she doing here if she'd quit, and with him no less? How did she get in? Did she have a key? Gina hadn't said anything about Donna turning in keys.

I threw on some leggings and a hoodie and headed down-stairs. I checked the alley door, and found it was unlocked. Someone had duct tape put over the lock so it wouldn't catch again. I tugged it off and shut the door, happy to hear the lock catch. I proceeded into the bar itself, but it was locked and dark-ened. Then I went to the office. I hadn't locked it, and the door was open a crack. I went inside and flipped on the lights. From what I could tell of my brief sweep of the room, nothing seemed out of place. Until I turned and my gaze swept across the lone gray filing cabinet next to the door.

The top drawer was slightly open, which was odd because I had been so focused on getting all the boxes unpacked that I hadn't even had a chance to clean out this file cabinet. I pulled it open. There were only a few empty files still inside. When I went to push the drawer shut, it refused to shut all the way. Something was stuck to the back of the drawer. I stuck my hand in and pulled out a brown paper bag. Looking inside, I found a baggy full of white powder. Cocaine.

I'd never done drugs in my life. I'd never even smoked so much as a cigarette, let alone weed. And yet I wasn't so naïve that I didn't know cocaine when I saw it. I knew beyond a shadow of a doubt that Cal didn't do drugs, for no other reason than he was on parole and subject to random drug tests. If Gina did drugs, she'd be too smart to leave her stash here. No, Donna planted this here. I knew who had put her up to it, Nick Palmer, Cal's stepfather. That's what I'd overheard them talking about in the alley, and that's why Nick had been in the office earlier.

It had to be the reason Donna was still working here even though she claimed to make better money at the Honeypot. She was spying on Cal for Nick. Donna must not have been moving fast enough for him and so he'd scouted out a place for her to leave the drugs, which meant one of them was going to call the police to search the place. If they found this shit here, Cal would go back to prison. I had to get rid of it. No. Not get rid of it. Give it back to either Donna or Nick. I ran back up to the loft to put my trainers on, when my phone rang, scaring the shit out of me.

"Yeah?"

"Hey, it's Mac. I'm just returning your call." I was so out of breath from sprinting up the steps I couldn't respond for a few seconds. "Kendall? Everything okay?"

"No. I need a big favor."

"Damn." Mac gave me an admiring look that made me flinch. "I didn't know you were such a ride or die chick."

We were sitting in Mac's purple Mini Cooper in the parking lot of the Honeypot with a paper bag full of cocaine on the center console between us. I'd driven because Mac's license had been suspended after her DUI arrest. She'd had me meet her at a storage facility near campus to get her car.

"I'm not!" I snapped.

"Then what would you call it? You're willing to risk it all for a dude you barely know. Damn that must be some good dick." She mumbled that last part under her breath, but I still heard her.

Instead of answering, I slumped back against the driver's seat as clarity dawned on me that this wasn't a good idea. What was I thinking? This wasn't my problem, and yet, it was.

"I know how it looks. But if the police find this," I nudged the paper bag, "in Cal's bar, he'll go back to prison and by default lose his claim to his mother's estate, and if that happens, I'll never get my fellowship."

"You act like your life depends on that fellowship. What would you be doing now if you had never gotten it?"

"I didn't get it. I got robbed, remember? Therefore, I'm about to plant a bag of coke in the car of my hot fuck buddy boss's evil stepdaddy's car so he won't go to prison, and I can move on with my life funded by a fellowship I earned and deserve."

We looked at each other and burst into uncontrollable laughter. There was nothing at all funny about the situation, but the laughter was burning off some of the stress.

We sat in front of the Honeypot and watched men come and go for over an hour. Finally, we saw Nick Palmer pull up in a black Beemer SUV and hand his key over to the valet.

"Cal told me he was broke," I whispered. "How does he have money to spend on strippers?"

"All he'd need is a handful of ones, and why are you whispering? He can't hear us."

"I know." I was nervous and stalling. The valet was already getting behind the wheel of Nick's SUV.

Men happily handed over their keys to the valet so they could slip into the club faster and not be seen. The lot was packed that night so I knew there must be some kind of big event going on, and I was hoping the valet would be too rushed and distracted to notice me going into the lot.

"How the hell are you going to plant this stuff if the car is locked?" asked Mac as I followed the valet and parked in the last row directly across from the back lot.

"That's where you come in."

"I was afraid you were going to say that," she replied grimly.

"As soon as he gets out, start flirting with him, before he has a chance to lock the car, and I'll stick the stuff in the glove box."

"What?"

"Oh, come on, Mac, it's the only way," I pleaded. I was

aware I was draining her goodwill toward me and making her regret reconnecting with me, but I was desperate.

"Fine," she snapped. "Come on, let's get this over with." We both got out of the car and approached the lot.

"What's he doing?" I asked.

"Looks like he's going through the glove box."

We both suppressed laughter as we watched the valet pocket whatever he'd found in the glove box as well as the cup holder. He even searched under the sun visors and the seats.

"Come on. Hurry. He's getting out." I ducked behind the dumpster next to the open gate leading to the back lot.

"Now would be a good time to start whispering," she replied. I stuck my tongue out at her, very aware of the weight of the bag of coke in the messenger bag slung across my body.

"Excuse me! Sir! Can you help me?"

The valet was a scrawny guy who looked barely old enough to drive let alone be working at a strip club. He jumped at the sound of Mac's voice and did a double take as he watched her walk toward him. Mac, being the knockout that she was, had no trouble getting his undivided attention in her deep V-necked shirt that molded to her chest like a second skin. The kid grinned at her as recognition lit up his face.

"Hey, you're Mackenzie Burk!"

Mac looked taken aback, but a big smile spread across her face. As much as I wanted to hang out and watch this interaction, the second the valet walked up to Mac, I slid past him and beelined it to where he'd parked Nick's SUV. Quickly and quietly, I opened the passenger side door, crouched down and opened the glove box, as my hand closed around the bag of cocaine ready to slip it inside.

As I reached to slide the package in, I spied something amongst the stacks of mail inside his glove box. It was an envelope with a handwritten name on the front, Samuel Callum Bennett Jr. I didn't hesitate. I plucked the envelope from the glove box and shoved the bag of cocaine into the back. I could still hear Mac offering advice to the valet who wanted to start his own YouTube channel. I closed the passenger side door and ran around to the back of the SUV. Now I had another problem. The only way out of the lot was the way I'd come in. How was I going to get past them without him seeing me? I looked around wildly and spotted a side door into the club itself and dashed across the lot and tried the handle. Thankfully, it was unlocked. I darted inside and was instantly hit by a wall of sound and flashing lights.

The lighting inside the club glowed red and a DJ was spinning a mix of hip hop and techno music. A large stage with a pole took up almost the entire center of the room with two smaller platforms with poles in the further corners. Nearly naked women danced on all three platforms surrounded by men waving money. Some dancers mingled amongst the seated clientele serving drinks or giving lap dances. A few of them led men through a doorway next to the bar labeled private for private dances and God only knew what else. It was crowded and loud, and it didn't take me long to find out why.

It was amateur night and women roamed around the club in a variety of outfits. There were cowgirls, cheerleaders, women in school uniforms, and there was even a woman in a catsuit with ears and a tail attached to her thong. They came in all different hues, sizes, and ages. There were women who looked like grandmothers as well as several who looked like soccer moms. All of them wore numbers pinned somewhere on their bodies.

What was motivating them to take it all off for money? I realized I'd answered my own question, money. People would do a lot more for less than these women would probably get tonight in tips. According to the flyer that had been lying on the bar, each woman had ten minutes to strut her stuff on the stage and remove as much or as little of her clothing as she wanted.

Dancers were allowed to keep any tips they made while dancing but had to pay the Honeypot a twenty percent fee and weren't allowed to take customers to the private rooms. Getting caught doing so would result in immediate expulsion from the club.

"Who are you supposed to be?" said a gruff voice in my ear.

I jumped and whirled around from where I'd been standing next to the bar. It was an older woman of about forty with very tanned skin and long dark hair that fell from a center parting. She was dressed in a leopard print string bikini and while her face looked older, she had the body of a twenty-year-old.

"Well?" she prodded when I continued to gape at her without answering. She had a gravelly smokers voice and hard blue eyes.

"I'm a... broke grad student," I practically yelled over the pulse pounding music. Now why the hell had I said that? She glared at me before looking me up and down and bursting out laughing.

"Yeah, I guess I can see that." My face burned with embarrassment. "Is this your first time?"

It took me a minute to realize she thought I was there for amateur night. I should have just left. I could see the entrance from where I was standing and knew Mac was probably waiting for me outside. Instead, I asked, "Does it show?"

"You look like you're about to throw up." She laughed and I smiled too.

"Is that how you felt the first time?"

"Me? Naw. I was born to dance. I started with tap at the Little Stars Dance Camp when I was four, then onto the Spangler Academy for Dance and Drama when I was twelve. I had a bright future. I was even a Ben Gal for a season."

"A what," I asked in confusion.

"You know, a Bengal's cheerleader."

"Oh, wow. You were a star. What happened? I mean not

that being here is... um." My voice trailed off, and I needed to leave before she sucker punched me.

But she only laughed again. "I'm not offended. What happened to me is the same as what happened to most of us working here. You come here telling yourself it's only going to be for a little while to pay for school or until you got your big break, then you get used to the money and the attention and next thing you know five years have passed and you're still here. Don't let that happen to you. If you're smart, you'll think twice if they call and offer you a job."

"I have a friend who works here, Donna?"

"Oh her." She rolled her eyes.

"You don't like her?"

She shrugged. "Most of the girls here are okay, but that one thinks her shit don't stink. Usually, the girls with the biggest egos have the least amount of talent."

"I heard she's dating a customer."

"Donna dates anyone who has enough money to keep her G-string stuffed full of cash." She wrinkled her nose. "She hooks on the side too."

Why did this not surprise me? I wondered if Phil knew.

"I heard she was dating a guy named Nick Palmer."

"That loser?" She snorted with laughter. "If she is, she's the only one who'll fuck with him."

"What do you mean?"

"I mean he's broke. Gabby, the girl over in the corner." She gestured across the room to a strawberry blonde clad only in a silver thong twirling on a pole on one of the smaller stages. I gaped at her athleticism as she worked that pole like a gymnast, landing in a split. "She took him back for a private dance and he tried to pay her with a pair of diamond earrings and not even a new pair. Probably something he stole from his wife."

"What? Really?" I feigned shock and surprise.

Cal had already told me Nick was selling his mother's

things as well as giving them away to other women. Did that
mean the bracelet I found had been given to one of the
Honeypot strippers who had then gone on to sleep with Byron?
Was he a regular here? I knew he was a liar and a cheat, but that
seemed unlikely even for my ex. But what the hell did I know?
I'd been with the man for three years and had no idea who he
really was. Why would a stripper set me up for Savannah
McCoy's murder?

"And what happened?"

"Got his ass kicked out. That's what happened. He was
barred for a little while until he came back with the money he
owed. This is a cash only establishment. If he'd wanted to give
her the earrings on top of paying her the cash, that would have
been okay. We don't barter here. This ain't the farmer's market."

"Wow." I looked beyond her to see Mac standing near the
entrance cupping her eyes and looking around the darkened
club for me.

I needed to go. This wasn't the kind of place a recovering
alcoholic needed to be, and I'd never meant for either of us to
come inside. Plus, she had no way home because I drove her car.
I had one last question. I pulled out my phone and saw I had a
few missed messages from Mac and one from my mother. I
ignored them and pulled up a photo.

"Hey, did this girl ever work here?" I showed her Savannah's acting headshot. She squinted at it.

"No. And I'm glad. She's pretty and would have taken a lot
of money out of my pocket."

"Thanks." I put my phone back in my bag not bothering to
tell her she had nothing to worry about from a dead woman.

"Well, I'm on in five. Nice talking to you, sweetie. Good
luck tonight and I hope I never see your ass in here again."

She was gone before I could assure her that she never
would.

TWENTY-SEVEN

ADDISON, OHIO

I dropped Mac off at her apartment. She told me I could bring her car back the next day, and then I went home and stared at the envelope I'd found in Nick's glove box. The envelope was unsealed, and as I took the folded piece of paper out, I told myself that if it had been sealed, I wouldn't have read it. I knew that was a lie.

To whom it may concern:

I, Lena Bennett, hereby testify that on the evening of Saturday, October 5, 2014, I engaged in a verbal and physical altercation with my husband Samuel C. Bennett Senior after he told me he was in love with another woman and was leaving me. I had been drinking heavily that evening due to a recent cancer diagnosis. After my husband asked me for a divorce, I picked up a nearby fireplace poker and struck him over the head once, rendering him unconscious. My intention at the time was not to harm him but to prevent him from leaving. In my inebriated state, the only way I could think to do that was to knock him down. However, the blow to his head caused a deep gash and lots of bleeding. I was

semi-hysterical and that is the state in which our son, Samuel
Callum Bennett Jr. found me in when he got home twenty
minutes later. Due to my incoherent and inebriated state and my
husband being unconscious, our son was left to deal with the
fallout and unfortunately was subsequently arrested. My
husband identified our son as his attacker for the sole purpose of
protecting me. Cal was convicted and spent eight years in prison
for a crime that he did not commit. As a result, he lost eight years
of his life and has suffered from the consequences of being a
convicted felon. This letter is a statement of the truth of what
truly happened and my admission of guilt in the attack on my
husband. I am confessing in order that my son's conviction be
voided, and he be able to re-enter society without my crime and
my and my husband's failure as parents weighing heavy on his
life. I will regret what I put my son through for the rest of my life
and don't want him to suffer for it any longer.

Sincerely,
Lena Bennett
April 10, 2022

Early the next morning, I put a pot of coffee on to brew as
Cal read the letter. When he was done, he put it back on the
island and stared at it without emotion. I let him process his
mother's words until he was finally able to speak.

"I've been trying to push that night and the last eight years
out of my mind for so long." His voice was soft.

"You don't have to tell me, Cal, it's okay." I patted his back.

"No. I need to get this off my chest. It's been like a weight
on my back, and I need to let it go."

"Okay."

"I'd been out that night and got home around midnight," he
began, and then took a deep breath and continued. "The house
was dark, and I just figured Mom and Dad were asleep. At least

I hoped they were asleep. They'd been arguing a lot, and I could hardly stand to be at home anymore."

"And?" I prompted when he stopped talking.

"When I walked in, I heard moaning coming from the living room. I went to check to see what was going on and found my dad lying unconscious in a pool of blood on the floor in front of the fireplace. He had this deep gash on the back of his head. I felt his pulse and he was still alive, so I called 911. Then I heard the moaning again."

"Who was it?"

"It was my mom. She was crouched in the corner. I didn't even realize she was there until she started up with that moaning again. She was holding the fireplace poker, and the front of her shirt was splashed with blood. My dad's blood."

"Did she say anything?" I asked.

"I asked her what happened and all she would say was that she had to stop him."

"And you ended up arrested for attacking him?"

"It didn't happen right away. The ambulance came and took Dad away. I'd taken the poker from Mom and made her clean up before they arrived. Then people started asking questions, wanting to know what had happened and how my father ended up with such a serious head wound. The police were called, and they knew something wasn't right. Then the next thing I knew I was being arrested because my father had identified me as his attacker."

"He was protecting your mom?"

"She had been in remission, but it came back. She'd been fighting cancer for so long and we both knew it would kill her if she'd been arrested. Dad already felt guilty, and I think he thought his wealth and position in the community would get me off. He hired me an expensive lawyer but..." His voice trailed off.

"You got eight years."

"Eight years of hell. You have no idea what it was like in there, Kendall. Constantly having to watch my back and not knowing when I might have to kill someone or be killed myself. I had to leave the Cal I used to be behind and become someone else, someone brutal and hard and violent."

His voice was thick with emotion and the tears he'd been so valiantly trying to fight finally broke free and soon his cheeks were wet. I was crying too, and pulled him close, squeezed him tight in a vain attempt to soften his pain. We stayed like that for a while until he finally started talking again.

"Dad died while I was in prison. He left me some money for when I got out as payment for my silence. Mom had remarried that slimeball Nick but bought this building for me to start my own business. I'd been out for a couple of months before I finally saw her again. She never once came to see me in Lucasville. She told me she couldn't stand to see me in prison knowing she was the reason I was there."

"But you got close again before she died?"

"Yeah," he said, wiping tears from his eyes. "I couldn't keep being angry at her if I wanted to move on, especially since her cancer had come back again and had spread. She was dying and wanted to make things right with me before she died. She left me everything in her will, which is why Nick is suing me."

"Did she leave him anything?"

"The car and everything else she'd bought him during the marriage and ten thousand dollars. Plus, he's allowed to live in the house for six months until he finds somewhere else to live."

"That's pretty generous considering how much of her money he ran through during the marriage."

The coffee machine finished brewing and I poured us both a cup. I really needed it since I'd gotten very little sleep the night before.

"He's still spending her money. If this drags on much longer, there won't be anything left to fight over."

We sipped our coffees in silence before he asked the question I'd been dreading. "Hey, you never told me where you found the letter. I thought you'd been through all the boxes, which one was it in?"

I sat my mug down on the island and let out a breath before launching into an account of how I found the cocaine and found the letter in Nick's glove box. When I finally looked up at Cal, his face was beet red. He slammed the coffee mug down so hard on the island it cracked and quickly began leaking coffee.

"You did what? Are you insane, Good? Why the hell didn't you call me?" He was so angry a vein in his forehead bulged.

I opened my mouth to try and explain when my phone rang. It was Mac.

"I've got to take this, sorry." I walked into the living room, grateful for the interruption, and glanced back to see Cal pacing the kitchen and looking murderous. "Hey, Mac. This isn't a good—" I began before she cut me off.

"I need you to drive me back to Columbus right now. It's an emergency."

I spent the next half an hour driving Mac home while she stared moodily out the window, evading all my efforts at small talk. When I picked her up, she'd told me her mom had called and ordered her home because her father had taken a turn for the worse and didn't have much time left. Mac's mood was unreadable. I couldn't tell if she was sad, mad, or indifferent and that just made me realize that while, according to her and my father, we'd been inseparable as kids, I didn't know the grown woman sitting next to me at all.

"It's the last house on the left." Mac perked up once we turned onto her street.

Mackenzie Burk's family home looked like a small castle complete with a turret and a lush, manicured lawn. I parked in

the circular drive behind a black BMW convertible, surprised
there weren't more cars in the driveway. I trailed behind her as
we made our way up the stone pathway to the front door,
staring up at the long pendulum lantern which hung down from
the ceiling of the front porch. A pretty, young, brown-skinned
woman dressed in all black with long burgundy braids that fell
to her shoulders opened one side of the black ornately carved
double front door. She looked me up and down and then wrinkled her nose like she smelled something bad and turned
to Mac.

"Who is this? Your mom's not going to be happy you
brought a guest home under these circumstances. She's barely
holding it together."

Mac grabbed my wrist and pulled me into the house behind
her, pushing past the rude woman, and into the spacious foyer
before turning to address her.

"It's your job to hold her together because you sure as hell
don't get paid to worry about what I'm doing. Just let her know
I'm home." Mac gave a dismissive wave of her hand and the
woman glared at both of us before heading up the winding
staircase.

"Who is that and what's her problem?" I asked, glancing up
the stairs after her.

"Sorry about that. She's my mom's assistant, Alayna. And
I'm pretty sure she was born with that stick up her ass." Mac
walked over to the bottom of the staircase, gripped the railing,
and looked up the stairs, hesitating. I didn't blame her one bit.
This had to be so hard for her and I didn't envy her.

"Well, you should probably go up," I prodded.

She merely nodded without looking at me and made her
way slowly up the stairs. I wandered into a large living room
just off the foyer. It was decorated with pale gold walls and had
one black accent wall that housed a large fireplace and a black
and gold marble mantel. The furniture was black leather. A

large sectional took up most of the room and a baby grand piano sat behind it. This room alone was easily the size of the entire loft back at The Hub. I sat on the sectional to wait for Mac and noticed how soft and buttery the leather was. There was an array of magazines on the square block of gold granite that served as a coffee table.

I grabbed an issue of *Essence* magazine circa May, 1998, encased in a plastic cover. It was the issue with Blessing Burk on the cover after she won her Grammy. She must have been about thirty and wore a shimmering gold gown with a high neck and long sheer sleeves. Her hair was styled in an intricate braided updo while her expression was haughty as she stared directly at the camera with elaborately made-up eyes of an Egyptian Queen. The caption under her picture read *Counting Her Blessings: Blessing Burk ushers in a new era of Gospel music*. Ironically, despite such high hopes for her career, she never won another Grammy and each new album she released sold fewer and fewer copies. She hadn't released a new album in years. She was, by all accounts, a one hit wonder. In the pile there was also the February 2010 issue of *Columbus Business Magazine* with Marcus Burk on the cover. The article declared him the king of luxury car dealerships.

Half an hour had passed, and Mac still hadn't come back downstairs. The house was eerily quiet, and I was restless and anxious to leave. I got a text from Cal asking if everything was okay, wanting to know when we could talk. I'd left him in the kitchen of the loft to rush to Mac's aid and hadn't talked to him since. I'd offered to drop Mac off and come back later to get her so she could spend time alone with her family. She'd insisted it would be okay if I came inside.

I walked back out into the foyer and spied a powder room. Once inside, I remembered the story Savannah had told me when she was pretending to be Mac, about that hideous family painting hanging in the bathroom because Marcus Burk hated it. As I washed my hands, I noticed that the large gold mirror on the bathroom wall wasn't quite large enough to cover the faded area where something else had once hung. No one else would have noticed it, but since Savannah had told me that story, it stood out to me. Figuring that most likely another mirror had hung in that spot, I dried my hands and went back out into the foyer. I ran into Mac coming out of the living room.

"There you are." She looked relieved. "I thought you'd left."

"How's your dad?"

"Comfortable. They've got him so doped up all he does is sleep."

"So, he's not... you know..." I couldn't quite figure out how to express what I was asking. Thankfully, I didn't have to.

"Death rattling?"

"Yeah, that's it."

"No. My mom exaggerated. She made it sound like he was going to be dying any minute."

"Will you be okay? I should probably get back to Addison. I can come back and get you tomorrow."

"No, you're not going yet." She walked away from me, and I had no choice but to follow her up the winding staircase.

"I'm not? And why is that?"

"You're staying for dinner, which should be in about an hour. You don't mind, do you?"

"Do I have a choice?"

"Not when I have my car keys." She waved said keys at me, and even though I was slightly annoyed, I couldn't help but laugh.

Mac and I went out onto the second-floor deck that over-looked the backyard and pool. There was a kitchenette at one end with a small fridge and a mini bar. Mac told me to help myself, so I grabbed a bottle of peach tea and a water for her.

"It must have been fun growing up in this house. I bet you had a lot of pool parties."

"Not really." Mac took a sip of water, her playful mood of mere minutes ago gone.

"Why not?"

"Dad was never home, so he didn't care what I did. Mom has always hated my friends and never wanted them over. The few times I did have friends here, she complained about us making too much noise and spent all her time watching everyone, afraid they'd break stuff or steal something, then no one wanted to come over anymore. Remember, we always used to play at your house?" she said and then clamped her hand over her mouth. "Sorry."

"No problem. I'm glad I have someone to fill in the gaps. What would we do at my house?" I finally felt like I was unlocking the secrets of my missing memories and wondered again for the millionth time why my mother was never willing to tell me this stuff. Until I'd reconnected with Dad, Mom had never once mentioned my friendship with Mimi aka Mac. If she had, Mac could have helped me fill in those blanks.

"Your dad would cookout and tell horrible jokes. And your mom..." Her voice trailed off, and I could have sworn I heard tears in her voice.

"My mom what?"

"Your mom was always so happy to see me." She turned so I couldn't see her face.

"Mac? You okay?" I reached out to touch her hand, and she flinched like I'd burned her and stood up abruptly.

"I'd better go see what's going on with dinner."

I stared after her wondering why she'd gotten so upset. I figured it must have something to do with her complicated relationship with her own mom. My mom had been kind to her, and she'd looked forward to receiving that kindness every time she'd come to our house. My accident and Dad's conviction brought an end to our friendship and those visits. I hadn't been the only one who'd suffered. Mac had lost something too.

. . .

While I waited for dinner, I dozed off in my deckchair and had
a dream I was falling end over end in an endless loop that
wouldn't stop. I woke up in a panic, not knowing where I was,
before remembering I was on the second-floor deck at Mac's
house. It was getting dark outside and at some point, someone
had put a throw over me. A quick check of my watch told me I'd
been asleep for almost an hour. Where was everyone? Once my
heart stopped hammering, I got up and headed out into the
hallway toward the stairs. That's when I heard it. The unmis-
takable sound of moaning. It came from a room at the top of the
stairs. The door was open a crack, and I stood at the door
listening and wondering if I'd been mistaken when I heard it
again. I realized this must be the room Marcus Burk was dying
in. Mac said they were keeping him comfortable, but he didn't
sound comfortable. It sounded like he was in agony.

    Against my better judgment, I gently pushed open the door
and walked inside the semi-dark room. The only light sources
were the digital displays on the heart rate and blood pressure
monitors he was hooked up to and a bedside lamp beside the
hospital bed he was lying in. Then there was the man himself.
If I hadn't known it was Marcus Burk lying in that bed, I'd have
thought he was a man much older than his mid-fifties. He
looked shrunken and gaunt, the cancer having eaten away not
just his strength and vitality but also his stature. He was bald
and gray stubble dotted his chin and sunken cheeks. He let out
another agonizing moan, and I took a step closer to the bed.

    "Mr. Burk. Do you need anything?"

    Where was his nurse? Surely, Mac, her mom, and evil
Alayna weren't taking care of him all by themselves. Then
again, there really wasn't much to do at this point except wait
for the inevitable. His gaze was fixed on the wall behind me,
and I turned to see what he was looking at and gasped. It was

the ugly family portrait that had been hanging in Savannah McCoy's house. It had to be the original. There was a display light illuminating it so Marcus Burk could see it, and not just see it. By the anguished look on his face, whoever put that painting on the wall had done it to torment him; it was probably all he could see whenever he was awake. That's when I realized he wasn't in physical pain. The IV bags of pain meds he was connected to were full. He was in emotional pain. I didn't hesitate. I walked over to the lighting fixture and turned it off instantly casting it into shadow.

"Is that better?" I walked back over to the bed and saw he was staring at me with wide fever bright eyes. His lips were moving. He was muttering something I couldn't quite understand. "What did you say, Mr. Burk?"

I had to lean over him with my ear near his mouth to hear what he was saying and still couldn't quite make it out.

"I'm so... appy."

Did he just say I'm so happy? "You're welcome, Mr. Burk. Is there anything you need?"

"What are you doing in here?"

I whirled around. Blessing Burk stood in the doorway, staring at me like she'd seen a ghost. She was dressed in a black shirt and jeans, and her hair was pulled back into a long ponytail that fell down her back. She had full glam makeup with impossibly long fake lashes and bright red lipstick. Large gold hoops hung from her ears. She was older than she was in that portrait, but I'd have known her anywhere.

"I am so sorry, Mrs. Burk. I didn't mean to intrude. Your husband was moaning, and I came to see if he was okay." I gestured toward the emaciated man in the bed. My words did nothing to wipe the look of anger and suspicion off her face.

"Who are you? You have no right to be in here. Are you a reporter?" Blessing Burk didn't know me from Adam, but why did I have the feeling she knew exactly who I was?

"No, ma'am. I'm a friend of Mac's."

"And where is my daughter? She had no right letting you in here. This isn't some kind of spectator sport that you can just come and watch. My husband is dying, and he deserves peace and quiet and dignity."

"Mom?" Mac appeared in the doorway, and her mother instantly shoved her out into the hallway and then stood inside expectantly while I exited the room.

"I am so sorry, Mrs. Burk. I meant no harm. It sounded like he was in distress."

"Oh, so you're a nurse?" Her anger was justified, and my face burned with embarrassment.

"Mom, chill. She didn't do anything."

"I should go. Again, I am so sorry, Mrs. Burk, I meant no harm. I'll see you later, Mac." I quickly headed down the steps.

"Kendall, wait!" She grabbed my hand when she caught up with me. I already had the front door open, and she shut it. "Please don't go. It's not you. You didn't do anything wrong. She's just upset. We all are."

"Which is why you need to be alone with your family, Mac. I shouldn't be here." I could tell by the determined look in her eyes that she wasn't trying to hear what I was saying. Why was my being here so important to her?

"Just wait. I'll be right back." I watched her walk back upstairs and realized I couldn't go anywhere because she still had the car keys. Was there a bus stop nearby? I could take it to the Greyhound Station and get a bus back to Addison.

Against my better judgment, I waited in the foyer, but it took almost ten minutes before both Mac and her mom came back. Fortunately for me, Blessing seemed to have calmed down and looked marginally more hospitable. She gave me a big smile that didn't reach her eyes, the kind she probably reserved for her audiences. She clasped both of my hands in hers; they were cold and clammy. It took everything in me not to pull away.

"Please forgive me, Kendall. We've just been so emotional with everything that's going on with my husband. You don't know how many people from the press have been trying to get into this house to get a picture of my husband on his deathbed once news of his illness finally got out to the press."

"There's nothing to forgive, Mrs. Burk. I was just so shocked when I heard him moaning like that. I was afraid something had happened."

"Will you join us for dinner?"

"Of course. Thank you." I said it with an enthusiasm that was as phony as Blessing Burk's smile and resigned myself to enduring the most awkward AF meal I'd ever experienced in my life.

TWENTY-EIGHT

BEXLEY, OHIO

Alayna, the rude assistant, also joined us for dinner. It was still quite warm out, and Blessing decided we'd eat on the back patio next to the pool. To my surprise, Blessing was the one who cooked the veggie lasagna that we had, and although it was good, the heavy mood in the house made it impossible to enjoy. I also noticed Blessing drink quite a bit. In the forty-five minutes it took for the meal to mercifully come to an end, she had three glasses of red wine. With each one she poured herself, Mac looked more and more annoyed. Alayna occasionally glanced at her employer impassively, seemingly unconcerned by how much alcohol she was consuming. Conversation was at a minimum, and I don't know why I felt like I had to remedy that, but I did.

"You have a beautiful home, Mrs. Burk." The compliment seemed to perk her up to the extent her whole demeanor changed.

"Thank you." Her face lit up with a smile that made me wonder if she was the same woman, I'd encountered an hour ago. "Marcus gifted me this house for our five-year wedding anniversary. Let me decorate it anyway I wanted."

She seemed proud and a little sad at the memory. No one was going to mention, least of all me, that it was common knowledge Marcus Burk's very public affair with an actress had prompted the gift of the house. Buying her this house was cheaper than a divorce would have been.

"You've done an amazing job." I took a sip of my water, purposefully avoiding alcohol for Mac's sake. I wondered how Blessing could drink so freely in front of her daughter who was struggling with alcohol addiction.

"This house was featured in *Columbus Homes Magazine* last year," stated Alayna nodding at her employer with a big fake smile while Blessing continued to preen.

That was the extent of the conversation for several long minutes while we finished our dinner, until Alayna brought out a tray of raspberry sorbet.

"Where did you and Mackenzie meet? I don't think my daughter mentioned that."

Blessing was staring at me so intensely it made me uncomfortable. She'd shoved her dish of sorbet aside and was pouring herself a fourth glass of wine. Even Alayna visibly winced as she watched her. Why was she asking me this? Didn't Mac tell her we were once friends when we were twelve and had met at Calvary Academy? Didn't she remember me from that time? Then I remembered what Mac had told me earlier about not having friends over and how we used to play at my house all the time. Had I even met this woman back when Mac and I were friends? I was about to mention Calvary, but something was telling me not to.

"We met at Bellbrook," I said instead.

"She knows that," interjected Mac. "She's just being extra."

"I needed to hear that directly from our guest because as you know, you have a very interesting relationship with the truth, daughter dear." Blessing knocked back half the glass of wine and stared at me expectantly.

"It's true. We met at Bellbrook." There wasn't much more I could say on the matter, and Mac and I both knew it wouldn't be a good idea to tell her mother the circumstances of our meeting. But why not just tell her where we first met?

"And you became instant besties, is that it?"

"Excuse me?" What was she trying to get at?

"It's just that this is the first time I'm meeting you, but here you are in my house, close enough to my daughter that she wants you by her side during a very difficult time for our family. I'm just wanting to know who you are. I think I have a right to know that, don't I?"

"Mom! Stop being so rude." Mac looked highly aggravated, and I held up a hand.

"It's okay. I totally get it. I'm so sorry if you feel like I'm intruding, Mrs. Burk. My name is Kendall Good, and I was born and raised right here in Columbus. My parents are Jackie and Ray Good, and the first time Mac and I met was back in sixth grade at Calvary Academy. So we aren't complete strangers."

I would have continued, but at the mention of my full name, Blessing abruptly stood up, knocked over the remainder of her wine and spilled it all over the table. We all jumped up and grabbed napkins to clean up the mess while the lady of the house continued to stare at me in alarm.

"Are you okay?" I took a step toward her, and she stepped backward, losing her balance, and fell onto the patio floor. Mac and Alayna rushed over to help her, but I could've sworn I saw Alayna push Mac's hands away as she helped Blessing to her feet.

"I'm going to take her to her room now. This has been a very stressful day for her." I watched them go in confusion, wondering what the hell had just happened.

"I am so sorry, Mac. This was a bad idea and I really need to go." I didn't wait for her response as I headed back into the house toward the front door with Mac trailing behind me.

"I apologize for my mother, that was out of pocket. I was so happy to have you here that I neglected to warn you that my mother is usually drunk by this time every night."

"It's okay," I told her, but it wasn't okay. Why did she react that way when she heard my name? It would be easy for me to assume that her behavior was caused by the impending loss of her spouse. But I had a feeling that Blessing's behavior pre-dated her husband's illness. Were both Burk women alcoholics because they lived with Marcus Burk? Was that why the sight of that portrait on the wall of his bedroom made him so distraught? Was it guilt over what he'd put them through? Or was it because alcoholism ran in the family? I wasn't about to ask Mac because it was really none of my business. I just wanted to go home.

I let her walk me to her car but had barely gotten within ten feet of it when I saw a huge problem. The front driver side tire was completely flat. *Shit!* Never had there been a time that I wanted to get away from someone so badly. Not Mac. But her mother, this house, and Alayna's rude ass. I was suddenly feeling so sorry for her having to grow up in this complete and total dysfunction. No wonder she had latched onto me so fast. I wondered if she'd ever had another good friend in her entire life.

As much as I wanted to leave, Mac talked me into staying the night. She said she'd have the man who serviced her family's cars come in the morning to change the flat. Thankfully, I didn't see Blessing again for the rest of the evening, or her little clone, Alayna. Mac and I hung out in her room, behaving like teenagers, trying on her clothes and shoes, listening to music, and eating all the snacks in the pantry. It had been so long since I'd done something like this like. Even Liv and I, as close as we'd become, had never done anything like this because Liv was such a neat freak. The thought of her space being cluttered with clothes and empty snack bags would be enough to send her into a nervous breakdown.

"I'm just gonna say it," she said, laughing, before popping a Sour Patch Kid into her mouth. "I'm glad the tire was flat because I haven't had this much fun in months that didn't involve a bottle each of Henny and Moet."

"Henny *and* Moet? That's hardcore."

"That would've been a low-key night," she said dryly with a faraway look in her eyes.

"How long were you drinking like that?"

"Probably since I was about fifteen or sixteen and found the key to my parents' liquor cabinet. Drinking seemed to work so well for my mom. I decided what the hell. Plus, I was hanging out with a pretty wild bunch of kids from school, and it just became a perfect storm of self-destruction."

"Was this your first time in rehab?"

"Are you kidding me? Try my fifth."

"Wow, Mac. I am so sorry."

"Why? It's not your problem." Her voice was so bitter I looked over at her thinking she might be mad at me, but she just looked sad. "Enough about me and my fucked-up problems. What about you? What secrets are lurking in the past of Kendall the Good?"

"What did you just call me?"

"Kendall the Good? Why?"

"I just suddenly remembered that's what they used to call me in high school, Kendall the Good. I hated it." I hated it because I was anything but good. In fact, my stealing was at its height when I was in high school.

"Well, it's better than Mac n' Wheeze."

"What?"

"I had asthma as a little kid but thankfully grew out of it by the time I hit middle school."

"That's just mean." I turned away so she wouldn't see my lips twitching.

"Yeah, but it was kind of funny." We both burst out laughing.

I was happy Mac was laughing, and I hoped I was taking her mind off her father and her mom's drinking problem. Was that why she hadn't put out an album in so long?

"What's up with that painting on the wall in your dad's room?"

"Oh, that." She frowned. "I remember when it got painted. Mom was hell-bent on having it done. Dad and I hated it. They argued the entire time we had to sit for it. The artist took his sweet time because he was getting paid by the hour. Finally, Dad refused to show up for the sittings and Mom had the artist paint the crown on his head crooked on purpose just to piss him off."

"That's messed up."

"No. What's messed up is her hanging it across from his death bed, so he sees it every time he opens his eyes. She's petty as fuck."

"It hasn't always hung there?"

"Hardly. It hung in the powder room in the foyer for years because my dad said the only way he could look at it was if he was taking a dump." She snorted with laughter, but my blood ran cold.

Savannah McCoy had told me the same story. How would she even know about that story if, like Mac had said, she'd only met Mac once when she'd hired her as a social media manager? There would be no reason to tell her that story during an interview. Had Mac lied to me?

"Earth to Kendall." Mac was waving a bag of Takis in my face, and I forced a smile and snatched it out of her hands.

"When will the guy be here in the morning to change the tire? I've got a class tomorrow at ten."

"Man, you really know how to kill a mood. I told him to be here at eight."

"Great."

"Hey. Check it out." Mac was waving a CD at me. "Look what I found!" It was Writing's on the Wall by Destiny's Child.

"Where did you get that?"

"It's yours. You loaned it to me the last time we saw each other. We had to listen to it at your house because I wasn't allowed to listen to secular music."

I didn't remember. I desperately wanted to because I needed to know who and what kind of person Mac really was. I knew she struggled with addiction. But were there worse things in her past, or her present for that matter?

"Why was your mom so freaked out when I told her my name? Didn't she remember that we used to be friends?"

Mac looked taken aback and her brow furrowed like she couldn't understand why I was asking. Then her face softened, and she shrugged. "You were my secret friend."

"Secret friend? Why?" I suddenly became agitated, possibly because all the sugar from the junk we were eating was hitting my bloodstream. Either way, my feeling that something wasn't quite right here had just amplified.

She sat down on the edge of her bed. "My parents controlled every aspect of my life. What I wore. What I ate. My hobbies. What music I could listen to and who my friends were. I was only allowed to be friends with the kids of their friends. I had to lie and say I was going to hang out with someone on the approved friends list when I came to your house. That's the real reason why we never hung out here." Her gaze shifted when she'd said that last part, and I got the weirdest feeling I'd just been lied to, again.

·   ·   ·

When I got up the next morning around six, Mac was still asleep. I had a pain in my neck and back from having fallen asleep amongst the oversized throw pillows on the floor. Mac was sprawled spread-eagle on her back a few feet away. I couldn't remember the last time I'd fallen asleep on the floor. My fumbling around in the semi darkness woke her, and she sat up and yawned.

"You can get in the shower first. I'm going to go check on my parents."

Since I'm not a morning person, I merely nodded and headed into her spacious bathroom and made a beeline for the shower. I stood under the large rain shower head as steam billowed around me for a long time. I lathered her expensive honeysuckle body wash all over and even used her shampoo to wash my hair, feeling like I was washing the weight of the world off my body. When I got out, Mac was in a robe and a pile of clothing, including jeans, a blue boat-necked long sleeved top and underwear, all with tags still on them, lay on her bed.

"These are for you. Stuff I got from brands that aren't my style."

"Thanks." I couldn't help but think how ironic it was that my wardrobe was getting a makeover in the form of unwanted clothes by two women I hadn't known a month ago. My former friendship with Mac didn't count because I couldn't remember it. "Everybody okay?"

"Dad's resting. His hospice nurse just got here and Mom's hungover and snoring. No clue where Alayna is. There's fruit, yogurt, muffins, and juice in the kitchen if you're hungry."

Mac disappeared into the bathroom, and I quickly dressed, braided up my still damp hair, and wound it into a topknot. I headed down to the kitchen hoping they had a coffee maker and was surprised and bit alarmed to find Blessing sitting in the kitchen with a mug of coffee. She wore black silk pajamas and fluffy black house slippers. Her hair was loose around her shoulders, and she wore no makeup. Her bare face was much older-looking with thin lips, deep dark under eye circles, and sparse almost nonexistent eyebrows. She looked awful. Had alcoholism done this to her?

"Good morning, Mrs. Burk," I said softly, trying not to startle her.

"Still here, huh?" She gave me an annoyed look, and I almost left the kitchen. Then my stomach growled. "Sit down and I'll fix you an omelet." She got up from the table and grabbed a skillet from the rack that hung over the kitchen island.

"That's not necessary. I can—" I was going to say have a muffin, but she glared at me, and I realized she didn't go out of her way for many people. I shut up and sat down at the table while she got busy chopping vegetables for my omelet.

Neither of us spoke, and I was just about to get up and pour myself a cup of coffee when she finally decided to talk to me.

"I need to talk to you about Mac."

"Mac? What about her?" Now I got it. Making me an omelet wasn't her being nice. It was a way for her to trap me while she said whatever she was going to say about her daughter.

"Look," she said, as she cracked eggs into a bowl. "People see my daughter online and think they know her."

"Meaning?" I didn't like what she was implying, but out of respect I paused so she could continue.

"Meaning, I know you consider yourself to be her friend. But there are things about her that you need to know."

"Like what?"

Blessing finally looked up at me. "Mackenzie isn't well. She—"

"You mean her depression and alcoholism? She told me all of that."

"I'm sure she told you. But trust me. She hasn't told you

everything." She poured the egg and veggie mixture into the skillet and started grating cheddar cheese.

"What else is there to know?" I wasn't sure I was ready for what she was about to say thanks to what Mac had unintentionally revealed last night about the portrait. I'd already convinced myself by the time I'd opened my eyes an hour ago that there was a reasonable explanation for Savannah knowing the story behind that portrait and where it used to hang.

"My daughter has a tendency to develop intense friendships. When those friendships come to an end, she has a hard time accepting it and can become quite obsessive in trying to hold on to that friend."

"Are you saying she's a stalker?"

"Stalking behavior has been involved in some of her previous friendships. But I'm just not talking about stalking. I'm talking about something worse."

"Are you trying to say that Mac is violent?"

"Did she tell you that she wasn't able to graduate with her high school graduating class?"

"No, she never mentioned that."

"Oh, of course she wouldn't. She couldn't march with the rest of her class because she was expelled. She and her best friend at the time had a falling out which led to a confrontation at school and Mackenzie slashed that girl's face."

"What?" The word came out as barely a whisper as my stomach clenched. Mac hadn't told me anything about this. But why would she?

Blessing sat a black plate with the piping hot omelet in front of me, but I'd lost my appetite.

"I really can't blame my daughter for how she turned out." She sat down opposite. "With me on the road so much and her father busy with his dealerships, and his other extracurricular activities, Mackenzie was alone a lot, and has a habit of latching onto people. So I blame myself and my husband for her neediness and abandonment issues. I'm just hoping to offset any future problems down the road for you."

"I don't know what to say." And I didn't. Instead, I stared down at my plate.

"I can tell that this comes as a big shock to you. I felt like you should know because I had a feeling she hadn't told you. If you walk away now, you probably won't see her again and there won't be any trouble."

"Thanks for letting me know, Mrs. Burk." I got up from the table.

"I know it's a lot to take in. I'm tired of cleaning up my daughter's messes and don't want you to be part of it."

I walked out of the kitchen, pausing to look back, and saw her sliding my plate with the untouched omelet across the table to herself, and began eating it, looking like a cat who'd just finished batting a mouse around.

When I got back up to Mac's room, I could hear her talking in the bathroom. I paused to listen at the door and realized she was filming a GRWM video. I was glad she was occupied because I had to go. I needed a neutral space to clear my head. Common sense told me that Blessing Burk probably wasn't the best source of information when it came to her daughter. It wasn't exactly like the two were close. Mac had told me she didn't seem to want her to have any friends. So the fact that she was trying to scare me off by painting Mac as some kind of obsessive stalker shouldn't have surprised me. But it was still time for me to go. Mac's father was dying, and she needed to be here. Maybe after everything with her family had settled down, I could revisit the whole Mac and Savannah thing. Right now, I just didn't have the energy for it. I had enough problems of my own without adding someone else's.

The room was a mess, and I at least wanted to clean up

before I left. I gathered all the pillows from the floor and put them back in Mac's walk-in closet where I'd seen her get them from last night. I wasn't sure exactly where she stored the pillows in the closet, but I spotted an empty shelf above where her many coats hung and lifted one of the pillows up, dislodging a tote bag in the process which fell to the floor.

"Shit," I said softly as I bent to pick it up and noticed the contents had partially fallen out. It was a T-shirt, stiff with dried blood on the front of it and a yearbook, the cover also smeared with blood. "What the hell?"

I sank down onto the large pink ottoman in the center of the closet. That's when I noticed that the yearbook was from Calvary Academy 2017, the year Mac graduated. Whose blood was on it and the T-shirt? I paused to listen and was relieved that Mac was still recording. Quietly, I flipped through the yearbook to the senior class of 2017. Before I even got to that section, I saw two cheerleaders in their black and yellow Calvary Bees uniforms posing on the football field with their arms linked, with the caption:

Mackenzie 'Mimi' Burk and Savannah 'Vanna' McCoy Bee-esties 4 Life.

Now it suddenly all made sense. The reason Savannah had known the story behind the Burk family portrait was because Mac had told it to her when they'd been friends. Best friends just like we'd apparently been. According to Blessing, Mac had slashed Savannah's face when she'd tried to end their friendship. Had there been another confrontation between them when she found out Savannah was impersonating her online? A confrontation that ended with Mac killing Savannah? Because I was pretty sure this was her blood on Mac's T-shirt. My stomach roiled and the scar along my hairline started to throb. I shoved the shirt and yearbook back into the tote bag and left the closet, taking the tote with me.

I spied the keys to Mac's car on her vanity table, snatched them up and grabbed my purse on the way out the door. I was relieved not to have encountered Blessing on my way to the foyer, or Alayna, who I hadn't seen all morning. I quietly opened the front door, hoping I wasn't triggering an alarm. I heard nothing beyond the soft click of the door as I pulled it shut behind me. An older black man in a navy jumpsuit was changing Mac's tire. He smiled when he looked up and saw me.

"Are you Ms. Good?"

"Yes, sir, I am."

"I'm Mr. Purcell. Ms. Burk told me you'd be using her car to get back to Addison. I changed the tire. I'm just gonna put a new spare in the trunk and you can be on your way."

"Thank you so much, Mr. Purcell. I really appreciate it." I reached into my purse to grab a twenty to tip him.

He waved my money away like I'd insulted him. I figured the Burk's must be paying him well to come at their beck and call when they needed their cars serviced. I opened the driver's side door and tossed my purse and the tote bag into the passenger seat just as I heard Mr. Purcell open the trunk. That's when I heard a loud gasp and the sound of something hitting the ground. I got out of the car just in time to see the tire that Mr. Purcell had been carrying roll down the driveway and into the street.

I ran around to find Mr. Purcell unconscious on the ground and the trunk open. Kneeling by the older man, I felt for a pulse, and to my relief, I felt one pulsing steadily under my fingers. Then I made the mistake of looking up. Alayna was curled up in the trunk of the Mini Cooper. Her skin was ashen and her lips were blue.

She was dead.

TWENTY-NINE
BEXLEY, OHIO

"If we're going to do this, it has to be today or it will be too late. How soon can you get here?" Mac whispered into her phone.

She was playing a recording of a past GRWM video in the bathroom so Kendall wouldn't overhear her conversation. If Kendall had any idea what was about to go down, Mac didn't know how she'd react. Mac listened to the voice on the other end, and the fear and uncertainty that accompanied it, and sighed in frustration. She'd been trying to arrange this ever since she'd gotten back from rehab and had thought she'd finally convinced them.

"I thought you knew that this was the only way."

Five minutes later, she got the confirmation she needed that their plan was a go. She was walking back into the bedroom when she heard the scream. Rushing to the window, she looked out to see Mr. Purcell on the ground behind her car. Kendall stared into the trunk screaming. Once Mac got outside, she stopped dead. Alayna was in the trunk. She was wet and only wearing her bra and panties.

"Is she...?" She reached out her hand toward Alayna to feel for a pulse when Kendall pushed Mac's hand down.

"She's dead, Mac."

"What the hell happened?" When she didn't get a response, Mac grabbed her arm. "Kendall! What happened?"

Snapping out of her trance, Kendall told Mac how she'd found Alayna when Mr. Purcell was fitting a new spare in the trunk. They both suddenly remembered the older man still lying unconscious on the ground.

"I think he hit his head when he passed out," Kendall told her.

Mac shut the trunk. She was surprised none of the neighbors had heard the commotion and come running over. Then again, there had never been any love lost between her family and the neighbors, and Mac wondered if they'd even call 911 if they saw their house on fire. How could this have happened? Who could have killed Alayna? She felt the beginning of tears fill her eyes. Not because she had cared about Alayna; just because she was dead didn't mean she suddenly liked her. But because she'd been waiting for this moment for years and now it was ruined. Once her secret guest arrived and saw the police were there, they'd take off and never come back.

"Help me get him into the house. Then we can call the police."

"But what about—" began Kendall, looking at the trunk.

"She's gone. There's nothing we can do for her. Now, help me."

Mr. Purcell was dead weight, but Mac and Kendall managed to get him into the foyer. As they passed the passenger side of the car, Mac happened to get a glimpse of what was sitting in the passenger seat. It was her own tote bag, the one with her bloody shirt and the yearbook she had taken from Savannah's crime scene. How did Kendall find it? Why hadn't she confronted her over it? Then it dawned on her. She'd been in the process of leaving without saying goodbye, and there could only be one reason. Kendall was scared of her now.

They made it into the foyer just as Mr. Burk's nurse, a heavyset white woman named Carmen, came down the stairs and rushed over to the prone man. The older man moaned. His eyes fluttered open, and he looked up at all their faces staring down at him and tried to sit up.

"Don't get up, sir," warned the nurse. She looked from Mac to Kendall, who spoke up to explain what happened to him. "We need to call an ambulance." At the sound of the word ambulance, Mr. Purcell became animated.

"No ambulance. I don't have health insurance." Against the nurse's orders, he sat up and winced gingerly, touching a knot that was beginning to form on the back of his head.

"We'll pay for it, Mr. Purcell. Don't worry," insisted Mac, wondering if this day could get any worse.

"I'm fine. I'm fine. Quit fussing over me. You need to be finding out who hit me."

"Hit you?" said Mac and Kendall simultaneously.

"I was just about to open your trunk to put your spare in, Ms. Burk, and someone hit me from behind."

Mac was grateful to learn that she and Kendall were the only ones who knew about Alayna's body. As far as she could tell, Mr. Purcell hadn't seen inside the trunk. She immediately got up and gestured for Carmen to follow her. "I'm not sure what's going on, but can you please take Mr. Purcell to the emergency room? The person who did this could still be lurking around."

Mac and Kendall watched as Carmen helped Mr. Purcell out to her van which was parked on the street, and then watched them drive away. Once they were out of sight, Kendall whirled around to face Mac.

"Did you do it?" She took a step back from Mac, looking at her like she was a stranger.

"Do it, as in did I kill Alayna? Because if that's what you mean. No. I didn't." Blood rushed to Mac's face and even though she knew why Kendall had to ask, it still stung. Kendall's eyes wandered over to the Mini Cooper.

"What am I supposed to think when you lied to me about how you knew Savannah. Is that her blood all over that shirt?"

Mac's head snapped back like she'd been slapped. Her breath was barely a whisper as she replied, "I didn't kill her. She was dead when I got there. I got her blood on my shirt when I tried to help her. It was too late by then."

The silence that hung between them was brutal as Kendall continued to stare at Mac like she was deranged.

"Your mom told me you attacked Savannah back in high school when she ended your friendship."

Kendall could have punched Mac, and it would have hurt less than what she'd just said. Mac shouldn't be surprised her mom had once again stabbed her in the back, but this betrayal took her breath away.

"Savannah attacked *me*! She thought I was trying to get with her man, and we got into an epic argument at school, and she slapped me so hard her ring cut my face and left a big scar on my cheek. I had to get plastic surgery. That was the end of our friendship."

"You hired her to be your social media manager? That makes no sense, Mac."

"My mom had always adored Savannah and blamed me for how things went down. I came home for winter break last year and found out my mom had hired her to be her assistant. That was before my dad's cancer diagnosis, and they were flirting with each other. Mom got mad and fired her."

"How'd she end up working for you?"

"I hired her to piss my mom off for always taking her side. I found out that, even after we'd stopped being friends, even after she attacked me and scarred me, Mom and Savannah stayed close behind my back. She was the daughter my mom had always wanted." Mac hated how her voice trembled as she explained all this but was grateful to see Kendall's eyes soften.

"Why run away from the house after finding Savannah's body? If you were innocent, you had nothing to hide, right?"

Mac threw up her hands in exasperation. Why couldn't she just believe her? "You have no idea how I grew up, Kendall. It was drilled into me at a young age that you don't embarrass the Burk family name, or it could ruin our brand. If things went wrong, there was someone my parents could call, and they'd fix it for us. That's why my DUIs never made the papers. Or my mom's drinking. Dad's numerous affairs were harder to cover up because scorned, pissed off women were harder to control. Not all of them would take the *shut up and go away* money they were offered after he ended things."

"So, why didn't you call this fixer after you found Savannah's body?"

"Because I'm not my parents," Mac said, louder than she'd meant to, making Kendall wince.

Kendall opened her mouth to say something when raised voices came from inside the house. There shouldn't have been anyone else there except Blessing and Marcus. They ran inside without hesitation. Once upstairs, it was clear the voices were coming from Marcus's room. Both women flew through the bedroom door, and that's when they saw her. She'd probably slipped past them as they were arguing in the driveway. And she had a knife to Blessing's throat.

THIRTY

BEXLEY, OHIO

"Mom? What are you doing? Let her go, please!" I couldn't believe what I was seeing. What was my mom even doing here?

"Jackie. This isn't what we agreed on. This is not the way to handle this." Mac took a step forward, and Mom pressed the knife closer to Blessing's throat.

"I thought you said our friendship was a secret?" I said, looking from Mac to my mom as my stomach knotted up. Panic was making me short of breath. I probably should have sat down. But I needed answers. "How would our moms know each other?" Neither woman paid me any attention.

"I tried to talk to her!" Tears of rage and pain filled Mom's eyes. "I've been trying to get her and her bastard of a husband to tell the truth for years. I thought things had changed now that your father is dying. I thought they might finally come clean. But she told me to get out of her house or she was calling the police."

Suddenly, the room turned airless, and I couldn't breathe. My knees began to buckle. Mac caught me and propped me upright. Had I just heard her right? Marcus Burk was my *father*?

"My father?" It came out in a whisper. My mom was so focused on Blessing, and the knife she held at her throat, that she hadn't even noticed my distress.

"This bitch is going to tell you what she did to me. What she did to us! Tell her!" Mom screamed in Blessing's ear.

"Jackie, we can get this all worked out," said Blessing. "We can get you the help you need."

Enraged, my mother shoved Blessing to her knees and yanked her head back, pressing the knife to her skin and causing a bead of blood to appear.

"Tell them!"

"Okay. Calm down." Blessing took a deep breath. "I was just trying to help you out, cousin. I was just trying to be there for you when you were so overwhelmed." Blood trickled down her throat.

"Help me? Bitch, you and this sorry son of a bitch stole my baby!"

"What baby?" I looked around the room and felt a touch on my back.

"Me," said Mac, looking shy and tentative. Mackenzie hesitated for just a second before she finally blurted, "I'm your sister, Kendall."

"Sister? What?" I took an involuntary step backward, looking around the room. They were all staring at me. No one but me seemed shocked by what Mac had just said. That meant everyone in that room had known Mac was my sister but me. "Please," I said, the word coming out as a sob. "Somebody needs to tell me what the fuck is going on here."

"She's telling you the truth, Kendall." My mom had finally looked at me. Tears filled my eyes.

"But how?" I was still so confused.

"Mackenzie was stolen from me when she was just three months old by my cousin and her husband."

"You abandoned her! You didn't deserve to be a mother!"

Blessing tried to get to her feet, but Mom tossed the knife aside and shoved her so hard she fell forward onto her face.

"Abandoned her! I would never abandon a child of mine! Ever! My only crime was to trust a bitch who was smiling in my face as she was slipping a knife in my back!"

"You're crazy! You were crazy back then and you're crazy now. Mac, baby, call the police." Blessing tried to get to her feet, but Mac stood glaring down at her.

"No. You're going to tell the truth for the first time in your miserable life."

"Mackenzie? Baby. Help Mama up." Blessing held out a hand to her, but Mac slapped it away.

"You're not my mom. You never have been. Why did you even want me? You never loved me." Mac's voice was thick with tears.

Blessing finally managed to get to her feet and stumbled into the nearest chair, which was next to her husband's bed.

"I didn't want a baby." Her voice was flat and devoid of emotion. "*He* did." She nodded toward the hospital bed. "My career was taking off after my very first album won all those Grammys. I was on a professional high. I wasn't about to ruin all that by getting pregnant and having to put my career on hold for a child, and he refused to adopt. He wanted his own child. That's exactly what he got. But not from me."

"He told me he loved me." Mom glared at Marcus's frail form lying in the bed and her eyes held so much pain at the memory. "He told me he was going to leave Blessing and that the four of us would be a family. But he lied! It was a big fat lie!"

"He may have loved you." Blessing got up to stand by Marcus's bedside. "But he wasn't about to leave the goose that laid the golden egg. My daddy's church funded his car dealerships. He wouldn't lose all that. So we put a plan in place.

Seduce my country ass cousin, Jackie. Get her pregnant. And take the baby."

"Oh my God," I said softly. Bile rose up in the back of my throat and I swallowed hard to keep from throwing up as I realized every single thing I thought I knew about my life had been a lie.

"When I got pregnant, Blessing threw me a baby shower. She was always taking such good care of me. I felt so horrible that I was pregnant by her husband, who I was in love with." She shook her head. "Then I had twins, and I didn't have a job and I was sick most of the pregnancy and everything was just so hard." Mom paused and ran a hand over her face, and it was like I was seeing the real her for the first time. The hurt and vulnerable woman, not the rigid and controlling woman she'd become after life kicked her in the teeth.

"Blessing was always there, right by my side, pretending she cared about me. I remember telling her how tired and run-down I was taking care of twins. My mom offered to help me, but she couldn't take care of both of you, so she took care of Kendall, while Blessing offered to take care of Mackenzie, so I could have a break. She even gave me an all-expense paid trip to Cancun and encouraged me to take friends with me. We had an amazing time, until it was time to leave, and I couldn't find my passport. My so-called friends had left me behind in Mexico. I tried to get back to the States. It took me six days to get home. When I arrived back in Columbus, I was served with a subpoena saying that I was to appear in court to face charges of child abandonment. They'd even paid my friends to lie and say that I knew I had children at home to take care of, but I just kept drinking and it was my decision to stay behind those extra days. They had more money and a better lawyer, and I lost custody of Mackenzie."

"Why didn't you lose custody of me too?" I asked my mom.

"Your grandmother had custody of you for a little while.

Until I got back on my feet. I was so afraid they'd come for you too, Kendall. But they never did."

"I didn't want one baby let alone two," blurted Blessing, staring daggers at my mom. "Twins weren't in the plan. Marcus wanted Mackenzie because she looked like him. Kendall looked like you. We figured it would be more believable that way."

I was incredulous and reeling from what I had just heard. Mac was my *sister*. And not just my sister, my twin. Had that been why I'd always been so drawn to her? "How were they able to get away with this and not have it become public?"

Mom let out a breath like someone had stuck a pin in her. Deflated, she leaned against the wall next to the horrible Burk family portrait.

"Mom?" I started to take a step toward her, but she held up her hand to stop me. Several seconds passed before she finally answered my question.

"They put a seal on it, so no one knew what they had done, and everyone assumed Mackenzie was their child. This bitch pretended to be pregnant, so everyone thought she had given birth to her."

"Did you know about all of this?" I asked my newfound sister, still amazed. She grabbed my hand and gave me a tentative smile.

"I didn't know when we first met back at Calvary. I just knew how much fun we always had together and how I felt like you were my sister even though I thought you were just my best friend." Tears were flowing freely down Mac's face. I squeezed her hand and nodded for her to continue.

"When your dad got arrested and you had to leave school, I was crushed. I got in an argument with my mom one day and she slapped me, and I ran away to your new house. I remember us listening to music in your room, then hearing shouts. We came out into the hallway and my dad was arguing with your mom. She said she would go to the media, and he hit her. Then you ran to help her, and he turned around..." Her voice hitched and she had to catch her breath. "I will never forget the look on his face as he backhanded you and you hit the wall and then fell down the steps. He didn't even go to help you because he was too busy attacking your mom. *Our* mom." She looked over at Mom. All the anger drained from Mom's face, and she smiled at both of us.

"Then he dragged me out of the house and told me if I ever tried to see you or contact you again, he'd make you pay. I couldn't understand why they were trying so hard to keep us apart until I was sixteen years old. I tried to sneak off to the Bahamas for spring break with my friends. I had already been told I couldn't go. So I got the combination to my dad's safe, and I got in there to get my passport. But I also found my birth certificate. Mackenzie Marie Burk born April 10, 1999, at 3:03 in the morning at Children's Hospital, Columbus, Ohio. The mother was listed as Jackie Reynolds and father was Marcus Burk. Underneath my birth certificate was another one. It was for Kendall Clarice Reynolds born April 10, 1999, at 3:24 in the morning. Mother, Jackie Reynolds, and father was left blank. But I knew it was Dad."

"We had no health insurance, Kendall, because Ray was in prison, and I was in school full-time." Mom glanced at the still unconscious Marcus Burk. "He said he'd pay your medical bills if I kept my mouth shut about what happened. I was so ashamed, taking his money, but I had no choice."

Almost as if on cue, Marcus Burk let out a moan and we all looked at him. His eyes were open and watery, and he mumbled just like he had last night. Again, I went to his bedside and leaned over him as his lips moved.

"I'm... so... appy." He stared at my mom and then I finally got it. He wasn't saying I'm so happy. He was saying, *I'm sorry, Jackie.* He must have thought I was my mom last night. In any case, those were the last words Marcus Burk ever spoke. His breath became labored, rattling around in his chest as he struggled to breathe. His eyes bulged and his back arched slightly off the bed with the effort before Marcus Burk went completely silent.

You could have heard a pin drop. None of us said a word. My mom's face was an impassive mask. Mac's eyes shone with tears as she walked over to stand by our father's bedside. Her face was awash with emotions that were at war with each other over her complicated and contentious relationship with her father. Anger, pain, and grief culminated in a sob that finally tore out of her throat. She put a hand over her mouth and looked at me. I instantly knew what she was thinking. She thought she was betraying me by grieving for a man who'd hurt me and our mother. But nothing was black and white when it came to feelings. I walked over to join her and grabbed and squeezed her hand to let her know I understood. I briefly glanced down at the still form in the bed and felt nothing at all. Blessing, who'd been oddly quiet during her husband's final seconds, threw herself on top of him.

"Marcus! Baby, no! Nooo!"

But Mac didn't give the woman who'd raised her a second to grieve her husband before asking.

"I know it was you who killed Alayna. Why?"

Blessing paused her dramatic wailing and lifted her head. Her face was hard and angry. Her mask had fallen off and what was underneath was ugly and without a trace of remorse. "It was an accident."

"She didn't end up in the trunk of my car by accident!" Mac raged. "What did you do?"

Blessing stroked Marcus's hand and didn't answer for several long seconds. "I talked her into going for a night swim with me. I got out and fell asleep in one of the chairs by the pool and when I woke up a few hours later, she was dead. She'd mistaken my wine glass for hers. Mine was mixed with Dopoxin, my sleep medicine."

"You mean you passed out drunk and left her in the pool and couldn't help her when she passed out in the water?" said Mac in disgust.

"It wasn't my fault."

"Then why hide the body? Why not call 911?"

"I think I know," I said as clarity finally dawned on me. "Your mother knew I was driving back to Addison in your car this morning. She told me all those lies so I'd be upset enough to leave without talking to you, Mac. What were you going to do then?" I stared directly at Blessing. "Call the police so I'd get pulled over with a dead body in the trunk?"

"Bitch!" Mom lunged at Blessing, and Mac had to grab her and hold her back.

"He changed his will!" Blessing jumped up from the bed. "He left everything to the two of you! Everything! After all that man put me through for years. The lying, the cheating, and the humiliation. He owed me! I made that man!"

"What are you talking about?" said Mac.

"Just what I said. I made him. After he ran through all of the money he'd made during his one and only season playing pro ball on drugs, liquor, and hoes, I was the one who came up with his origin story of how he was a home town hero who'd started his own dealership when an injury ended his career. I was behind everyone thinking he used that money to start his own business. In reality, he was broke. So I begged my daddy to invest in his dealership. Neither of you little bitches deserved what I worked so hard for all these years. I figured if you were out of the picture, my daughter would share with me."

"Did you kill Savannah too?" I asked. "Were you the one behind the scavenger hunt?"

"I loved Savannah like a daughter. When I hired her to be

my PA, I made the mistake of not having her sign an NDA because I trusted her. But she was running to the tabloids selling them stories about all our business. I could have overlooked that and forgiven her if she hadn't started flirting with my husband. So I did what I had to do to protect myself." With that, Blessing Burk charged through Mom, Mac, and me like a linebacker, knocking us sideways and sending my mom to the floor.

By the time we helped my mom – our mom – to her feet, Blessing was halfway to the front door. She ran out of the house toward Mac's Mini Cooper, jumped inside, and took off. A few minutes later, while we were still reeling, we heard a distant crash. Whether she'd crashed into the tree on purpose, we'll never know. Although, I for one didn't think so because she'd been wearing a seat belt. In either case, by the time emergency services arrived, the car was engulfed in flames. Blessing couldn't be saved.

THIRTY-ONE
ADDISON, OHIO

Two days later, Cal helped me move in with Mac. Even though he had the letter from his mom, overturning his conviction would be a lengthy process and he'd decided to close The Hub temporarily. In the meantime, Nick Palmer had dropped his claim to Lena Bennett's estate. He had been pulled over on his way home from the Honeypot with a bag of cocaine in his glove box. He had much bigger fish to fry now, fighting a drug charge that could land him behind bars for quite some time.

I helped Cal clean out his mom's house to put it on the market. The house was mostly empty as Nick had been selling off everything. The downstairs wasn't bad, but the bedroom Nick had shared with Lena Bennett was the worst hit of all. He'd spent most of his time in this room and it was littered with fast food and condom wrappers as well as his dirty underwear, a few random pairs of women's panties, a couple of bras, and an unmade bed with stained and disgusting sheets that reeked of his signature body odor and cologne.

"How could he bring women here? It's worse than a drug house." I held my breath as I used gloves and tongs to pick up the debris.

"Look." Cal waved a pair of pink rhinestone encrusted cat-eyed glasses at me before putting them on. I laughed but something tugged at my memory.

"Were those your mom's?"

"Naw. My mom wore contacts. These wouldn't have been her style."

I continued to work but then I froze. "Hey, give me those glasses."

"Sure." He tossed them to me.

I unfolded them and looked at the left tip and saw the initials LB engraved on the inside and my heart sank into my stomach. LB. Just like the initials on the bracelet I found that had belonged to Cal's mom, Lena Bennett. I'd wondered why a man would give his side chick a bracelet with his wife's initials engraved on it. He would if his side chick had the same initials as his wife.

"I gotta go." I pulled off my gloves and headed downstairs with Cal calling after me.

"Where are you going? What's wrong?"

I didn't answer.

I tossed the bracelet and the glasses onto her coffee table. Liv glanced at them and smiled.

"It took you long enough to figure it out, but you got there in the end."

"I found the bracelet under Byron's bed. I thought whoever lost it was sleeping with him too. But you were sleeping with Nick Palmer, Cal's stepfather. He gave you his wife's bracelet."

"Byron?" She threw her head back and laughed. "If there's one thing you should know about me, Kendall, it's that I've never been into boring dick. That's your thing. It must have come off when I was looking through your diaries after we had dinner at your place. I knew you kept them under the bed. I had to work fast while you were arguing on the phone with Mommy."

I ignored that last part. "Oh, so you like the married dick, huh?" Who was this chick? I'd considered her a friend since freshman year.

"Nick was a means to an end. That end was to screw you over. I met him at the gym. Who do you think convinced him to contest his widow's will? Me!" She stared right back at me like it was no big deal.

"But why? What have I ever done to you, Liv, beside be your friend?"

She shook her head and let out a harsh laugh. "You've never asked me how my dad died. Weren't you ever curious?"

I just stared at her. It was true that I'd never asked Liv about her dad. Probably because I didn't want to answer any questions about my own dad. Why was she bringing this up now? "I... I just assumed he'd been sick."

"Oh, he was sick all right. Not physically. Emotionally. He killed himself." She said it so matter-of-factly, that I honestly didn't know how to respond. Liv continued, seemingly taking delight in my discomfort. "You see he was the accounting manager at a big accounting firm, Waters, Rogers & West."

As soon as the name of the accounting firm came out of her mouth, my body involuntarily tensed in alarm. Heat flooded my face and my nails dug into my palms. As much as I wanted to run out the door, I was frozen to the spot unable to look away from Liv's face. Because I knew what she was going to say next.

"One of the accountants he supervised was this hotshot asshole who thought the world owed him, and over the course of several years he embezzled millions from the firm's clients."

"Liv, I..."

"Shut up!" screamed Liv. "I'm not finished!" She was breathing heavily now and had to take a few seconds to regain her composure before continuing. "This asshole ended up in prison. But because it happened on my dad's watch, the firm fired him. Twenty years down the tubes. Plus, he got black-balled and couldn't get another accounting job. He refused to get help, not that anyone was willing to help him. My grand-mother hated him because she thought my mom married beneath her and everyone else avoided him like the plague, afraid his bad luck would rub off on them. He just sat around in his underwear all day watching TV and drinking beer." Tears flowed freely down Liv's cheeks now. She angrily wiped them away.

"Until one day I came home from school and the house was filled with gas fumes. I couldn't get either of the garage doors open and had to run to our neighbor's house. When the fire department got there, they found him in his car in the garage with the motor running. There was a letter in the passenger seat next to him. The firm was denying his unemployment claim. We had no money and were about to lose our house. All because of what your dad did."

"But, Liv," I began tentatively. "My dad paid for his—"

"Shut the fuck up!" she screamed in my face, and I flinched away from her.

I was both afraid of her and ashamed of what my dad had done. I wondered how many others were collateral damage because of his embezzling. Then, a thought occurred to me. "Did you know who my dad was all along? Have you hated me all this time?"

"No," she said in a voice devoid of emotion. "I mean, yes. I figured out pretty quickly after we met who you were. Good isn't exactly a super common last name, and it was easy to figure out after I met your mom. I'd seen her on the news in the court-room during your dad's trial."

"Why pretend to be my friend if you hated me so much?"

"That's just it." She sank down onto the chair next to the coffee table. "I didn't hate you at first. I made myself get to know you to prove you weren't a thief like your dad. But you were, weren't you?"

"You read my diaries."

"You think this is about some petty theft?" She glared at me in disbelief.

"Then what? What did I do?" My voice, thick with tears, was barely a whisper.

"You are unbelievable." She shook her head. "You weren't the only one that applied for the Bennett Fellowship. You didn't know that, did you?" I stared at her in disbelief with my mouth hanging open, and when I didn't respond, she continued. "Of course, you didn't because what's going on in anyone else's life is of no concern to you because you're too busy thinking about yourself."

"This was about the fellowship?" Was she insane? Looking into her wild eyes, and witnessing the cruel twist of her lips, I realized she couldn't have been anything but crazy. It was like watching Dr. Jekyll turn into Miss Hyde. "Who are you?"

Liv jumped up from the couch. "I'm the one who deserved that fellowship more than you did!" she shouted at me, causing spittle to hit my face. "My GPA was better than yours, and I participated in more extracurricular activities than you ever did. All you did was work in the library and a few community charities. You were so mediocre. I couldn't believe it when they gave my fellowship to you! First, my father died because of what your father did and then you stole my fellowship! I'm just taking back what's mine!"

I was so taken aback I was speechless. Liv glared at me, breathing heavily. All I could do was push forward. "What did Savannah McCoy have to do with the fellowship? Why kill her?"

She grinned. "I met her when I took Spanky to the park, and she was there with her dog, Biscuit, and I could see that she was upset. Before I knew it, she'd told me all about how she was working multiple jobs at the Playhouse and as a social media manager and her big dream was to be an actress. Her agent had just dumped her and the influencer she'd been working for ended up in rehab, and her mother had fired her. She was behind on her rent and needed the money. And that's when I got the idea. With you expelled for academic fraud, the Bennett Fellowship would be awarded to me next semester."

I continued to gape at her as she spoke, feeling sick to my stomach. "Where'd you get the money to pay her and for her to offer to me?"

Liv shrugged and I wanted to slap her. "I never told my grandmother that I was a GTA now and getting free tuition. So when she sent me the check for my tuition for the year, I had an extra $35k just lying around. I paid Savannah to approach you as Mackenzie Burk, the chick she was already working for, because I knew you used to be a big fan. I told her to hire you to take her class for her. I used my access as a grad student to add Mackenzie Burk's name to the Psych 101 class I was teaching online. I was so busy I had no idea you'd told Savannah to switch sections until more than a week into the semester when I noticed her name was no longer on my class roster. And the section she'd switched to was cancelled for low enrollment, ruining everything."

"And you killed her for that?"

"That was never the plan!" she shrieked at me.

"She still ended up dead, Liv! Why?"

"When I told her there was no reason to continue after the class got cancelled, she demanded more money, or she was going to the dean, and I was all tapped out. The money I got from my grandmother all went to pay the both of you. There was no more. Obviously, I couldn't have her going to the dean. I needed a way to fix the problem. What better way than to set you up for her murder? I got the idea for the scavenger hunt when I saw the pic she posted of her and Byron. Then you told me how you'd slapped Kayla, and it just all came together from there because it showed you had a capacity for violence against your ex's sexual partners."

Now, it was my turn to jump up from the couch. I rushed toward her, backing her up against Spike the boa constrictor's tank. "Let me get this straight. You mean, because for once in your privileged life you didn't get something you wanted, you made it all *my* fault, and an innocent woman died? And for the record, what happened between our fathers was not my fault. I didn't make my dad steal that money any more than I made your dad kill himself. You have no right to punish me for what two grown ass men did when we were both kids! And why did you even need the fellowship when your rich grandmother paid your way through college?"

She shoved me away and I went stumbling backward almost toppling over the coffee table before I was able to stop myself. "Money can't buy respect, you stupid bitch! And that fellowship will open professional doors for me that my grandmother's money never will!"

"But you made a mistake." I watched her eyes widen in surprise. "I never tried on the black Luciano Silva's. They didn't fit. I just held the box and tried on another brand. My prints were never on the shoe you used to kill Savannah."

"So, what?" She shrugged. "Everyone thinks Blessing Burk killed Savannah. You were the one who said she did."

Neither Mac, Mom nor I had told the police Blessing had confessed to Savannah's murder. We'd told them exactly what she'd said, which was *I did what I had to do.* And the police were so eager to close the case, they assumed it was a confession. That's what had been all over the news and social media for days. But why had Blessing said what she'd said? Why allude to killing Savannah?

"You need to go now. I have a test to study for. Not all of us woke up yesterday an heiress with a rich boyfriend."

"And not all of us are going to jail."

"What?" The frown on her face turned into panic when she saw my phone.

"I've been live-streaming our whole conversation. It pays to have a sister who's a social media star. Looks like more than 100,000 people just listened to you confess to murder." I opened her apartment door and Detectives Delaney and Wallace stepped inside, and I headed down the hall to the sweet sounds of Liv's screams of outrage.

THIRTY-TWO

COLUMBUS, OHIO

Marcus and Blessing Burk were buried on a rainy Saturday afternoon four days after Liv's arrest. I hadn't wanted to attend. I went for my sister's sake because, despite Marcus's actions, Mac had loved him to the extent that he'd allowed himself to be loved by her. Blessing hadn't lied. He had left everything, his businesses, his cash, and even the house that Mac had grown up in, to the two of us. I wanted no part of anything to do with him and planned on opting out of my share. Mac talked me into doing something good with the money although I'm still trying to figure out what that is beyond buying my dad and Cora a bigger place for the restaurant.

So I sat with my sister in the front row of Blood of Christ ministries church in Columbus to watch a stranger and a murderer be laid to rest. Blessing's father, Pastor Augustus Grimes, gave them a beautiful eulogy that neither of them deserved.

And I finally found out why Blessing had alluded to killing Savannah that horrible day. Mac and I were at the repast at her grandfather's house after the funeral. She'd been quiet and subdued all day, and I thought it was because she was grieving for the only parents she'd known. I was wrong.

"I have something to tell you." She led me away from the house to sit in the vast garden.

"What is it?" The haunted look in her eyes concerned me. But at the same time, I wasn't sure I wanted to know.

"Blessing killed Alayna on purpose. It wasn't an accident," said Mac, giving me an anxious look.

"What? Why do you think that?"

"When she said she did what she had to do to protect herself, she was talking about Alayna not Savannah."

"How do you know that?" I eyed her skeptically. "Why kill Alayna?"

"I went to check on her after that disaster of a dinner that night and overheard them arguing. Blessing had fired her and was threatening to sue her if she broke her NDA. Alayna was hysterical and threatening to tell the media her big secret."

"Her big secret? What big secret?" Though technically, Blessing Burk had been a woman of many secrets. One more shouldn't have surprised me.

"Blessing couldn't sing anymore. Years of alcohol abuse had ruined her voice. On the rare occasions when she performed in public, her microphone was turned off. She lip-synced while one of her backup singers sang for her. That's the real reason she hadn't made an album in years."

"How did Alayna find out?"

"She was always snooping around, being nosy. She found some old contract Blessing signed for her last tour where it was in writing that at no point during her performance was her microphone to be turned on. Didn't take much to figure out why."

"But it still could have been an accident," I insisted.

"Not when she'd been told by her doctor not to mix her sleep meds with alcohol. She never did. She didn't even really need sleep meds when she was passed out drunk most nights. So there was only one way Dopoxin could have gotten into the wine glass Alayna drank from."

We were both silent for a while before I let out a slow breath. "Wow. That is so fucked up," I whispered. Mac merely nodded in agreement while staring off into space. "Here." I pulled a small package wrapped in brown kraft paper and tied with red twine out of my purse and handed it to her.

"What's this?" She took it giving me a curious look.

"I was going to give this to you when we got home. But figured now was a better time. Go ahead. Open it." I watched as she peeled off the tape, careful not to rip the paper, to reveal a 4x6 black leatherbound diary. She quickly flipped through the blank pages and rolled her eyes.

"You got me a diary? Why?"

"Because I'm worried about you, Sis." Since Blessing and Marcus' deaths Mac's emotions had swung so wildly between extreme anger and deep sadness that I was getting whiplash and was afraid she'd start drinking again. I knew there had to be more going on with her and I'm glad she'd finally confided in me about Blessing's secret. "This was going to be my next diary. I don't need it anymore. But I think it could really help you."

"How?" She gave me a skeptical look.

"Keeping a diary is like having a confidant you can tell everything to who won't judge you no matter how sad, angry, or crazy you might sound. It helped me after my accident and since you're my twin, I refuse to believe that keeping a diary won't help you, too." I gave her a goofy smile and she burst out laughing,

"Fine," she said with a sigh. "I'll give it a try."

"That's all I'm asking. Just try it for a few months and see how it goes." We sat in silence for a minute then I got up and held my hand out to her. "Come on. Let's go back inside."

"I'll be in in a few minutes. I want to sit here for a little while."

"Okay. See you inside." I walked back into the house knowing we'd both take Blessing's secret to the grave. Not to protect her reputation, but so we could finally put this nightmare behind us and move on with our lives.

Mac watched her sister head back into the house and let out a sigh of relief. Kendall had believed her. But her hands still trembled. She set the diary down on the bench and stuck her hands into the pockets of her blazer. Her fingers encountered the thing she'd been keeping with her since the night Alayna died. She pulled the empty bottle of Dopoxin out of her blazer pocket and stared at it. Yes, Blessing occasionally took Dopoxin to sleep on the rare nights she hadn't been drunk. But this bottle of Dopoxin was Mac's. It was what she'd used to try and kill Blessing. She had no idea Alayna had drunk from Blessing's wine glass. She wasn't supposed to die.

When Mac had gone to check on her after dinner that night and overheard their argument, she'd waited until after Blessing agreed to keep Alayna on and had left the room. As soon as Blessing spotted Mac, she'd exploded, demanding to know why she'd brought Kendall into her house and that she wanted her gone by morning. That's when Mac finally dropped the bombshell that she'd been holding on to for years. She'd known Blessing was her stepmother and not her real mother, and that Kendall was her sister, and she wasn't going anywhere.

Of all the ways Mac thought Blessing would respond to that admission, she never thought she'd laugh. But that's what she did. She laughed until tears streamed down her face. Disgusted, Mac turned to go. Then Blessing dropped her own bombshell.

"Does your precious sister know you're the one who really shoved her down those stairs?"

Mac whirled around. Her mouth was suddenly so dry she could barely get any words out. It was like she was being strangled. "Wh... what did you just say?" How could she have known what happened? She, her father, and Jackie had kept that secret for twelve years.

"Your daddy told me what you did after I questioned him about why we kept getting bills from the Children's Hospital."

Mac closed her eyes, trying to shut out the image of Kendall broken and bleeding at the bottom of those stairs. Everything had been fine. She and Kendall had been listening to Destiny's Child in her bedroom, laughing and having fun, when they heard the shouting and had run out of the room to see what was going on. Her father was attacking Jackie, and Kendall flew at him. He backhanded her away from him. Mac ran to help her, but Kendall had pushed her away.

"This is all your fault!" she'd screamed at Mac. "Get out of my house! I hate you!"

She hadn't meant to do it. She was standing at the top of the stairs and her hand flew out. Before she'd even realized what she'd done, Kendall was falling and had landed at the bottom of the stairs with a sickening thud. Marcus and Jackie immediately shoved past Mac and ran down the stairs to Kendall. Jackie was sobbing and Marcus was shouting at her as Mac just leaned against the railing staring down at the scene below her in shock.

"Answer me!" Blessing shouted at her, snapping her back to reality. "Does she know it was you who pushed her that day?"

Mac didn't answer. Couldn't answer. Instead, she turned to go, but Blessing had more to say.

"Well, I think it's time she knew the truth, don't you?"

Mac whirled around again. "You stay away from her," she said through gritted teeth. Her hands had curled into fists. Her voice was low and menacing. But Blessing only laughed again.

"Or what? What are you gonna do?"

Mac rushed across the room to where Blessing was sat on the edge of her bed and got right into her face. "I'll kill you." Blessing's mocking smile never left her face, but she thought better of saying anything else.

Mac left the room realizing she couldn't trust a drunk to keep secrets. She should have never brought Kendall to this house. If her sister ever found out what really happened that day, Mac would lose her forever and she couldn't let that happen. Not when she'd been given a second chance to make up for what she'd done.

Later that night, Mac put the Dopoxin into the wine decanter on the counter, right before Alayna took it out to Blessing by the pool. There had only been one wine glass on the tray with the wine decanter. Alayna was supposed to leave for her night off after taking the wine out to Blessing, which meant Blessing must have offered her the wine, then watched Alayna pass out, stripped her and put her in the pool to drown before putting her in the trunk of Mac's car. Mac didn't think Blessing had meant to set up Kendall. She'd put Alayna's body in her car to let her know she knew that drugged wine had been meant for her. She'd effectively killed two birds with one stone—protecting her secret about having lost her voice, and sending Mac a message—and Mac had inadvertently helped her. Blessing had never counted on Jackie showing up to confront her about what she and Marcus had done all those years ago. In trying to run from the past yet again, she'd been killed.

Mac would have to live with how she'd contributed to Alayna's death for the rest of her life. But she'd been carrying around secrets for as long as she could remember. What was one more?

Mac finally got up, grabbing her new diary from the bench, and went back into the house to join Kendall. On her way through the kitchen, she tossed the empty bottle of Dopoxin into the trash.

EPILOGUE
COLUMBUS, OHIO

Two Months Later

Life was slowly getting back to normal, or at least the new normal. My mom had even had dinner with me, Mac, and Cal at Cora's and was able to apologize to Dad for the lie she'd told so many years ago. I'm hoping she'll be able to move forward with her life now and maybe even find a partner to share it with one day.

I received my fellowship money from Lena Bennett's estate, but I turned it down. It no longer felt right to take it after everything that had happened. It went to the next person on the list, which wouldn't have been Liv. Ironically, she'd been tenth on the list. Instead, I was going to be a graduate teaching assistant next semester and teach Psych 101 classes. With Liv in prison awaiting trial, I was taking over her classes and it felt right. I didn't know what the future held for me and Cal. But for now, things were damned good. And my hoe phase, which never really was a hoe phase, was officially over now that I was in a relationship. Mac and I are trying to make up for lost time, which was why in the first week in November, I went with her to the airport with only a winter coat, a pair of boots, and a passport per her instructions.

"Don't you think you're taking this whole surprise thing a bit far?" We were standing outside Columbus International Airport.

"You're a grad student. And you don't know the definition of a surprise? Girl, bye!"

I burst out laughing. "Where are we going? And please don't say skiing. I tried it once and almost broke my ass."

"No," she replied coyly as she grabbed my hand and pulled me behind her into the airport. "Not skiing." She grinned at me. "Try the northern lights."

"Iceland? We're going to Iceland!"

"Sister dear, I am taking you to the land of fire and ice, waterfalls and volcanoes, the blue lagoon, glaciers, and black sand beaches! And we are going to have the time of our lives and everything we need will already be in our room when we get there. Are you ready?"

I squeezed her hand so hard I'm surprised I didn't break it as tears filled my eyes.

"Bet!"

From the diary of Mackenzie Burk:

November 1, 2023

Dear Diary,

These last couple of months with my sister have been better than I ever imagined. Yet sister is such an inadequate word for what Kendall is to me. She is my twin. My other half. My better half.

With Kendall, I am finally whole, and I refuse to let anyone tear us apart again. Not Jackie. Not Ray. Not Cal. No even Kendall herself. Because I can't go back to being half a person. I can't go back to being incomplete. And I am terrified of what I might do if Kendall leaves me again.

A LETTER FROM THE AUTHOR

Dear reader,

Thank you for reading *Her Pretty Lies*. I hope you enjoyed Kendall's story. If you'd like to hear about my new and upcoming releases, you can sign up for my author newsletter.

www.stormpublishing.co/angela-henry

If you enjoyed this book and could spare a few moments to leave a review, that would be greatly appreciated. Even a short review can make all the difference in encouraging a reader to discover my books for the first time. Thank you so much!

What if you'd hit rock bottom and a stranger offered you a lifeline? But accepting it not only went against everything you stood for, but could ruin your future if you got caught? Would you do it? That's the question I want readers to ask themselves as they follow Kendall's journey.

Human nature has always fascinated me. Why do people make choices that go against their best interests? What were their reasons? Writing mysteries and thrillers gives me the opportunity to create complex stories and characters whose situations and motivations lead them to unexpected places and often deadly choices making us question our own humanity or, at the very least, ask ourselves what we would do in the same situation.

Thank you for being part of this amazing journey with me, and I hope you'll stay in touch – I have so many more stories and ideas to entertain you with!

Angela

facebook.com/authorangelahenry

instagram.com/angelahenry_autho

tiktok.com/@angelahenryauthor

Made in the USA
Columbia, SC
21 May 2024

35996716R00164